Lest Angels Weep

Detective Liz Moorland
Book 5

Phillipa Nefri Clark

Lest Angels Weep

An important note...

This series is set in Australia and written in Aussie/British English for an authentic experience.

Like to discover more about Liz, other titles, and Phillipa's world? Visit Phillipa's website where you can subscribe to her email newsletter. www.phillipaclark.com.

Prologue

Branonville, Victoria. 1971

Even in the dead of winter, night took its time coming, dull sunlight casting long shadows of the church onto the red dirt of the graveyard. Once it was dark, the warmth would leave the air abruptly and chill the ground and everything on it.

Janie squatted against a headstone, praying for that darkness. Unless they carried torches, she'd be safe. She knew this place.

Her shoulders ached and her wrists burned from being tied behind her back all afternoon while those boys... those demons... drank beer and taunted and planned what to do with her. That they'd not harmed her other than to tie her up was the only thing which might stop her from telling her uncle once she got home. If he knew, he'd load a rifle and kill each of them and that would put him in jail forever. She couldn't bear that.

I can do this myself. I will find a way to punish them all.

There'd been a huddle among the young men which

resulted in a short argument and then a lot of laughter. Only the youngest of the group was uneasy. His eyes kept flicking to her and he was the one whose voice had raised in protest.

She'd expected the worst as all of them approached her chair, the younger one brandishing a hunting knife.

If they were going to kill her they'd better be quick. But what if their intentions were more sinister than a quick death? Bile had filled her mouth, its acid making her throat raw.

The knife had cut through the rope like butter and breathing foul fumes of alcohol, he'd leaned close to her ear. 'Run fast. Or hide.'

'What?'

'Stop talking, bitch.' The oldest one – the one who'd grabbed her earlier today as she'd tended the new grave – sneered as he loaded a gun. She recognised the kind. A 22-calibre rifle. Like her uncle's with six bullets.

Terror swirled for a second then she was out of the chair and outrunning their staggering attempts to stop her. Their shouts and threats faded behind as her legs raced along a bush track. But in her panic and confusion she'd chosen the wrong direction. Away from the safety of her home.

And now she was here. At the grave where she was taken.

Her heart hurt. Their loss was raw; her family's. Days old. Earlier, she'd picked wildflowers. Been talking to the headstone like it meant something. Shed some tears onto the parched ground. Then hands had come from nowhere and held her like a vice.

She had to decide what to do. These were just stupid boys who thought themselves better than anyone else in town. Police wouldn't do a thing. She wasn't hurt as such but shaken enough. Anyway, they hadn't followed her.

Slowly, she straightened until she was standing. Not moving other than her head, checking. They weren't here and at least she could breathe. Her fingers played with the pendant from her mother. A gift when Mum was diagnosed. Precious and one she always wore. Touching the form of the angel gave her courage. A whisper which was always in the air... *you can do anything, sweet child.*

She reeled back, falling, grasping her stomach, the wind knocked from her lungs.

Then came the sound. A bang. Like a car backfiring. Echoing.

Voices.

They were coming.

Her feet didn't want to work as she dragged herself upright. There was blood on her hands. So much blood.

'There she is!'

The church was close and she stumbled up the steps and fell against the door. It gave, spilling her onto the floor. This time she couldn't stand so she crawled. Across the timber boards to the darkest corner.

Surely they won't desecrate the church? They all worship here.

Pain came in waves and she vomited.

Unable to clean her mouth as dizziness hit, she shuffled a little further away, her back to the cold stone wall.

The doors were flung open and she tried to make herself small but the movement ripped new pain through her abdomen.

'Silly little bitch. Did you really think you could hide for long? Against men?'

'Mate, maybe we should let her be. She looks bad and—'

A slapping sound. A small cry from someone.

I'm going to die. I can't leave him. Them. Please God. Please hear me pray. Please send someone to help me.

Maybe she blacked out for a moment. The dizziness was making her see things.

Had those awful people gone?

Was her little brother really here... sobbing for some reason? And her uncle as well.

She wanted to ask why they were crying.

Instead, she closed her eyes.

1

As shuddering turbulence hit the Cessna for the third time in ten minutes, Liz Moorland questioned her recent life choices.

She hadn't *had* to fly up.

Phoebe had recommended driving.

So did Candace, who made things worse with a weird story about a near death experience in a charter plane over Iceland.

Reuben had raised his eyebrows but kept his own counsel.

Pete enthusiastically offered to come with her.

Meg muttered something about being better off commandeering one of the helicopters.

Only her old mentor – Vince Carter – agreed that speed was of the essence.

Speed was one thing. Arriving alive quite another.

'Not long now!' The pilot – a thirty-something, long-haired man called Joey who was the only other occupant – turned in his seat to grin at Liz. "Heading through the storm cell which will reach Ouyen late tonight. Bit bumpy."

A bit? And why aren't you concentrating on flying this piece of tin?

The left wing dipped alarmingly and Liz grabbed the armrest.

Joey smirked but faced forward again and the little plane evened out.

The scheduled landing time was still twenty minutes ahead in the outback town of Ouyen. It wasn't her final destination but would provide a hire car and hopefully a meal before she drove an hour or so to Branonville. Meg had helpfully suggested Liz didn't drive at night, sunrise or sunset, and didn't stop for anyone.

'There's rumours of unnatural occurrences,' Meg had warned. "Disappearances after seeing strange lights moving erratically in the sky.'

'Aren't you a scientist?' Liz had asked.

'Science is an ever-evolving thing, Liz. What seems bizarre or impossible one day is simply a discovery waiting for a measurable explanation."

Probably just a fleet of small planes with cowboys as pilots bobbing about in the sky.

In a couple of hours the sun would be setting and by then she'd be at the motel so any disappearances would be Liz getting a decent sleep. After she'd taken a look at the scene of the crime which brought her here.

Finally below the heavy clouds, the turbulence settled and Liz drank in the view. Red land as far as the horizon other than a few darker areas around a distant snaking river. The far north-west of Victoria was the opposite of the bustling city of Melbourne where she lived and usually worked.

Driving here would have taken six hours or more. Thanks to the details of the suspicious death being sketchy and already a couple of days old, the trail was at risk of going cold. Her job was to assess the use of Operation Nobody's resources.

'Be a bit longer. Hold up at the airport.' Joey called to Liz.

"Not the bad-guy kind of hold up.' He found himself amusing. 'Be funny if it was, with you being a cop and all. We could fly in and arrest them. Pity it's just a delay thanks to a backlog and that's gotta be funny on its own. Not like we're landing at Heathrow.'

'So how much of a delay?'

'Ten mins. Maybe twenty. Get you on the ground in time for a beer at the local.'

A beer sounded good. But one with her team would be better. At least her original team.

An impossible wish.

Liz opened her tablet rather than give the memories a chance to slide in. The whole reason she'd taken lead on this was to get out of Melbourne. Get away for a while from the brick building which housed Operation Nobody.

The information she had was basic, to say the least. A report of a body found on the grounds of a church. Specifically, on top of one of the graves, clearly placed there by the description, with no sign of how. And no idea yet who the person might be. Meg was already drilling down for further details and hopefully once landed, Liz could reconnect to the internet and download whatever she'd found during the flight.

The case was odd on its own but local police would normally have been left to deal with it.

Her team was alerted for one reason.

Decades ago, two other bodies were found in uncannily similar situations. Two male corpses, each face down on a specific grave. The same one as this latest death. Investigations took place and were abandoned due to lack of evidence and accidental death being favoured despite certain unusual aspects of the cases.

More likely it was all too hard for whoever was in charge.

Liz loved her job. Being a police officer was all she'd ever wanted and she worked damned hard to do well. But she wasn't naïve about the sprawling organisation that paid her wage. Not everyone was honest and the amount of past corruption she'd seen was depressing. Cops were human first and foremost, honest or dishonest. It wasn't long ago she'd seriously considered quitting Homicide. She and Pete. Then Ben Rossi swept in and offered both positions in his new covert team.

And now he's gone. What the hell are we supposed to do without him?

The churning in her gut had nothing to do with the plane. Motion sickness wasn't something she'd ever experienced. No, this clawing of nausea sat firmly between anxiety and anger.

Neither were useful.

She gave up on the tablet and stared through the small window. Somewhere down there was a killer. That was almost a given. But was there a real connection to the cold cases? Was a serial killer still at large or could this be a copycat? Either way, they needed stopping before anyone else died. For the first time since heading for the airport she wished she'd brought Pete along. Even with his endless complaints and opinions.

Joey's ten or twenty minute delay turned into forty minutes of making large circles in the sky and then the hire car booked by Candace had a flat tyre. While it was changed, Liz tried to access the app for Operation Nobody. That was fruitless. She phoned Meg.

'Oh thank goodness, you're alive!'

Liz grinned. 'The plane was late, that's all.'

'Duh, I know. Been tracking you since you climbed into that thing. Why would anyone fly in anything other than a... well, actually, flying sucks unless you are a bird.'

'No wings here.'

'Of course there are, because you are an angel,' Meg sniggered. 'And I did suggest taking a helicopter which would have dropped you virtually at the crime scene.'

'Since when can I just call a chopper as if it's an Uber?'

'An excellent question.'

Liz waited but no answer came.

'Thanks for caring but I'm safely on the ground. I can't get into the app.'

'Leave that with me. Is it dark?'

'Not even close.'

'I can see you're stationary and haven't left Ouyen so I'll book you into a motel for the night.'

'Um, no. The car is almost ready.'

There was an exaggerated sigh on the end of the line.

'Meg, I seriously am able to drive myself a few kilometres no matter the conditions. I promise to be aware of kangaroos and strange lights in the sky.'

'You are mocking me.'

'I am.'

'Lovely. Alright then, I've reset your tablet and phone so log in and all will work.'

Meg didn't sound the least bit offended. She would probably be at her desk with its three screens and two keyboards, mug of coffee and goodness knows what else.

'I've dumped more information into the case files. One is the active case which is lacking a lot of details. The other file has everything available on the cold cases. Everything I can access, anyway. And it is woefully inadequate.'

'And I have a contact to meet?'

'You do. The town has a one-officer station but comes under the jurisdiction of Sanston which covers thousands of square kilometres and has six officers. Can you call me once you're on the road? I wouldn't mind some fresh air soon. On the roof.'

The roof was the only part of the building not wired for sound. When Ben Rossi set it up, along with Dr Candace Carroll – the resident criminal profiler and psychologist – and Meg, the consensus was that team members needed a safe place to talk. Away from prying ears, even those they worked for.

'Everything okay?'

'Yes.'

'People around?'

'Yes.'

'I need to pick some food up and will call when I'm out of town.'

'Cool. Watch for roos.'

'Yes, ma'am.'

'That's Queen ma'am to you.'

With the paper cup recently filled with hot chips now empty beside a half-full coffee, Liz ran a hand across her salty lips then phoned Meg. The car was navigating to her accommodation first and then would take her to the site of the crime. Alleged crime.

'Perfect timing. I just stepped onto the roof.'

'You're alone?'

'Hopefully. I see you are a few k's out of Ouyen.'

'And it is still light. In fact the sky is so big and so blue I doubt night ever falls.'

'Have you never been out of the city?'

'Not for a long time. Too long.' The last words sounded wistful. Liz loved the city but missed being immersed in the natural world. Other than some recent cases in a few rural locations, it was years since she'd been any real distance outside Melbourne and never so far into the outback.

Her car braked. She hadn't touched it but its sensors picked up something ahead.

'What just happened?'

'Now, Meg. Surely you can see what I can?'

'Very funny. You slammed on your brakes so was it a kangaroo or some scary hitchhiker?'

'A pig. Feral, I imagine.'

'Keep going because they'll turn on you in a second.'

Speeding up again, Liz glanced in her side mirror. The creature was out of sight. 'You can mark me safe from wild boars. What's up?'

'Nothing. And everything.'

'Just a suggestion but talking to me might help. At least, help me understand because I can't see your face. So come on. Give.'

The hesitation told Liz more than any words. The team had been left to its own devices for a couple of weeks since Ben's last day in the office, which was earlier than he'd planned after welcome news of his wife, Ellie's, pregnancy.

'We have a new leader, Liz.'

Although her instinct was to pull over, knowing Meg was watching on satellite kept her driving. Her heartbeat increased. She'd been offered the position and declined. Until she properly dealt with the past year of issues from her father, she wasn't about to lead the team.

'Candace?'

'I wish.'

'Reuben?'

He'd make an excellent head of the team. Calm under pressure. Highly skilled with firearms and hand to hand combat.

An intelligence background which gave him an edge over the average cop.

'Wrong again.'

'Are we playing guess the leader? Okay, is it you?'

Meg burst into laughter.

'I guess not. Tell me its Pete.'

'It's Pete.' The sniggering continued.

'So, not Pete. That leaves Phoebe and Jeff who would both rather quit than take the reins.'

'And they're civilians.' Meg's voice sobered. 'The powers that be decided to put both teams together which is what Ben expected. But he'd planned to stay to ensure the merger was smooth.'

Only a few months ago, Operation Nobody learned of the existence of a second team designed in a similar way and funded by the same source. Although both team leaders knew what was going on, they weren't allowed to discuss each other's existence with their own people, as part of a bigger experiment feeding into a still-unknown higher command. Each team operated under similar guidelines and budgets but was different in some respects. For example, only Nobody had a dedicated criminal profiler and forensics lab.

And only the other operation had helicopters.

It was the recent events around the desperate chase for Liz's father which had them work together during a dangerous situation and they'd done little more than communicate via ops, so this was new for both sides.

'Are we moving?'

'They are.'

'We get their boss?'

'We do.'

She took a moment to finish the almost-cold coffee, racking her brain to recall the snippets of information from

Ben but nothing came to mind about his equivalent in the other team.

'It isn't as simple as it sounds though,' Meg continued. 'Two of their people and the boss will move to our building. They are keeping another five people at the other location which is near Essendon airport because two are helicopter pilots.'

'When does all this happen?'

'Starts tomorrow.'

I shouldn't have come here. This is a big change for my people.

Her foot came off the accelerator.

'Does everyone know?'

'Not as such but there's a briefing first thing tomorrow. And you'll get an invitation to join by video which is why we're talking now. Candace knows though, so call her if you need more intel.'

'She knows the people?'

'Some more than others from the little I've gathered. Transparency is the issue for me although I could easily start some discreet checks on them.'

Meg sounded hopeful, making Liz grin.

'You want me to authorise you to snoop for dirt about our new team members?'

'And the boss.'

'Ben trusted them, Meg. We'll be fine.'

'I was counting on you to demand answers!'

The humour in Meg's voice was covering something. Anxiety, perhaps? Meg was one of the most practical and calm people Liz knew, always the one who'd use logic under pressure. But the past few months had taken a toll on everyone. Meg couldn't be immune.

'And I'm counting on you to keep an eye on the others. Pete, mostly.'

'I'm surprised he hasn't hassled you yet. He got the all-clear this afternoon for full duty. And he is itching to load up a BearCat and take the long drive north.'

'Good news about the clearance. He probably won't get his wish because all I can see is red dirt for miles and will probably be home this time tomorrow.'

'Yeah, sure. Right, I'm going to collect everyone and take them to the pub.'

'Have one for me.'

'We all will.'

After the call ended, Liz accelerated. She was here for a reason and whatever went on back in Melbourne was out of her hands. Calling Candace was pointless because she'd find out soon enough. Had she wanted to step into the role managing Operation Nobody, Ben had assured her she'd have not only his support, but that of a small committee which the team ultimately answered to. The window to make that decision was short. Far too short when she hadn't had enough time to process the senseless loss of a brilliant cop, serious injury to Pete, and deaths of three people who had all – to varying extents – done unthinkable harm to others. She'd been deep in interviews and debriefs after unloading every bullet in her sidearm into her own father when the deadline passed.

There are better people for the job. Ones who don't lose officers.

It was a bad way to think. Multiple sessions with Candace gave her tools to manage the worst of the fallout but it still felt like any decision would be wrong. There was a haze around her which refused to clear. Right now, getting to her accommodation for the night was the first step. Then she could take the next.

2

One look inside the booked room had Liz strongly considering sleeping in the car. The six-room motel was the worst she'd ever seen. Or at least, her room was. There was no sign of recent cleaning of any kind. The toilet was heavily stained and had only the remnants of a roll of paper. An unmade bed. A smell Liz couldn't identify and wasn't sure she wanted to.

The back seat of the hire car held a whole new level of appeal.

She left her belongings in the car and pushed open the door of the office which was at the furthest end of the row.

The man who'd just checked her in had disappeared and she tapped a bell on the counter. He'd barely acknowledged her on arrival, pushing a form in front of Liz and taking payment up front.

She rang the bell again, twice.

'Hold your horses. Something wrong with your room?' He shuffled out of a back room, patting his top pocket for glasses which were on his head. 'Best in the area.'

'Couple of things. Can you help me with directions to All Hallows?'

He found the glasses, shoved them on, and peered at her. In his late sixties, maybe a bit older, he was unshaven and despite looking clean, smelled a bit off. Not unlike her room.

'Strange place to wanna visit. Unless... you a cop?'

'I am.'

'You here to solve the murders?'

Before she could answer, a hand was suddenly shoved over the counter to shake.

'Gordy. Gordon Brain. Thought you were a blow-through.'

Taking her life into her hands – one hand, anyway – Liz shook. Thank goodness she carried sanitising wipes at all times but there wasn't enough to make her room liveable.

Gordy glanced at his open ledger. 'Do ya mind moving? Gotta feeling room six was waiting for my cleaner.'

'Not to be rude but I wouldn't be leaving a five star review for that room.'

He chuckled, showing two missing top teeth. 'We're not even rated. But I can put you in a different room for the night.'

'Appreciate that.'

'You got one of them navigation tools on your phone?'

'I do, but a paper map is best if I'm on foot or out of internet range. Would you have one I can buy?'

'Give you one. Bit stained though. Coffee cup sat on the last one I have.' He reached for a folded map and opened it. 'You'll need both sides. This one,' – he showed her a town map – 'good for getting around the main streets, but for that church you need this side.' Gordy laid the map on the counter, shoving aside the bell to make space. 'This is us.' He circled a spot. 'Keep going on this road. Now it'll seem like it leads nowhere but guarantee it saves time.'

Sure, that fills me with confidence.

His pen kept moving. 'Road'll narrow. There's a one-lane bridge and straight after that, take a left. Another half mile or so and the church is on the right. You won't see much of it from the gate. There's two. The one on the right is private property and you won't be welcome. Should find the other open, unless Connor has it taped up.'

'Leading Senior Constable Connor?'

'She expecting you?'

It was debatable. The police station wasn't attended when Liz briefly stopped after spotting it on the road to the motel. One of the team back in Melbourne would have spoken to the officer to confirm Liz's arrival but she didn't really mind either way. Looking at the scene on her own was fine for first impressions.

'Thanks, that's really helpful.'

'Shall I move your suitcases into the other room?' Gordy folded the map and handed it to Liz.

'Still in my car.'

'Office closes in an hour but here's the key to room three. Just go in when you want.'

'Thanks again. Best takeaway?'

'Pub. Or there's Thai on the other corner from it. Or the wine bar.'

'The wine bar?'

Out here?

'Yeah, we call it that.'

'Supermarket?'

'Closes in an hour.'

Back in the car, Liz was torn. If room three wasn't much better than six, she'd want cleaning supplies. And bottled water and snacks in case she worked through the night. Her watch buzzed a message from Meg.

> The senior constable is waiting at the
> graveyard. Shall I tell her to stand down?

Liz almost laughed. She'd heard the term 'stand down' often enough from her bosses and generally ignored the instruction.

She quickly replied.

> Be with her in a few minutes. Thanks.

Decision made, she followed the directions on the map. Gordy had done a good job, other than not mentioning the road with the bridge was not only dirt, but peppered with deep potholes. It was closer to fifteen minutes when she came upon two gates, both rusted and decades-old. One was closed with a heavy chain wound around a post. She nosed the car through the other driveway, whose gate might not have moved in years by the growth of weeds through its wire, and missing the top hinges.

Once the graveyard was in sight, almost shadowed by a stone church, Liz slowed to pull behind a police car parked to one side of the track. Stepping onto a bed of dried gum leaves and scrawny grass, she locked the car through force of habit after collecting her phone and sunglasses. There was nothing else she'd need for the moment. Ahead, a uniformed police officer approached down the middle of the track. Headstones rose from unloved ground across an acre or more structured with no rhyme or reason. No carefully laid out paths or fresh flowers. Too many lost souls.

The weight of loss and hopelessness gripped her stomach.

'Found the place okay?'

'Leading Senior Constable Connor?' Liz extended her hand. 'I'm Detective Sergeant Liz Moorland.'

Their hands gripped in a firm shake. The officer was only a bit younger than Liz, she estimated. Black hair forced into a tight bun. Brown eyes giving nothing away. Sunglasses pushed back on her head.

'You've got quite the reputation, detective.'

So she'd looked up Liz's record. At least until the day she'd moved into Operation Nobody and became virtually invisible. 'Liz is fine. What have you got for me?'

'Call me Kath. Everyone does. What I've got probably won't interest you more than it has any other senior officer. No offense, ma'am.'

'None taken and its Liz.'

'I'll show you.' Kath gestured to the left of the church. 'Furthest part of the graveyard.'

They began trudging across what was little more than hard dirt with the occasional tuft of grass.

'The body was found three days ago.'

'Who found it?'

'Him.' Another wave, this time toward the church. 'Erik Piper. Poet.'

The name wasn't familiar. Liz's recent cases had plenty to do with art, and she enjoyed a good fiction book, but knew little about poetry other than the classics she'd studied a lifetime ago. Liz stayed close to the senior constable who weaved through headstones, clearly familiar with the way to go without accidentally stepping on a resting place. This was like no other graveyard or cemetery she'd ever visited. And she'd been to more than she cared to think about.

Kath abruptly stopped and put her hand on Liz's arm. 'Wait.'

A snake crossed in front of them, body winding and leaving a track in the sandy topsoil.

'Okay. He's off to do his thing now.'

Liz liked snakes. Better than most people. At least you knew if they were likely to bite. Her phone buzzed and she ignored it. Time to talk to the team later.

The headstone Kath finally led them to was unassuming. Small. No engraving. Four stakes in the ground around it formed a perimeter.

'Have to remove those. Had police tape but nobody respected it.'

'So the scene was compromised before a crime scene room could process it?'

Kath snorted. 'Sorry. What crime scene room?'

Where the hell do I begin with this?

Liz glanced at the church. Perhaps 'hell' wasn't the most appropriate word.

'Start at the start, Kath. I'm listening and I *will* take you seriously.'

A glimmer came into the other woman's eyes. Curiosity, perhaps, of why a city detective would fly up here when the local cops didn't care enough to respect a potential crime scene.

'I was first here. After Mr Piper. Checked vitals. Established the person was deceased. Searched carefully for any identification because I don't know them and Mr Piper claims he'd never seen them.'

'No ID?'

'Nothing. Bit of a mystery.'

'What then?'

Kath crossed her arms as she gazed at the grave. 'Made calls. Asked for detectives. And a crime scene room.' Her eyes shot to Liz's. 'Told to tape the area and keep people away. My senior officer arrived a couple of hours later. I'd covered the body with one of them pop up cabanas to shade it but still... never forget the smell after too many hours in the heat.'

'And then?'

'Senior officer arranged a pick-up to come from the hospital, for the morgue there. Another hour wait. I'd spent all the waiting time taking photos and making notes. Scouring the area for evidence. And sending interested parties away.' Kath shook her head. 'Used to things taking time but whoever had died... they deserved more than I had the resources to give.'

'Single officer station here?'

'Yep. Mostly that's fine. We aren't the crime capital of the world.' Kath smiled. 'Shouldn't complain.'

Yes. Yes, you should. But I bet nobody would listen.

Although Liz had only ever worked in the city, she had plenty of cop friends with eclectic backgrounds and stories of being the solo officer in a large regional area. Much seemed to depend on chain of command and demographics when it came to resources. It wasn't right. Policing was hard enough without the inevitable challenges of distance and understaffing of a placement like this.

'And the body is where?'

'Still at the hospital morgue while enquiries are made. Believe they've taken fingerprints and a DNA sample but they can be weeks. Months.'

'Not with me here.' Liz cautiously circled the marked area. 'Three days. How many people do you think have been here in that time?'

'Enough to leave too many footprints and mess with anything which might have helped us.'

'And further? In different directions?'

'Graveyard is old and out of the way, if you hadn't picked it. Maybe two or three regular visitors a week. Keeping Mr Piper away was harder than anyone because he's angry about it. The intrusion.'

Turning to gaze at the church, Liz was already making plans. She needed to talk to this poet but the first priority was speaking to Meg.

'Kath, do you mind if I make a phone call? I'd like to get some expert help.'

'I'll be in my patrol car. Still catching up on paperwork.'

'I'll come and find you soon. And Kath? You've done well.'

With a shrug, but also a half-smile, the other officer headed toward her car.

Meg didn't answer her phone which was virtually unheard of. Neither did Jeff, the forensic scientist seconded from a private lab for a few months. And when she tried to reach Candace, the call was answered by Reuben.

'Has everyone else vanished into the ether?' Liz joked. There was music and conversation in the background. Lots of it.

'Playing a fierce game of pool. I knew Meg is competitive but she has nothing on Candace, who gave me her phone to hold. And as for Phoebe...'

'What, wait? Phoebe's there with you? At the pub?'

Reuben chuckled. 'Sure is. She just bought us all a round.'

'You're teasing me.'

'Not at all. Here, I'll take a pic.'

A moment later a message popped up and sure enough, there was Phoebe wielding a pool cue with either skill or bravado while most of the team watched on.

'I take it back. Gone less than a day and you all show your true colours.'

'Would rather you were here, Lizzie.'

His tone lowered. Some strange emotion tugged at her. They'd built a connection, Liz and the ex-intelligence officer, despite their different life experiences. He'd been there when she'd emptied her gun into her father. Caught her when she collapsed. Let her cry more than once in his arms and never expected even a thank you. They'd saved each other's life from violent criminals and shared unspeakable sadness.

'Still there?'

'Hmm.'

'How's the town?'

'Haven't seen too much yet and am out at the crime scene. Bit of an issue with lack of services and care, for that matter. Other than the local officer.'

'What do you need from me? From the team?'

'Fast-tracked forensics on the body, first and foremost. The deceased had no identification and from what I read on the plane, there's no abandoned vehicles within a fair radius nor reports of newly missing persons. I'll need a background check on the man who found the body.'

'Jeff and I are going back to the hub once we've eaten.'

'I thought you were playing pool? Why not stay and relax a bit?'

He chuckled. 'And show my workmates I have zero talent with a pool cue? Nah, I'm going to clean out the pantry and fridge at work to ensure there's space to add whatever our new friends like to eat.'

Of course you are.

'So much for a briefing in the morning,' Liz said.

'Meg got off the phone to you earlier and realised Pete had been within earshot on the roof the whole time. She had a word with Candace and now we know. Well, we know to expect company at some point.'

'Better than secrets.'

'Much better. Do you want me to call once I'm back at work?'

'I'll call. No idea where I'll be.'

'Looks like our meals are done. Don't worry how late you phone.'

'Be up to your elbows in tofu?'

'At the least.'

When the call ended, Liz was smiling. Few people saw her. Properly saw her. Reuben did and whether it was a good thing or trouble waiting to happen, remained to be seen.

3

Night was closing in, casting long shadows of the trees from the last of the light as Liz and Kath stared at the grave.

'Who is buried here?'

'I don't know.'

'How can you not know?'

Liz squatted close to the headstone but there was no inscription. She took some photos and zoomed in. Not even the trace of one.

'The church records don't include this particular grave. Either it wasn't recorded or the details have been removed.'

'Who has the church records?' Liz stared at the building in question. 'It isn't active?'

'Not for a long time.'

'Mr Piper owns it?'

'No, he lives in the priest's accommodation which you can't see from here. Built just after the church and rented out after the congregation stopped attending and the last priest left.'

'Is it unlocked?'

Kath's eyes widened. 'The church? Been locked up forever. Nobody ever goes inside.'

The hairs stood up on the back of Liz's arms. She needed her team. Pete, specifically. Of everyone, he'd be finding a way in. And he wanted to be here. And Meg.

'When did that happen? The closure of the church?'

'Maybe mid-80s. Soon after the earlier deaths, anyway. People weren't exactly loyal to this church, or the priest. One or both. There'd already been a lot moving away to a newer church in the next town west. But the catalyst was the unsolved crimes here. Right here.'

'Who does own it?'

'I guess the church still might.' Kath's phone beeped and she checked it. 'Good grief.'

'What?'

'The usual. Old man McGregor needs escorting from the pub.'

'Like a hand?'

Kath grinned. 'He'll curse at me in Gaelic, sleep once he's in the car, then stumble into his house. Happens a few times a week and he has nobody who cares much. Nothing nasty about him but I'd better sort it.'

Liz walked back to the patrol car with her.

'What time can we meet tomorrow?'

'I'm at your disposal, detective. Sorry, Liz. Usually at the station by seven unless I'm in the car. Message me if you like?'

'Any issue with me wandering around a bit?'

'Out here?'

With a short laugh at the disbelief in the other woman's voice, Liz nodded. 'I might be more accustomed to city life, but I'm not bad at looking out for danger.'

'Like the snake, earlier?'

'Good point and ever since that, I've used my eyes more.'

They reached the patrol car and Kath turned to look squarely at Liz. 'Not just your eyes. Use every one of your senses then add intuition and draw on what the landscape tells you. Have you touched the earth yet?' She opened the door. 'Don't stay beyond dark. Not on your first night. And you have my number if you need me. Any time.'

As Kath drove away, Liz squatted and scooped up a handful of warm, red soil. Millions of particles of ancient land. She turned her hand and opened it.

Touch the earth. Learn from it.

'What can you teach me? Can you help me find a killer?'

She'd once worked on a case with a First Nations tracker. Her role was merely as one of hundreds of police and volunteers searching for a lost toddler in Gippsland. The fear was the child had washed off a beach but the calm and solemn man called Ollie believed otherwise. While those around him hurried and stomped everywhere, he stood, his eyes missing nothing. Most of the others went ahead but Liz stayed nearby, ready to follow his lead. The connection between Ollie and his environment was a different kind of relationship than Liz had ever seen. He made measured choices in direction, stopping often to study the ground or the terrain around him. The child was located safe. It was an unexpected lesson in observation which she'd never forgotten and over the following years she learned to trust her instincts, even the ones which were merely a prickle at the base of her neck and nearly always meant she was being watched.

Like now.

Letting the soil spill through her fingers until nothing was left, she straightened. Rotating a slow step at a time, Liz scanned the area. From here the church loomed over the land and she had to spend a moment focussing on the building before seeing the figure of a person.

He blended well with the stone behind him and stood still. Very still.

Perhaps a hundred metres separated them. A long way to see details but he wore a long robe of some kind. His hair was white and below his shoulders. Anything else was a blur and short of using her phone camera to zoom in on him, the rest was guesswork.

'Erik Piper? I'm a police officer. Might I have a moment of your time?'

Liz walked in his direction, trying to get eye contact but having to work her way around and between graves. By the time she'd cleared them, having looked down a couple of times on the way, he'd vanished.

Was he even here?

A scent lingered. Weed. She wasn't seeing things.

The change from dusk to total darkness was abrupt. Liz was back in her car, the doors locked and headlights on as she retraced the earlier drive. She'd decided against searching for the man on her own. Kath was right about not being out here in the dark. Not until she'd found her feet and had a better idea of what she was up against. It was likely to be the local resident, Erik Piper, who had wandered across to smoke a joint and see who was disturbing the peace. To live in the old lodgings of a long-abandoned church with only snakes and graves as neighbours was unusual. Perhaps he was eccentric. Or a murderer.

She drove past the motel and turned onto the main street of the town. There were half a dozen shops on either side, most closed, including the small supermarket. The pub was a typical building of its era. Two floors. Stone and wood structure. Lots of open doors around the public bar and customers sitting at tall tables outside. It was the busiest part of the street.

Across the road was the Thai restaurant with a handful of customers in a small waiting area for takeaway.

A couple of shops down, the so-called wine bar was open and Liz parked between it and the Thai place. She was hungry. The wine bar was an eclectic little space with an upright piano where a woman with bright red hair sang a seventies ballad. Pretty well, actually. There was a bar with stools and a couple of small round tables. On a wall a blackboard had a short list of wines and something about tasting plates.

It might be good for another night. Right now she'd rather take something back to the motel and phone the hub before it got too late.

Opening the door to the Thai restaurant made her stomach growl. Spices mingled with scented candles on either end of the counter. The menu was long and dishes cheap and Liz over-ordered. There'd been a microwave in the first room and a fridge, so hopefully room three had at least those so she could warm up leftovers for breakfast.

She waited outside, curious about the town.

Once the three hospitality venues closed for the night there'd be nothing left open. Even the petrol station on the corner of this street and the road to the motel closed at eight.

What happens then? Does it become a ghost town or is it when the real action begins?

Branonville wasn't particularly known for having a problem with drugs or alcohol and was relatively low-crime. That was according to the brief Liz read on the plane, in between turbulence. The population was aging. Youngsters tended to move away after leaving the tiny school. There was little to attract newcomers. It was a sad story reflected across many of the country's regional settlements.

And like almost every town, the pub was the centre of attention once evening came. Plenty of cars... mostly utes and

SUV's. And as many women as men from what Liz could see. Upstairs was accommodation with only one light on. Either everyone else was downstairs or there was just one guest. It was the only other option to stay locally apart from the motel. No Airbnb's around here.

The night air wasn't much cooler than before dusk. There was no breeze. Nothing to break up the humidity.

A tap on the window from inside alerted her to her order being ready and she went in to collect it. The restaurant itself was almost empty. Only one couple were at a table, deep in a serious conversation. All the other people were here for take-away and Liz had watched several migrate from the pub to collect Thai, then climb into their cars and leave.

Kath would have a field day breathalysing people.

Except, for a tiny community with one cop, it would likely create more issues than solve any. City cops had it easy by comparison. Follow the rules. Get back-up quickly. Have less connection to the people.

Liz let herself into room three a few minutes later, dropping the bag of food onto a table and going back to the car to retrieve her luggage and briefcase. Those went onto the bed and she locked the door and looked around. Despite it being years since the walls were painted or décor updated, it was clean and tidy. There was a bar fridge, microwave and a small desk. The bathroom had fresh towels. A huge improvement on room six.

Inside the fridge was half a dozen bottles of water, all chilled. And a couple of beers and a bottle of wine. A note said the water was complimentary and the alcohol would be charged with the room, if opened. Liz helped herself to water and was half-tempted by the beer. For now she needed food.

4

While eating Liz had typed a report on her laptop, for the team, for her own information, and probably to submit to her new boss. Whoever he was. She ignored the rising irritation about how the change-over was being handled. Her job was to evaluate this crime and the past ones and make a decision about the team getting involved. Not worry about the structure of Operation Nobody.

She made note of her observations of the grave in question and those around it. Of Kath's various comments concerning the events of the day and following days after finding the body. And the sighting of the stranger near the church.

Stomach finally full, she cleaned up and put a surprisingly small container of leftovers into the fridge and took another water.

Rather than sit at the desk, she lounged on the bed and dialled Reuben.

It rang a few times. Had he changed his mind and was still at the pub? She went to hang up just as he answered.

'Hey, Liz. Just making some tea.'

'What kind?'

'This one is a mix of hibiscus and mint and before you tell me those don't go together, I thought the same. Until I tried it.'

Liz was smiling, imagining Reuben in the kitchen at the hub, carefully measuring tea leaves into his favourite pot.

'You find the most interesting things to eat and drink.'

'Do I?'

'Is Jeff around?'

'Somewhere. Lab, I think. Shall I take you there?'

'As long as it doesn't mess with your tea ritual.'

'Ritual?'

'Turn the pot three times clockwise, twice counter-clockwise. Let it rest for precisely two minutes. Pour slowly. In two sessions. Let the tea cool for one more minute. Then sip.'

'Do you really watch me so closely?'

'Not personal, mate. I need to know the strengths and even more importantly, the weaknesses of my team. I watch everyone. Equally.' The last two words were delivered in a sinister tone.

His laughter lowered her stress levels. The banter between most members of the team was priceless. There was an easiness which came from familiarity and from dealing with the extremes the job threw at them. She'd always had this with Pete McNamara, her sometimes-partner back in Homicide days and a member of this team. But being part of a covert room introduced the need for a whole new level of trust and camaraderie and despite two awful misjudgements of past members, everyone was on, or close to, the same page.

Which makes the looming changes more confronting. We just found a balance.

'In that case I shall break my predictable ritual and pour my tea now, after only a few seconds. But I warn you, if it doesn't taste good...'

'Sure. Blame the person who is sitting on a lumpy bed in a one-horse-town.'

'What's it like up there?' Reuben was on the move from the sound of background footsteps. 'Is the motel okay?'

'Typical of a small motel, I guess. Interesting owner though.' She quickly went over the earlier conversation with Gordy. 'It was odd how his demeanour changed when he worked out I'm police. Extra friendly and helpful whereas often it goes the other way.'

'We'll do a background check on him.'

'Thanks. I've got a bit I need help with and will send an email shortly. But I have some forensic questions which I'm hoping Jeff can answer. How is the team?'

'Last seen they'd split into two groups. Half playing pool in a desperate attempt to beat Phoebe even once, and the others watching and making commentator-style narration of the whole thing. I'm just going to juggle the phone to tap in the code to the lab.'

Operation Nobody was housed in the back streets of an inner suburb of Melbourne, one which was predominantly industrial and had as many buildings empty as filled. The old, plain brick exterior hid a fit-out worthy of a slightly futuristic movie. The area referred to as the hub was within reinforced walls and teched-up to the maximum. There was a well-stocked kitchen, several overnight rooms for staff to use, a couple of offices, and a large room which included a round table and conference area as well as space for games and relaxing.

On a different floor was the purpose-built lab. This was Meg's doing and recently, had become Jeff's domain. He was on loan from a private, cutting-edge forensic science company and completed the skillset of the team perfectly.

'Hi Jeff, I have Liz on speaker.'

'Our intrepid explorer? Our preferred leader?' Jeff did a fake gasp. 'Did I speak aloud? Anyway, you missed a fierce tournament tonight.'

'So I heard.' She'd also heard what else he'd said. It was nice he'd seen her as a potential team leader but her job now was to support whoever had been given the job.

'Shall we chat on video, Lizzie dear?' Jeff asked. 'I had my hair styled today and I'm keen to show off.'

Laughter bubbled up and she couldn't contain it. Jeff was completely bald. Somehow she managed to tap the video icon despite the camera shaking as she laughed and his face appeared, deadpan.

'You don't like my new do?'

'Actually, now you mention it... you've changed your parting.'

Reuben snorted in the background and Jeff ran a hand over his shining dome. 'What are your questions?'

Returning to the laptop, Liz gave the men a brief overview of the last few hours, finishing with the odd sighting. 'I saw a man standing by the church but he'd disappeared by the time I closed the distance.'

'Did the senior constable recognise him?' Reuben asked. He was on screen as well now, taking the occasional sip from his teacup.

'She'd gone to escort a drunk pub patron home.'

'And left you there in the dark?'

'It wasn't dark when she left, Reuben.' Hopefully her tone was firm enough to let him know she didn't need his judgement or protection. Not this time.

His eyebrows flicked up but he didn't reply.

'So I'm wondering, Jeff, how long it would take to get fingerprints processed from this unfortunate victim? IDing them is crucial.'

'Overnight if I can get clear images. End of tomorrow at latest.'

'There's DNA samples.'

'That's harder. If I know where it's been sent I can intercept and do a quick turnaround.'

Liz tapped a note to contact Kath next.

'What chance do we have of collecting any viable trace from on and around the grave where the body was placed?'

'Are you certain this was a murder and that the crime scene was elsewhere?'

'No. Not to either. But Kath says yes to both. Kathy Connor, the leading senior constable. She's smart and observant and frustrated by the lack of resources and interest from the higher-ups. Until we get access to the images taken we can't be sure but it sounds like the positioning was too precise and strange to have been a natural death. Oh, and the body was in full sun for several hours before she was able to erect a canopy.'

Jeff narrowed his eyes. 'In the right hands that isn't an issue, Liz. Who is doing the autopsy?'

'Another question I can't answer. And I'm not going to harass Meg tonight.'

'I'll make some calls, lovey. It would help if I was there, of course.' Jeff's eyes widened. 'Never done a road trip with the team. And I can bring a mobile forensic lab. Just a small one, you understand. But enough to get ahead of the game.'

Liz was already formulating the ideal team for this crime but until the briefing tomorrow with new management, she had no idea what authority she still had.

'The other thing, Jeff... if we can locate any trace from the original deaths, the ones from the eighties, is it worth looking at them?'

He nodded. 'Solving old cases is becoming more possible every year. Technology gives us insights we would only have dreamt of even a decade ago. Half a decade. You get me any kind of sample and I'll do my best to give you answers.'

That was the reassurance she'd needed.

'I'm going to chase up those fingerprints and DNA and send both of you emails once I have something. Call or message if you need clarification.'

'And I shall make a list of what I need to pack,' Jeff said. 'Sunscreen. A hat. Snacks and—'

'Okay, okay, I get the hint. We will talk tomorrow.'

'Goodnight.' Jeff winked. 'And I'll bring my own pillow. Always prefer it to those in seedy mot—'

With another laugh, Liz cut the connection.

Before anything else, Liz sent a text to Kath's number requesting access to a copy of the fingerprints as a priority, info about the DNA, and also for the photographs taken of the scene. She had no idea if the senior constable would reply tonight but before she could get as far as begin an email to Reuben, the reply came.

Let me know where to have the fingerprints sent.

Liz replied with Jeff's name and email address.

Will contact my boss about the rest. If he needs to confirm with you, may I pass on your phone number?

. . .

He should have it but feel free to give it to anyone who needs it.

My phone is always on.

Candace, who'd stepped into the senior role after Ben left, had been in touch with the Sanston police station. There'd been sufficient notice and information from Operation Nobody to make the local powers-that-be aware of Liz's attendance. That they'd not arranged a senior officer to be available either when Liz arrived or even better, at the crime scene, was either a sign of a short-staffed station, or a lack of interest.

Just like the deaths all those years ago. Is someone lazy or are they involved?

Liz opened the fridge and helped herself to a beer.

She wasn't about to rule out local police involvement in the murders, whether protecting the killer, ignoring vital information, or actually having committed them. Her level of trust had taken a hammering lately and police were human. Not beyond reproach.

After sending emails to Jeff and Reuben, Liz opened the file on the current case. She'd originally read it in Melbourne after one of Meg's clever programs intercepted a newspaper report and cross-referenced the data with hundreds of cold cases. There'd been enough similarities for the system to flag it to Meg, who dug around more and then highlighted it for the team. The timing might not have been perfect, but the case matched their criteria.

Finally swallowing a mouthful of beer, Liz scanned the report, the visit to the crime scene fresh in her mind.

Kath Connor had prepared the report which was added to by a senior officer and a brief from the local medic who'd been present at the body collection. There was as much missing – such as photos – as was included.

At 7.45am today I received a telephone call from Erik Piper. He identified himself only by his first name and sounded agitated or distressed and struggled to speak coherently. Once I established he wasn't in imminent harm, he told me he'd found a dead man on top of a grave. I advised him to retreat to the side of the church and I would leave immediately and he was not to touch anything. After finishing the call I contacted emergency services, requesting an ambulance. I then called Sanston for back up. I arrived at the graveyard at 8.02am. Mr Piper was sitting on the ground, leaning against the church wall. I called for him to remain there while I checked the body.

I approached the scene with caution but it was apparent the person was deceased. It was a white male I estimate to be aged between sixty and seventy years of age. He was face down on top of a grave, his knees pulled under himself, hands clasped under himself, specifically between the ground and in front of his chest. He wore shorts, a polo shirt, socks and work boots. There was a regular watch on his right wrist. Checking vitals confirmed my assessment. His neck displayed irregular bruising. A careful search of his pockets provided no identification.

His watch, clothes and shoes might yield valuable forensic information so should be sent to Jeff.

While waiting for back up I spoke to Mr Piper. He was angry at his morning being interrupted and only supplied a short statement at that time. He'd not heard nor seen any other people or vehicles since the previous afternoon, when Mrs Georgio attended her mother's grave for a time as she regularly does.

'What are you, Mr Piper, some kind of self-appointed caretaker?'

The rest of the report aligned with Kath's description of erecting a shelter and taking notes of her observations. One part was particularly interesting.

I was unable to ascertain how the body reached the grave. There were no obvious signs of drag marks or obvious footprints other than Mr Piper's boots and mine in the immediate vicinity. Although there are areas of grass/rock, much of the graveyard is surrounded by soft soil which should help find which direction those responsible for placing the body came from. I requested a crime scene room.

Liz wasn't certain of the closest police station with crime scene officers but even if it was several hours away, they should have been called in. Bruising around the neck was enough to warrant their attendance instead of the scene being mismanaged.

And bruising around the necks of two men found on the same grave, three years apart, decades ago, had been similarly ignored because both were declared to have died from natural causes.

Sure, all three just happened to die of natural causes while visiting the same grave.

Somebody in or around the tiny town knew exactly what was going on.

Nobody had talked back then and so far, nobody was talking this time.

Yawning, Liz closed the file and resisted the urge to revisit the cold cases. Tonight she needed sleep. With the expected video briefing tomorrow, she'd need an early start. And a clear mind. She poured the rest of the beer down the sink.

5

Unable to sleep once light streamed through the only bit of curtain Liz had failed to close, she showered and dressed and was in her car before seven, not bothering to sample the packet-coffee beside an old kettle and not ready to think of eating.

The road to the church was easier to navigate in daylight and she remembered the way without using a map. This time, she got out of the car at the dual gates. The air was warm and filled with scents of trees and absolute freshness.

The condition of the other gate was almost as bad as that to the church but showed signs of recent use. Grass and weeds didn't grow through it and there was a rut in the narrow dirt road, worn down by it being opened and closed many times. There was a chain wrapped around it and the post with a padlock. Erik Piper didn't want visitors. Or perhaps too many people had confused his driveway with that of the church.

There was nothing to see other than trees and scrub which hid whatever was beyond a small rise. Only the top of the steeple of the church was visible proof of its existence.

Why would anyone build a church so far out of the town?

40

Back in the car, Liz drove to where she'd parked yesterday and for a moment, she gazed at the building. There was little to differentiate it from any Catholic church she'd seen, other than the setting. Here it looked ridiculously out of place. Surely the land and sky and water and creatures inhabiting them needed no human interface with a god? Yet in the city, nobody would think twice about it being part of their everyday life.

Her phone rang and she tapped it to answer.

'I see you are back at the graveyard,' Meg said.

'You sound chirpy for someone who was out drinking last night.'

'More playing against a hardcore pool champion than drinking. That woman is ferocious.'

'Did you win?'

Meg huffed. 'Only one person won... every game! She is now offering tuition. For a fee.'

'What on earth did you all do to Phoebe? Some experimental drug you and Jeff concocted to bring her out of her shell but accidentally gave her superpowers?'

'Maybe she's always been like this around us but is terrified of you.'

'I am pretty scary.'

They both laughed. Pheobe was an introvert, a mix of quiet ideas and critical thinking, and one of the smartest people Liz knew. She owned a true crime podcast with a massive international following and her work was valuable to Operation Nobody.

Climbing out of the car, Liz began walking toward the church.

'The meeting is at nine. Apparently the new boss will be in the hub and there'll be live streaming for you and a couple of his people.'

'Okay. Once I'm done here I'll go see Kath Connor and

then find somewhere quiet to tune in. Are you there now? In the office?'

'I am. And Reuben is making breakfast for everyone else who will arrive soon. Liz... we don't know what to expect.'

The worry in Meg's voice was uncharacteristic. She was a tough cookie. An over-achiever who never gave up when it came to uncovering the truth about a crime. And she'd been around members of the team for a long time, first working for Ben Rossi in Homicide and then in the hub.

'We've all gone through changes in leadership but you have to keep in mind how important and unique this team is. A lot of money and structure was allocated in the inspector's will and we have the benefit of his foresight. Particularly after solving the murders of his parents.' Liz took a breath. 'That was the only target we had to meet in order to secure the ongoing funding and we did so.'

'At terrible cost.'

'I know.'

Liz reached the grave. 'I'm concerned, Meg. Stressed. I feel I've let our little team down by not stepping up. But every one of us is strong and I keep holding onto the goal of us as a cohesive room, rather than wallowing in feelings about this.'

There was the tiniest glint of something at the head of the grave.

Liz frowned and squatted for a better look.

'That's actually good advice. Look at the goal, not the emotions. I like that a lot.'

'I might have just found something.'

Meg's voice was immediately back to normal. 'Don't touch. Show me.'

After taking a few photos, Liz sent them to Meg and straightened. 'Got them?'

'Mm, mm. Okay, so metallic in appearance. I'd say it is the tip of something. Like an iceberg.'

'The kind of iceberg which doesn't melt in heat and humidity?'

'Focus, boss. Do you have an evidence bag?'

I'd feel naked without them.

'Actually, I need more images first. Hang up and I'll call right back.'

'Oka—'

The line was dead.

A message beeped. An invitation to join a video call in just under two hours. She accepted.

Meg's call straight afterwards was something new. A grey screen with one prompt. 'Click the okay icon please.'

Liz obeyed, expecting Meg's face to appear. Instead, there was a grid of sorts.

'I've been playing around with a new idea. Point the camera at the object please. And just hold it there for a bit. Yes, that's perfect.'

Nothing changed on the screen. Except... the grids began to narrow then widen, then change from a few dozen to half, then half again, until only one remained.

'Got it.'

'Got what?'

'Can't you see? Bother. Back to more programming. Basically, this helps identify anything which comes into its vision. Well, not anything. Not yet. But metals, plants, animals, some people, gemstones. Stuff.'

By now Liz should be accustomed to Meg's brilliance, yet once again, the forensic analyst took her by surprise.

'Still there?'

'Yep. So, what am I looking at?'

'It'll be an hour or so to get a full report so go ahead and carefully bag it. And please collect a fair bit of the soil around it. Do you have any police tape?'

'No.'

'Can you get the leading senior constable to put some up?'

'That I can do. How far around the area?'

They spoke for a few minutes about the logistics then rang off.

Wearing disposable gloves, Liz carefully cleared a small area around the tiny object, taking photos as more of it became visible. The glint had come from the silver it was made from. Had she not been looking directly at the spot the sun would have moved on and once again shadows from the church and trees and taller headstones would have disguised it.

What poked out of the ground was just a link, perhaps two, of something such as a jewellery chain. But as she gently brushed soil and debris away, more came to light. A lot more. Almost afraid to breath, Liz revealed the complete piece. She sat back on heels to stare at it.

This was a silver chain with a pendant. And the pendant was an angel.

'Liz, Jake, Darcy, Helen... thanks for joining the call.'

Candace Carroll held court in the still-to-be-named room at the hub where the team often gathered around the big table for meals or briefings, but also regularly relaxed in the other end of it listening to music or playing table tennis or cards, or reading from a well-stocked library. Whatever the room was, it worked.

Liz was in her motel room at the small desk. She'd run out of time to reheat last night's leftovers but had relented and made a coffee using a sachet of the generic granules. She'd had worse.

Small boxes on the computer screen housed two men and one woman as well as Liz.

Around the table were new faces as well as her own team... other than Meg, who must be managing the camera.

Pete waved madly at her image and she grinned. The sooner she got him up here, the better.

'We want to welcome you all to our hub,' Candace continued. 'As a quick introduction, Jake and Helen are helicopter pilots while Darcy provides ground support. Liz, for anyone who hasn't met her, takes lead on most operations and specialises in cold cases, homicides, and missing persons.'

Interesting way to describe me. You forgot killer. And isn't there a name for people who kill a parent?

She slowly reached for one of the few items on the desk and held it in her palm, squeezing hard. The stress ball was a gift from Pete, who had a collection thanks to his long stint in hospital after Liz's father mowed his motorcycle down with a huge 4WD.

'I'd like to hand things over to our new senior officer, ably stepping into Ben Rossi's role and bringing considerable expertise in a range of areas.'

And that told me nothing. Do you not like him, Candace?

The doctor was expert at hiding her thoughts. At least, most of the time. It was little tells which gave away there might be more going on. Candace Carroll was an exceptional part of the team but had refused to consider taking the top job. She was a civilian who had become invested in the strengths she brought to the team's unique investigations. There was more to her. Much more – such as being a wonderful cook and host of memorable dinner parties. But being boss of the hub was not on her list.

The focus turned to a man who looked familiar to Liz.

She'd definitely met him and although a sense of sadness dropped, the time and place escaped her.

On the surface he fitted the boring profile of the average manager in the country. White, male, fifties. Liz didn't really care for 'average' or statistics. She judged people purely on how they behaved. What she'd loved about Ben Rossi was his commitment to his team. To his people. Anything less wouldn't wash.

'Good morning. Thank you, Dr Carroll. And thank you to Darcy, Helen, Jake and especially, Liz, who I am aware is involved in a time-sensitive case. Your attendance is appreciated and I'll keep things brief. We do have several additional team members currently on a case so they will join us in the next few days.'

He gazed around the table.

'Ben Rossi is someone I deeply respect and admire. We've spoken at length about his work and that of you all, and I want to assure you that I'm not here to make wholesale changes or mess with the brilliance of the team. On the contrary, my intention for the next month is to work with each of you in turn so I can best understand your roles.'

And I still can't remember your name or how I know you.

She texted Pete.

> Do you know him?

> Yes. Don't you? He ran a taskforce targeting people trafficking a while back. Superintendent Fletcher.

· · ·

The last time Felix Fletcher made a public appearance was more than a decade ago, but even so, Liz should have connected the dots. She had met him under tragic circumstances but that was even longer ago. If he was now their boss, then she had a lot of questions. Liz put the stress ball down. He was a decent cop and a fine leader. Wherever he'd been for all these years would have an explanation and it now made sense that Ben was willing to step aside without apparently having a clear line of succession behind him. The default would always have been the leader of the sister team when he came with such a pedigree.

'Today I'll touch base with everyone, personally here, or by phone elsewhere. If you have pressing questions then prepare them. My approach is open-door and I believe in trusting the team and the processes.'

Liz had plenty of questions and requests and once off the call would make a list. Her world revolved around lists at present. She wasn't quite at the point of trusting her memory or instincts and abilities.

Thanks, Dad.

Her fingers found the stress ball again.

'Meg will forward my contact details shortly to those who don't have them. Dr Carroll has agreed to act as 2IC on a permanent basis however we will formulate protocols to ensure she isn't overwhelmed with queries and admin instead of continuing her excellent work to date.'

Candace stared at her hands. That wasn't normal. There was a disconnect between the two and while the comments on the surface were flattering, Liz suspected a hint of condescension was hidden in the words. Candace was rarely, if ever, 'overwhelmed'.

'I wonder if you'd like a trip up here, lady?' Liz whispered.

'Thank you all again for being here this morning. I'll let you all go. Helen, I know you have a reccy flight imminent so be safe.'

Helen – who on the small screen appeared to be mid-thirties with a thick, black braid of hair – raised a hand in acknowledgement.

'And Liz? Once you have my mobile number, please text me with a suitable time to talk. I've no intention of interrupting your investigation and will make myself available at your convenience. Alright, everyone go back to your normal work and we'll talk soon.'

He settled back in his chair, eyes elsewhere. It was a bit awkward. Some of the team started talking to each other, as one by one, the other people on the screen in their little boxes disappeared. And then there was nothing to see.

6

Pete slipped out while others huddled around the new superintendent, hurrying through the empty main rooms of the hub before taking the stairs to the roof. He stopped twice as pain reminded him his body would never be the same as it was a second before a huge black vehicle had powered out of an alley, straight into his motorcycle, with the sole intent of killing him.

For a while he'd believed it might as well have succeeded.

Weeks in hospital followed by rehab took a mental toll as much as physical. As a man who didn't know how to stay still for long, it was a peculiar torture. He longed to be out in the bay on his jet ski. Or chasing down a perp. Some nights he'd wake at two a.m., thinking for a moment he was safe in his childhood bedroom and that his mum was only a wall away. Hushed voices from nightshift nurses would return him to reality with a thud of his heart and he'd almost choke on a sob.

The cloud over his future as a cop was darkened by Ben Rossi's need to move on. Pete was newly home, using a crutch thanks to a hairline fracture in his femur which had initially resisted discovery, when the boss tapped on his door. They'd discussed it at length over a bottle of scotch and an oversized Uber delivery of junk food. In reality there was nothing to talk about as Ben's decision was made the second Ellie's life was threatened. That it was by Liz's insane father was Ben's biggest worry because he knew Liz would find a way to blame herself. Ellie's pregnancy provided a new way out. Didn't stop Liz from overthinking it though.

He reached the roof and closed the fire door, leaning against it to catch his breath. While he was officially fit to work, some days were better than others. He'd spent too long at the gym before dawn and was paying the price.

The sky was grey, ready to rain. He didn't care as this was the best place on the property to talk without being overheard.

As he made his way to the wall on the edge, Pete dialled Liz.

He put the phone on the top of the wall and leaned his arms either side, gazing down at the street. As usual it was deserted. Yet not all that long ago, Kyle Moorland took up residence down the road, able to watch the activity around the hub and form some patterns. He'd gone as far as to dress as a homeless person and taunt the team with his proximity.

Clever. Far too clever.

'About time you called me,' Liz answered.

'Tried last night. Twice.'

'Wait, what?'

He was sure he'd rung her.

'Are you sure? Or were you drunk, dude?'

'Yes. Probably both.' He checked his outward calls. 'Right. Scrap that. Turns out I called Carter.'

The laughter through the phone lifted his mood.

'Dunno why he wouldn't answer.' Pete rolled his eyes at himself.

'No idea. Would have nothing at all to do with your history of mutual hate and relentless insults.'

'But I saved his life. Remember how I shot that creep who was after him?'

'Lyndall saved his life. You saved Lyndall from answering difficult questions about the said creep's demise.'

Fair enough. But I'm still proud of landing my shot precisely where she landed hers.

'Meg and Reuben and Jeff are busy with secret forensic and research business. Expect a few calls and emails soon.'

'Excellent.'

Liz sounded a bit off. Worried or uncertain. She was alone up there. No real back up if a killer was out hunting.

'This case... the real deal?'

'I wish I knew for certain,' Liz said. 'Yesterday there wasn't nearly enough time to take a decent look at the area and this morning I only had half an hour with Kath before the video call. She's a solid cop and up against it with resources and support. Pete, that's what's got me wanting to dig around more. There's something not right but I've not yet spoken to the higher-ups here.'

'They haven't reached out to you?'

'No, and they have my number.'

'A cover up?'

'Mm.'

He grinned. What he admired most about Liz was her instincts. Her knack of pulling little pieces of information from different sources and seeing patterns or suspicious behaviour. Unlike forensics, it wasn't a perfect science but he'd follow her hunches over anyone else's facts, any day of the week.

'Did Reuben circulate the email I sent last night?'

'He did. And I know our new boss has seen it because after the video call ended, he said he expects this case to be a priority.'

'He did?'

At last there was some relief in Liz's voice.

'So who do you need up there?'

Pete almost held his breath. His desire to get back in the field was almost unbearable yet somehow he controlled the natural urge to blabber on about the skills he'd bring until he wore her down.

Wearing her down was no longer on his to-do list.

She'd had enough of being used and he had to make himself useful instead of woeful.

Geez, mate. Talk about pathetic. Remember your own history and be proud.

He'd had a long conversation with Candace on his first week back. She wasn't treating him like a patient but as a colleague and friend. Her advice was to use the time he'd be behind a desk to work out what he wanted in the future. There was a chance at that point he'd never see active duty again. And Pete wasn't the person to accept a backward step. So he'd worked on himself. Questioned his goals and considered alternatives. Along the way he found a place of acceptance, if not peace, about his future. He'd be okay. There'd be other options.

'I've just got a text from Superintendent Fletcher,' Liz said.

'Do you want to call him now?'

'No. I want you to help me decide the team to request. If you all leave in the next couple of hours, we'll have enough daylight to do a proper sweep of the crime scene once you arrive.'

Pete's eyes closed for a moment. He wanted to pump the

air. Or tell Liz she'd make a good decision. She'd included him. His eyes opened.

'Thanks, boss. Okay, let's talk it through.'

Liz walked the half kilometre or so into the main street and ordered a coffee and something she'd not expected here... a breakfast burrito. She sat at an outside table sipping her drink while she waited, watching the world go by. The world of this tiny town.

It wasn't busy although all the shops were open. Only the restaurants and pub were closed. Polar opposites of last night.

Pete had surprised her. Expecting him to immediately nominate himself to join her team, instead he'd put forward well-considered ideas. They were pretty much on the same page with one exception but this might all be a pointless exercise if Fletcher didn't agree. She'd replied to him with a suggested window to have their discussion, giving herself enough time to think and formulate her approach. And eat.

'Hi there, here's your brekkie! Would you like another coffee?'

The young woman who'd brought a delicious looking plate out, smiled.

Liz had ordered takeaway but this was probably better.

'I'd love another. That is the best coffee I've had in ages.'

'You just made my day. And the coffee is on the house.' Sweeping the cup off the table, the server went inside, humming.

And that just made my day.

The food was good and Liz demolished it by the time another coffee arrived.

'I'm happy to pay for the coffee.' Liz had already taken care of the other items when ordering.

'Not a chance. Enjoy the sun because in an hour it'll be too hot to sit in it.'

Waiting for the young woman to go inside, Liz left a decent tip with the condiment tray holding the notes down.

She took the coffee with her, ready to talk to the new boss. Food and coffee had made all the difference... and the brief interaction. She'd spoken to so few people in the town but each time was positive. Even the somewhat odd Gordy – once he'd realised she was a cop – was pleasant. The town deserved answers.

Back in the motel room, Liz spent a few minutes reviewing her notes. Brushing her hair. Checking that when she started the video call that the background didn't include her unpacked suitcase or other mess.

Then she dialled.

It was almost instantaneous that the call was answered and the new boss's face appeared. He was far too close to the camera as he tapped at some setting then suddenly came into focus as he settled back in his chair. Then he looked to his left, mouthing something to whoever had caught his attention.

'Liz, sorry about that. Getting my head around things here and Reuben just offered me a coffee so I'm not about to knock that back.'

Wait until he offers to cook for you. You'll never want to leave.

Ben had loved the impromptu meals and he'd gone. But then again, his wife owned an Italian restaurant beside the sea. Liz pulled her head back into the right place. 'He makes good coffee. Are you settling in?'

The man on the other side of her screen pulled a face... a comic expression which almost made her laugh.

'I haven't even had a real tour yet other than a couple of the main rooms and the bathroom. Saw the kitchen as I hurried through. But every single person here is welcoming and friendly which is more than I expected.'

'Did you expect hostility?' Liz kept her tone even, her brain sorting through the signals she was picking up. 'You ran our sister team. Ben knew and respected you.'

'Not hostility. No. But Operation Nobody has been through the mill and that tends to build bonds. Here I am, a complete stranger, stepping into the office of the man who had built the team from the ground up and had your complete trust.' He sighed. 'Ben left big shoes to fill.'

What was she meant to say? Agree? Acknowledge his own status?

'We've met.' His eyes peered at the screen.

'Yes, Superintendent Fletcher. It was following the Anzac Day attack many years ago. A gunman at a peaceful gathering.'

'First of all, I only answer to Felix. And yes, I remember. Sergeant Vince Carter put himself in the line of a gunman to protect everyone.' His eyes narrowed. 'You were hurt.'

'Slightly. Bullet grazed me, that's all.'

'Vince is a good man. Decent cop and human.'

'He is.'

Reuben returned with a cup of steaming coffee, placing it on the desk and waving at Liz before retreating.

'Sir... Felix? May we discuss the case I'm observing?'

After picking up the cup with both hands, he nodded. 'Meg provided me with a brief about this new death and the similarity to the cold cases. The addition of the find of the angel pendant solidifies the importance of switching from observing to investigating. Is that in line with your thinking?'

Liz drew in a long, slow breath before nodding. 'I'm keen to talk to a number of people. The man who lives in the church

residence. Senior police. Work more closely with the local officer. Have a proper look at the immediate and greater site.'

'What do you need from me? Or should I say, who do you
need?'

'Pete. Meg. Reuben. How many people am I permitted to
request?' Liz smiled. She'd like the whole team. But Jeff had
already said he could only bring basic equipment so was better
off in his own lab. Phoebe wasn't on her radar at present. The
podcaster's strength was her huge audience and network of
clever people and at this point, there was nothing to broadcast.
And Candace, while always an asset, could manage any queries
remotely. Those people she had yet to meet in person were too
much a wildcard.

'Done. When?'

'When do I want them?' Exactly how accommodating was
the new boss? 'Soon.'

Felix looked serious. 'How urgent though? I can get people
to you by helicopter but I expect you need at least one Bear-
Cat? Or a forensic room?'

The unrest Liz had felt since Ben left finally took a
backseat.

'A BearCat is perfect, thank you. Meg can kit it out to bring
what she needs in order to communicate findings with Jeff.
Reuben and Pete will both know what we're likely to want up
here. I can manage until they arrive.'

'But having on-the-ground help sooner would make a
difference.'

It wasn't a question and she wasn't about to ignore the offer.

'Yes. And if I have a choice it is Pete.'

'I'll arrange it. Is there anything else you need?'

'Access to the church. Or at least, your approval for me to
do whatever I need to get inside.'

A slow smile softened Felix's stern features.

'Do what you must, detective. Every decision will be supported, so go ahead at your discretion.'

And I can have that in writing?

This was good. Liz nodded at the screen. 'Thanks, Felix. I'll book more rooms where I'm staying?'

'Book away. Thanks for the chat and we'll talk later.'

And just like that the call was over.

7

She's been inside the room for close to an hour. I heard the click as the door locked. What could be keeping her there for so long? One of the curtains is partly open. Dare I move closer? Catch a glimpse of whatever she's planning?

I dig my nails into my palms because the risk of exposure is too high for now.

Later, once I understand her patterns, I'll do what needs doing.

But why does anyone care this time?

It wasn't like this before. Or the one before that. Those were easy to misdirect. To manage the narrative. No big city cops snooping around. Asking questions. trespassing on sacred ground.

The door opens and she steps out, looking around.

I sink back to blend with the shadow of the trees.

She's pretty... for a cop. Looks like she can run and maybe even fight a bit. Fit. Best she loses interest and goes home so we don't need to put that to the test.

Once she's in her car, I move to mine.

Keeping a good distance back, I trail her. It seems like she's returning to the grave. How often must people intrude? Bad enough they took his body away instead of leaving it for the wild dogs and rodents to devour.

Her car goes past the turn-off.

I ease off the accelerator, keeping her just in sight. Too far away for her to think anything of traffic on the quiet stretch. Another kilometre and she goes into Brown Horse Road. This makes no sense. Or is she just sightseeing?

If she's off somewhere else, I'll go to the graveyard.

As I do a U-turn, the chain hanging from the rear-vision mirror sways and I unloop it. For a moment I stop the car and hold the pendant against my heart. Then I kiss the angel and slide it all into a pocket.

8

With Meg and Reuben on their way in the BearCat, Liz decided against driving to Sanston to chase down a senior officer. It could wait until the team had a chance to collect more information and go armed with well-formulated questions. She'd packaged the angel pendant to return to Melbourne with the helicopter so Jeff could get to work on it.

Can't believe we have helicopters on call now.

She also couldn't quite believe the new boss was so generous with resources but only time would tell if this was a one-off to get everyone on side with him.

Liz drove out of town in the general direction of the church, but taking a different route. She'd spent time on Google Earth, patching together a mental map of the landscape and other properties abutting the twenty acres the church and graveyard occupied. Before leaving the motel she'd emailed Meg with a screenshot, asking her to find who owned what, especially the church grounds.

Rather than turning the usual way, she drove another kilometre to Brown Horse Road. As nice a name as it was, there

60

were no horses – brown or otherwise – in sight, but rather bush-land on one side and open, flat fields on the other. There was a crop growing. Wheat was one of the region's few reliable staples.

Each time she passed a gate, Liz slowed. There were a dozen or so on the left, with fields and most houses set a long way from the road. On the right there was not even one driveway or any sign of habitation. Somewhere behind the dense undergrowth was the church.

The road split in two and she took the right fork. After a few hundred metres she pulled over on the shoulder and checked the screenshot she'd shared with Meg. The church was still somewhere to her right. According to Google Earth, there was a house between, although almost completely obscured by vegetation. And about half a kilometre ahead, this road ended.

Liz continued to the dead end and parked facing the way she'd come.

There were just two gates in sight and like the ones to the church and the poet's house, they were almost side by side. One was well cared for. The gate itself was electric with a panel to tap in a code. Here, the grass was green and short and a small garden of roses trailed along a timber fence. The driveway was in good shape with no visible ruts. No sign of a house. The driveway was flat for a hundred metres then dropped away.

The comparison was stark with the second gate which was at least two metres high and built from mismatched timber planks. Around it the ground was almost barren. There was a chain with a heavy padlock wrapped several times around a gap in the planks and a solid steel upright post. Barbed wire fencing looked almost new, three strands deep.

And then there's the sign.

Liz took a few photos and sent them to Meg with a message.

. . .

You did put a bolt cutter into the BearCat?

The sign was large and attached to one side of the fence.

DO NOT ENTER
TRESPASSERS WILL BE SHOT

'Even if I bring cake?' Liz muttered. This property had gone to the top of her to-visit list for once the team arrived. Most likely the owner was nothing more than a recluse or possibly someone growing something illegal, but the signage invited a discussion.

Before setting off again, Liz made notes on a shared document. This one was accessible by every member of the team, including Felix Fletcher. She kept it brief, mentioning her observations from the drive so far. That was enough for now.

She took her time following the route back, making certain she'd not missed a driveway or glimpse of buildings.

Although Liz wanted to return to the graveyard, there was little point until Pete landed. Instead, she drove as far as the bridge but instead of turning left to the church, continued on the narrow, rutted excuse for a road. Slowly. The poor car juddered and creaked on the corrugated surface and Liz almost missed a break in the undergrowth. She couldn't exactly park here, so she backed up and idled. If there was any fencing, it was well hidden. No gate. No sign this was private property rather than a track through public land.

A check of the screenshot from Google Earth seemed to confirm this was a trail winding in the general direction of a narrow body of water called Carver Basin. Some distance in, it crossed with similar tracks and one of these appeared to lead close to the grounds of the church.

Now wasn't the time to explore it and not in a hired SUV. The BearCat would make short work of the poor surfaces and had superior navigation tools.

And people who bring skills I don't have.

A glance at the clock and Liz reluctantly turned back. Pete would arrive in under an hour and she still hadn't arranged accommodation for the team. Something told her that trying to squeeze the four of them into one ordinary motel room wasn't an option and Pete would complain if he had to share.

'Not exactly five star, is it?' Pete dropped a suitcase on the end of the bed in his room before checking the facilities. It didn't take long.

'If you don't like it, I'll ask if room six is still available.'

His eyes actually lit up and for a second, Liz was tempted to lead him down the wrong path. But then she'd have to put up with hours of him voicing his disappointment.

'Is that the best room?' He asked. 'Let me get my bag. Reuben can have this one.'

'Your choice entirely, but first I should show you a pic I took when I was originally put in there.' Liz scrolled through her photos then turned the phone.

'Hang on... is that bed unmade?'

'Hadn't been cleaned since who knows when. Smelled like crap as well.'

'And you thought I'd prefer it? Oh. Oh, right. This is a Liz-life-lesson for Pete. If Pete complains, give him something to really complain about.'

'Smart man.'

'Why aren't we staying at the pub?' He rechecked the mini bar. 'Noticed one when we flew over. Meals and grog easily accessible. Pool table. Music.'

'Because of all of those things. And I thought you would be off the idea of playing pool for the moment.'

He made a groaning sound and shook his head.

'Are you coming to see the graveyard or do you need time to unpack, iron your clothes etc?' Liz opened the door with a grin. 'The instant coffee is awful, by the way.'

'Why are you being so mean?' Pete wasn't the least bit put out and after sweeping up the door key from the edge of the bed, followed Liz out. 'Anyone would think you regret inviting me here.'

'Oh, I do. But you have an important role.'

At the car, she tossed him the keys.

'You wanted me for my driving skills?'

'Just get in, dude.'

Liz directed Pete along the route to the church, offering small warnings about a pot hole here or a sharp turn there. In between, she told him about her drive earlier and the dead end with the ominous sign. 'I've got Meg onto it for some background info, but testing the whole no trespassing without being shot thing is high on my to-do list.'

'Mine as well, now. Reuben will have stocked up the BearCat with some decent armoury and protective gear so I'm up for it. And we'll be careful, Liz. No rushing in or dropping our guard.'

She couldn't look at him. If everyone thought she needed reassurance about their ability to stay alive then how could she lead them? And why the hell would anyone follow her after she'd lost people only months ago? Pushing down a lump in her throat, Liz vaguely gestured at the bridge and muttered directions.

Pete pulled up in the graveyard driveway and pointed to the other gate. 'Is that where our main suspect lives?'

'That's where the man who found the body lives.'

'Yes, but did he find the body because he already knew where to look?'

He had a point and it wasn't something Liz hadn't considered. That and the odd behaviour of the man had her senses tingling.

'We'll speak with him later but first I want to show you the crime scene.'

'Best news all day. Let's go visit dead people.'

Glad he'd dressed for the environment – hiking boots, lightweight pants, a loose shirt, and wide-brimmed hat – Pete quickly remembered the importance of watching his step by almost tripping on the tip of a buried rock.

'Better than the snake yesterday,' Liz mentioned.

'Great. If the killers don't get you, the wildlife will.'

Pete knew his way around red dirt land. But it had been years. Decades. He stopped near the grave Liz was squatting beside and drew oxygen in through his nostrils, not for breathing but to smell. Faint notes of eucalypt from the abundance of nearby trees mingled with the freshest of air and an earthiness found nowhere else. Almost as good as the sea spray when he was on his jet ski.

'When I arrived yesterday, most of the barrier tape was gone. Pulled off the stakes. As you can see, I've got Kath to redo it because I'd rather not have curious people touching anything. Not after finding the angel.' She gestured to the spot where she must have found it. Newly turned earth with bits of weed. 'I don't know how long it was there, Pete. And I haven't checked the photos I took to remember if I did all that damage, or if the ground was already a mess.'

That was a worry. Liz had a sharp memory.

You have to be tired. Exhausted.

'We can check later. Jeff will sort its age and all that clever stuff he does with tests. Do you remember if the clasp was intact?'

Or have I just made it worse?

But Liz nodded. 'Yes. As in, yes I remember and no, it wasn't. The chain was broken at the loop which goes into the clasp. My gut said...' She straightened and ran a hand through her hair, biting a lip.

Pete crossed his arms, staring at her. 'Said what?'

Better than anyone in the world, he trusted her gut. The annoying little voice in his head which reminded him about Vince Carter's bond with Liz was quickly dispatched to the part of his mind he kept for irrelevant information.

'I'm not convinced the angel pendant was on the body. The recent body. The broken chain indicates someone pulling on it while on another neck. Or held in a hand, maybe. It might be as simple as someone visiting the grave in the past and accidentally catching the chain and dropping it.'

'You don't believe that.'

She looked him in the eye. 'No. I feel it was the result of some violence. A fight to the end.'

Sobering.

'So the crime scene might be here after all?'

They both stared at the grave with its rough surface of earth, weeds, and tufty grass.

'Not exactly well tended, this graveyard,' Pete said. 'I

noticed a couple of graves with flowers and some grass growing on top but most are like this. Old. Forgotten.'

'I've asked Senior Constable Connor to compile a list including the names of those buried here, living relatives, who manages the graveyard and other connected questions. She's doing that today in between other duties.' Liz turned to look in the direction of the church.

'We can help. Once Meg's here, she can shortcut a lot of the red tape, if not all. Can we go inside?'

'Thought you'd never ask.'

Liz set off without waiting for his answer.

'Guess that's a yes.'

9

Having Pete here was more of a relief than Liz had expected. His typical comic approach to any situation was oddly calming even if it deliberately masked his keen intellect. There wasn't much the detective missed when he found a case interesting. And he was already asking good questions and making observations which lined up with her own. It gave her a bit of faith in her judgement.

There'd been a conversation about this with Candace at the doctor's beautiful apartment. It was weeks after the events of the night which had shocked the team and still haunted Liz's dreams. She'd just been cleared of any wrong doing, yet the knowledge she'd not face charges for the death of her father or involvement with that of three other people at the old mansion didn't help. Over their dinner on the balcony, they'd talked only of other things. A bit about Candace's past work and lots about Liz's recently found niece and grand-nephew, two unexpected joys among the weight of mistakes.

Candace wouldn't let Liz help take the empty plates inside, returning in a minute with a bottle of red wine and two glasses.

She poured without asking if Liz wanted one and handed it over. 'This is an exceptional drop. I do have an entire story about my first visit to the winery if we have time later.'

'Tell me now.' Liz picked up the glass of deep red liquid and tapped Candace's. 'To origin stories.'

'It can wait a little longer.'

Silence settled on them as they sipped. The balcony overlooked the Yarra River, black velvet beneath and between city lights. Peaceful, despite the proximity to Melbourne CBD. Liz loved this view. She'd put in an offer on an apartment two floors down and facing the same way, but the wait for agreement was dragging on.

'Once you live here, we can do this more often,' Candace said.

'Are you reading my mind? I was just wondering how long before I hear if I've offered enough. They're probably checking if I'm a suitable person to buy in this building.'

'I'm sure you'll be fine. It is a nice apartment and you'll turn it into a real home for yourself in no time.'

Liz wasn't so sure. She'd rented her last apartment for almost two decades and done hardly a thing to make it more than a place to sleep.

'It will get better, Liz. The doubts you feel now are completely normal. Not just about the apartment but your future. Let yourself feel. But also, give yourself some grace. Time to heal.' Candace reached over the table and gazed directly at Liz. 'The only person putting unrealistic blame and pressure on you, is you. Practice kindness.'

How do I practice kindness for myself when I don't believe I deserve it?

'Earth to Liz. Is there a key or do I get to break in?'

Pete grinned at her and Liz mentally shook herself back to the present.

'No key but rather than damaging the place, shall we walk around it for a proper look?'

'Spoil sport.'

For good measure, Pete rattled the heavy wooden door at the top of two steps. It barely moved.

'What do you know about the church so far?'

He started around the side of the building and Liz followed.

'Too little. Old Catholic church. Built more than a hundred years back. And has been closed for a couple of decades. Perhaps longer.'

Liz stopped and when Pete noticed he turned back with a questioning look. She gestured toward the brick wall. 'This is where someone was standing last night, watching me. No time to even get a photo of him because while I was avoiding stepping on graves and watching my feet, he vanished.'

'A ghost?'

'Be serious. Most likely just the neighbour who sounds nosy and possibly possessive of the grounds here.'

'The dude who found the body. Why wouldn't he simply wait and speak with you?'

'Another excellent question and one I'll happily ask him when we visit his home.'

They continued along the long wall with a series of windows too high to see through. Most were clear but a couple had stained glass. Liz wasn't religious but found the architecture of churches and the stunning fittings quite fascinating. Stained glass in particular. The grandness of this building was almost jarring against the ancient landscape.

Turning the corner, both stopped at steps about halfway along.

'Cosy,' Pete said.

There was a covered porch of sorts with an old table and

chairs. This was beside another door, one less imposing than the front. From the steps, a footpath of concrete pavers led away.

'Do we follow the path or check the door?'

'Door first, Pete.' Liz climbed the steps and almost put her foot through a rotting timber plank. 'Um... carefully.'

He watched his footing and reached for the handle then drew his hand back. 'We should dust.'

'I don't have a kit.'

'I do. Two minutes.' Pete jumped down the stairs and jogged away.

Liz had travelled fairly lightly, expecting to call on the local police for anything she didn't have on hand. With the well-equipped BearCat on its way there'd be all kinds of crime scene tools but when she'd left Melbourne, it was only to assess the situation. She took photographs of the porch and furniture and door then turned her phone in the direction the path took. About fifty metres away was an outhouse and the path went around it and disappeared. The path probably led to the original house belonging to the church.

She sent a text.

> Hi Kath, I'm at the church with a colleague. Wondering if any prints were taken around the doors or internally after finding the body? And the past bodies? Liz.

Pete appeared, carrying a backpack he'd thrown into the car earlier. He set it on the table and unzipped the main pocket.

'Meg has drummed into me the need to be ready for anything on a field trip. I've got a few useful items in here. Ah, here we go.' He extracted a small box and opened it, revealing a mini version of a standard dusting kit. 'She prefers her fancy tech way of taking prints and the like but that is beyond me.'

'This will do fine. And we might do the front door too, although you've had your hands all over it.'

'I'm in the system so easily discounted.'

Liz's phone beeped and she read Kath's response aloud.

> Church was fingerprinted in 1984 but not since. I have requested all the files be sent across.

> Are you planning to enter the building?

'Wait a couple of minutes before replying,' Pete said. 'We'll open the door first then you can honestly say we aren't planning on it.'

Liz couldn't help smiling as she tapped a reply.

> Yes. Only to take photos for now.

The response was quick.

> Be careful.

'Odd.'

'What?'

'Kath said to be careful.'

'Makes sense.' Pete was dusting the door handle and surrounds. 'You already put a hole in the deck.'

Yet something felt off.

Careful, how? Give me a call.

While Pete continued working, Liz watched her phone for a reply. There were a stack of notifications from the app the team used but nothing coloured yellow, which would require her immediate attention. Meg had a system for everything. But no reply from Kath.

'I'm done so we can kick down the door now.'

'Not funny.'

'What's up?' Pete finished packing the box.

'Nothing really. Asked Kath to elaborate and she's not answered.'

'Which could mean she's driving or arresting someone or has gone to the loo. So, boss? Shall we check this place out?'

With a groan, the door gave up under the onslaught from Pete's foot. He'd made a good argument for a few well-placed kicks after it had opened enough to see through a crack.

'See, just stuck,' he said. 'And nothing a bit of pressure couldn't fix.'

'A bit?'

There were a dozen or so shards of timber scattered around the doorframe. Pete shrugged and stepped over them.

The air inside was cool. Almost cold. Liz stopped a couple of feet in to give her eyes a chance to adjust to the semi-dark. The high windows allowed little light through. Perhaps when the sun was higher, but not for now. She inhaled and almost coughed on dusty air.

'Do you have your kit?'

Pete was halfway to the front door.

'Yup. I won't touch anything without dusting.'

'Don't open the door without me, please.'

Liz followed him until she was in the middle of the building. She turned to look back, the shadows focusing into shapes. To her left was a room with one door, which was closed. On her right, old pews were stacked against the wall leaving one side of the church empty.

'Come and see this, Liz.'

Pete was squatting, his attention on the lower part of a stone wall. He had a small UV torch in his hand, slowly sweeping the light over a metre or so. Ribbons of dark staining mingled with large dots of something lighter. He straightened and stepped back, continuing his exploration.

'Oh my god, look at that,' Liz said. 'It's like blood and other bodily fluids.'

He shot her a glance. 'And this was never investigated?'

'I can't answer that, Pete. There's nothing in any of the information we already have. And this looks old. Not that I'm an expert.'

'Meg will know.'

'How far does this go?'

Pete continued walking backwards a slow step at a time and when there was no more trace to see, plotted its perimeter.

When he'd done, both took multiple photographs, Liz using the team app to send directly to Meg.

'This whole place needs locking down for a full search,' Pete said. He put the phone and torch away and headed for the door to the room at the back. 'What were they doing here? Human sacrifices?'

Liz caught up. 'Catholic church so probably not. But then again, who knows what goes on behind closed doors?'

Dusting kit out, Pete gave her a look. 'We all know what goes on behind closed doors... far too often. I grew up Catholic. You think I never saw things I shouldn't have?' He began dusting the door handle.

'Pete... do you need to talk?'

'Nothing to say. I was the kid the priests and teachers left alone because I already had a reputation. And I tried but couldn't protect everyone.'

What the hell? How long have I known you and this is new information?

'Reputation?'

He glanced over his shoulder with a look of pure innocence. 'Not like I was known for punching school bullies or anything.'

'And how old were you?'

'Excellent question, detective. First offense was probably around seven, maybe eight.'

A well of emotion rose and it was all Liz could do to push it down again. Caught between admiration for a naturally protective and courageous kid, and sadness for him being forced to grow up way too fast, she had an unexpected urge to hug her partner.

If Pete suspected anything, he kept quiet, finishing the job with quick efficiency and not for the first time, Liz was a bit frustrated with the man who had such a good mind and heart, yet played court jester rather than just be himself. And now she had one more piece of the puzzle which was Pete McNamara.

'Done. I hope there's a skeleton with a white collar behind here.'

Pete's head was down, concentrating on labelling what he'd just finished. Not having an opinion either way, Liz pulled her phone out and it was her peripheral vision which caught the smallest movement.

She turned to her left just as one of the front entry doors clicked shut.

'What was that?'

'Someone opened the door. Go out the back, Pete.'

Hand on her holster, Liz sprinted to the front of the church, hearing the back door creak open again.

It was just a parishioner. Or a visitor. Someone looking for directions.

Think what she might, Liz's heart raced and she took a breath before opening the same door.

10

Pete was out of the door, off the porch, and around one corner of the church before his brain caught up.

What if I can't catch them? What if I fall?

Cleared for active duty he might be but chasing a potential perp across unknown ground could be his downfall. He'd completed and passed every test thrown at him to get back in the field but kept secret the pain he'd suffered for two days straight afterwards or how many ice packs and painkillers he'd gone through to recover.

He jogged along the length of the building, eyes moving across the landscape. There was no movement anywhere. He'd chosen the wrong direction. At the front of the church he stopped long enough to see Liz running in the direction of the hire car and then he sped up again. The dirt beneath his feet was solid and flat. There was nothing wrong with his muscles or tendons and the bone was fully healed. Avoiding a chase was against every fibre in him.

Ahead was no sign of another person, only Liz, who he was

slowly closing in on. And not because he was faster – she'd always been able to outrun him – but because she was slowing down.

He did the same and caught up near the car.

She was panting. 'Lost... sight.'

Pete dropped his torso forward, hands on knees, drawing in air. Nothing was bent out of shape. Nothing hurt any more than usual.

'Sorry, mate. Didn't mean to make you chase after me.'

'Needed a stretch.' He straightened. 'Can you ID them?'

With a shake of her head, Liz turned and began walking to the church. He went with her.

'They were miles ahead by the time I got through the front door,' she said. 'Too far to tell anything other than that they were fast. Possibly scared.'

'Tell me exactly what happened because all I heard was you saying someone opened the door. I glanced over and it was shut.'

'Yeah. Only opened a crack before they must have realised there were people inside and scarpered off. Have you noticed signs of a squatter?'

'No. Not that we've seen the whole of the building yet but we can now. The door to that room is ready to open and I'm keen to see what's behind it.'

They closed and locked the front doors behind themselves and took a moment to drink bottled water. Pete still felt fine. Just hot and thirsty now. Maybe it was time to start trusting his body again. He tightened the lid on the bottle and nodded toward the door to the room.

'There's a lock on it. Another kicking job?'

Liz rolled her eyes at him. 'So you've forgotten how to pick a lock. I'll get it open without the destruction.'

'But I like destruction. Chaos. Mess.'

'I know. We all know.'

He chuckled and took all of thirty seconds to unlock the door. His smile faded as a dreadful stench assaulted his nostrils. 'What the hell?'

'Should you say that in here?' But Liz's nose was wrinkled in the same disgust.

Pete collected flashlights, handing one to Liz before turning his on. He held it aloft, sweeping light through the room, quickly checking there was no death in here. It sure smelt like there was.

'We should wait for Meg,' Liz said. 'Except... what if there's a body under that mess?'

She gestured to a corner where a pile of flattened cardboard boxes were piled halfway to the low roof. The room was six or seven metres square at a guess and fully enclosed with a flat ceiling and no windows. And no ventilation by the look and smell of things. Liz flicked her light over the floor, which was the same timber floorboards as the rest of the church. Pete found his black light and did the same and sure enough, there was trace present. Blood, if he was right.

'I'll take a quick look if you can keep the black light on please. Just in case the trail leads to a body.' Pulling gloves and shoe covers from a pocket, Liz slid them on. 'Prefer not to add more contamination in here from the rest of the building or grounds.'

'Be careful, Liz.'

'Only doing a welfare check. Can you keep your light on the boxes for now?'

It only took a few minutes for Liz to confirm they were alone and no deceased bodies were in here. She stepped out of the room and removed the gloves and shoe covers.

'The smell seems to be old clothes, and there's a box of tinned food which has some open. Did you notice the bedding?'

She gestured to one corner. 'Looks newer than everything else in here. There's a sleeping bag and cushion.'

'Maybe we chased off the owner.'

She nodded. 'Possibly. A squatter?'

'A killer?'

Liz gave him one of her looks and he shrugged. His theories didn't always match up with hers... or anyone's... but were part of his investigative process. It made sense at this stage to consider anyone who wanted to keep a distance from the police. And double points for those who lived close to the scene of the crime. Squatting counted as living. Just in someone else's property.

'I'll go and call Kath and arrange to get the church taped up. Would you update the app on our progress, please?'

Not waiting for him to respond, Liz headed for the back door.

Pete gazed around. The weight of his childhood was heavy on his shoulders. Ghosts from another church. Another time. And in his experience, ghosts were best kept at a distance.

While Liz was dialling Kath, a patrol car appeared along the dusty driveway and pulled up behind the hire car. Liz glanced behind, expecting Pete to be close. He was nowhere in sight. Hopefully he wasn't breaking into anything else behind her back.

Kath climbed out the driver's side and the passenger door opened.

The man who stepped out was very tall and slim and wore a uniform.

Ah, the bigwigs are making an appearance.

'Detective Sergeant Moorland, this is Sergeant Barnaby Hobson.' Kath had waited only until they were all within speaking distance. 'He is my direct boss and works out of the Sanston station.'

Liz extended her hand and when the sergeant took it, his palm was damp and offered little pressure in return. She somehow resisted the urge to wipe her right hand on her pants. Close up, he was in his early sixties, perhaps more. There was an air about the man which got her senses on alert. And she trusted her senses. Mostly.

'Detective. Apologies for the delay in meeting with you. We've had a number of pressing cases and I'm sure you are aware our region is large.'

Liz glanced at Kath. The officer stared at the ground, her hands stiffly at her sides.

'I have quite a few question, Sergeant Hobson.'

'So do I.'

Planting his feet, he crossed his arms.

'Please, go ahead.' Liz said.

Give me an idea of who you are as a cop.

'You weren't inside, were you?'

'The church?'

'Yes, the church.'

'Did you happen to see someone in a hoodie and shorts on your way here? Along the back roads?' Liz directed the question to Kath, who immediately looked up.

'No. Only passed a couple of cars, owned by locals. Nobody on foot.'

'Why?' The sergeant hadn't moved.

'Someone opened one of the front doors of the church and when they saw us, took off on foot.'

'So you were inside. That's private property, detective.'

'Not exactly.' Pete wandered up, hands in pockets. 'Our intel says the Catholic Church still owns it and although there's no priest or congregation, they have an open door policy for worshippers and those in need of sanctuary.'

'And you are?'

'A bit busy.' A moment dragged and then Pete finally offered a hand. 'Pete.'

'Just Pete?'

'It's what I answer to.' He winked at Kath, whose lips turned up at the corners for an instant.

An uncomfortable silence fell and the sergeant looked ready to pop a vein. Pete had that effect on people when he wanted to be annoying.

'I have a team arriving in the next few hours who will assist the investigation,' Liz said. She gazed steadily at Hobson. 'We'll work closely with Leading Senior Constable Connor and need to speak to any other officers and emergency personnel who attended the scene. In the short term, access to the body, possessions, and all the forensic evidence which was collected will be a good start.'

The tension was palpable. Kath's eyes were again looking down. Hobson emanated irritation. Or stress. All this did was turn on Liz brain... it raced with questions. What had really happened here and who knew what? Why was the person in charge of the regional police station not supporting his solo officer? And why was she afraid of him?

If that's what it is. It looks that way.

Hobson drew in a long breath through his nose. 'Connor will liaise with you to make that all happen. How many people make up this team of yours?'

'Four, including me. At least for now.'

'Why would you need more than four for an accident?'

Pete wandered to the hire car. 'So the victim accidentally got run over by something, then accidentally got to a grave and accidentally died in the same position as two previous accidental deaths?' He opened the driver's door and looked back with a comic expression. 'Can't get my head around so many accidents happening to one poor dude. Oh. Actually, three dudes. Because this death is eerily like those in the last century.'

Kath nodded imperceptibly but she kept her mouth closed.

Hobson's colour had heightened which was incredibly interesting. Either he didn't like being challenged or he knew something.

Or both.

Pete wanted lunch so Liz got him to drop her at the motel and take the car. She stood under the shower for a few minutes, visualising the tepid water washing away the touch of the creepy sergeant and the stench from the room in the church. There was no doubt for her that there were sinister forces at work behind the scenes. Until Meg and Reuben arrived and they could begin to dissect the data, there was little more Liz could do. She'd update her report and probably phone Candace and that was it.

Knocking on her motel door with a handful of takeaway bags a few minutes after she'd dressed, Pete had other ideas.

'I've been thinking. We need to start some conversations with local residents.' He stopped in the middle of the room. 'Some of the townsfolk are pretty friendly.'

Liz moved her laptop to give him space to put the bags down.

'How much food did you buy?'

'Enough. Anyway, there's bottled water in this one and snacks in this.' He moved the two in question onto the end of her bed. 'See, just one bag with our lunch.'

'Thanks, mate. I'm hungry, now I can smell food.'

'All good.' He began extracting the items. 'There's wraps. Really decent sized, too. No idea what's in them but they looked okay. And cookies for after.'

'From the café?'

'Yeah. Had a chat to the young woman behind the counter. Ruby.'

Taking one of the long cylinders of foil, Liz kept herself from smiling. Pete had a way with people when he wanted something. And sometimes he was genuinely himself. The real Pete McNamara.

'Anyway, she asked if I was another cop and knew the cool chick she'd served this morning. The one who had a breakfast burrito and two coffees.'

'Oh, *that* Ruby. What did you say?'

Cool chick?

'That I only hang around with cool people.' He grinned and tore off one end of foil. 'Gossip spreads fast here and she'd heard a crack police unit was up from Melbourne.'

Between Kath and Gordy, it didn't surprise Liz. The grave-yard death was something which would concern anyone.

'Do you want to speak with her officially?'

'Not specifically Ruby, but shop owners and staff often have a good insight into local politics. Who hates who. What deals are done over a coffee with a server being part of the scenery. Are their secrets to be told... that kind of thing.'

He had a point and kept talking.

'If this death happened in the city we'd send uniforms to speak to anyone in the immediate area. This needs to be treated the same way.'

Another good point.

Liz ate the wrap – filled with cream cheese and roasted pumpkin and spinach and other yumminess – while she plotted a course of action. If Pete was keen to 'chat' to people, then she'd let him. But nothing was happening before the rest of the team arrived and they had a chance to talk. Perhaps the town itself would be their best resource. It meant treading carefully. Planning their moves.

And being sensitive to people who might well know the victim... or the victims from the past.

11

Liz gave Meg and Reuben twenty minutes to settle into their rooms and freshen up. They'd arrived in good time, mid-afternoon, the BearCat a welcome sight turning into the carpark.

They met in her room, the men bringing chairs in from their own rooms and they sat in a circle of sorts.

'I've been here just under twenty-four hours,' she started. 'Hopefully I've kept you all up to date with what I'm seeing and thinking.'

'You've done... okay. I mean, you could have done better.'

All eyes turned to Meg.

'What? I created a wonderful app with many wonderful features and most of them aren't even used to ten percent of their capacity.'

'Perhaps we need more training, Meg. I agree the app is incredible but there's a lot I don't know still.'

Meg tilted her head then nodded. 'I'll create some tutorials. And, after this case what if I schedule a half day workshop for everyone and we'll try out the groovy stuff together. Practical experience is better, I think.'

Good on you for taking criticism and turning it into action.

'With the two teams merging, that's a brilliant idea,' Reuben said. 'I love gadgets and intel and stuff and want to explore how to get the most out of our app.'

'Consider it done.' Meg tapped on her phone then put it away and looked around. 'When can we see the crime scene?'

Pete and Liz spent a few minutes talking about their earlier visit to the church. It was one thing to add info to a shared app but quite another to talk person to person.

'We have a whiteboard with us. Not huge, but we can at least use it as a visual way to keep everything in one place.' Reuben had been quiet for much of the conversation. 'At the very least it might be useful to cross off any tasks you set us and no offence about the app, Meg, but sometimes the act of writing and running a line through something has a certain satisfaction.'

Meg raised both eyebrows. 'Which is still my preferred approach to big picture problems. You should see my office at home... actually, can that. No, you shouldn't.'

'I've seen it,' Pete said. 'You showed me after a few rums one evening.'

'Darn. I did, didn't I.' Meg rolled her eyes. 'That's what happens when a friend appears uninvited on your doorstep with an expensive bottle of liquor tucked inside the sling for their broken arm while using their good arm to manage a walking cane.'

Reuben poked Pete's foot with his. 'Exactly how many of us did you do that to?'

'Anyone who answered their door, mate.'

Everyone laughed other than Liz. It had taken weeks for her to be in the right headspace to talk to Pete. Really talk to him. After spending every moment possible at the hospital until he was completely out of danger, she'd been consumed by guilt over the reason he was so damaged. Her father had done this. Had a decent attempt at killing the police officer who'd been Liz's partner on and off for years. And was closer to her than most people.

'Pity Liz doesn't like rum,' Pete teased.

She met his eyes. There was only friendship and respect in them. No blame or doubt.

Not like my own reflection in the mirror.

Liz changed the subject. 'The whiteboard will be great thanks. I'm going to ask Leading Senior Constable Connor whether there is a room we can use in the police station. Something lockable and accessible just by us. If not, we'll use this room.'

It wasn't ideal, dragging the team in here all the time.

'I'm keen to go back to the graveyard and the church. Get your opinions, Meg and Reuben.'

'Suits me,' Meg said. 'I've brought some fancy gear. Not as much as I'd like but Jeff gave me something to test. It might help with the grave in question and possibly the trace you found in the church. Oh, there'll be a chopper up in about three hours to pick it up and anything else we care to add.'

'In that case, let's head there now. If there's time, I want to speak with the elusive neighbour.'

They drove out in the BearCat which made short work of the poor quality roads. Pete took the wheel with Reuben beside him, giving Liz a chance to catch up with Meg.

'I heard from Jeff that he should have some results – including the pendant – by tomorrow,' Meg said. 'Not only is he looking at trace but also the age and history of where it has been over the years. Possibly even its maker.'

'Like he found with the earring from the cellar in our last case?'

'Precisely. He enjoys jewellery testing.'

'We have so many new fingerprints to send back to Melbourne from the doors of the church and other areas.'

'I can scan those. Much quicker.' Meg looked out the window. 'This is so beautiful. Never been up this way but you were right about the big sky. So blue over the red soil. Just spectacular.'

Liz agreed. The area was more than anything she'd seen on television. More in every way.

'Is Candace alright?'

Meg's eyes turned to hers. 'She's off her game. Not in any way which will compromise the case but something is really bugging her and I reckon Felix Fletcher has a lot to do with it. When I get some free time I'm planning on deep diving into his history.'

'I met him years ago. After the Anzac Day shooting.'

'I know.'

Of course you do.

'I should ask Vince Carter. He remembers everyone from his time in the force.'

'Except that was a terrible part of his life. No, go do your own research and let me know what you find.'

Meg looked pleased.

'Graveyard or neighbour first?' Pete turned around as they neared the church.

'Graveyard. Best we get Meg doing her thing.'

They parked closer than Liz previously had, almost in front of the church. Meg and Pete unpacked the gear she wanted while Reuben wandered to the grave with Liz.

'Thanks for getting up here so fast,' Liz said.

'Thanks for including me. I think everyone on the team...

the original team, that is, wanted in. Maybe not Phoebe so much though.'

'Phoebe lives for her podcast and I'm not about to disrupt that unless really necessary.' She glanced at Reuben. 'This is about the merger? Everyone wanting to abandon the hub?' Liz smiled to soften the question.

'Partly. And partly because this is the first case which is completely outside of the city. And probably there's an element of wanting to work with you again.'

Unsure what she thought of that, Liz kept quiet.

'How long has the police tape been here?'

They'd almost reached the grave and while Liz stopped, Reuben slowly circled the boundary.

'Today, which is take two. Kath had one in place which was pulled to pieces by persons unknown. Or possibly known.' Liz gestured toward the church. 'The local resident. Or the squatter. And I'm not discounting curious visitors nor whatever officials were involved in removing the body and doing some version of an investigation.'

'Oh my sweet lord... what is this? Certainly not a serious crime scene. In fact, the lack of respect at this crime scene is seriously criminal.' Meg was aghast. She had bags in each hand while Pete followed with the portable evidence table she'd had made and a couple of boxes with carry handles. 'Just put the boxes down anywhere and can you quickly build the table?' She lowered her bags. 'I'm going to take some preliminary photos.'

While Pete dutifully constructed the table, Meg pulled a camera with a long lens from one bag and began taking images.

Liz turned away to check some messages which had buzzed through but before opening the phone, her eyes landed on the same man from last night. She was certain it was him. Long robe, long hair. Staring at her.

'Mr Piper, a moment, please.'

This time he wasn't going to vanish.

She lowered her voice. 'Reuben, fancy a quick chat with our new friend?'

He quickly looked in the same direction. 'Yup.'

Erik Piper stood on the top step of the church entrance. He folded his arms as they approached, certainly not appearing ready to flee but nor to be a friendly witness.

Liz and Reuben stopped a couple of metres from the bottom step. 'Mr Piper?'

'Who are you?'

The voice was a surprise. The accent, the timbre, was English. Educated, upper class English.

Reuben flashed a badge. 'Detective Sergeant Reuben Barnes and Detective Sergeant Liz Moorland.'

'From the city.'

'Yes.'

He nodded slightly as though confirming this was important.

'I didn't see what happened. To the victim. Nor hear anything.'

'We'll need a full statement, sir,' Liz said. 'You found the deceased and we have some questions which—'

'I answered Kath's questions.'

'And we have our own to ask. Would now be a good time or would you prefer to arrange to come into the station?'

The man shrugged and dropped his arms. 'Neither. But you can come to my home tomorrow morning. Ten. Precisely or I won't answer the door. Perhaps you can bring something for morning tea.'

Liz wasn't certain she'd heard correctly but Erik Piper's expression hadn't changed. There were deep furrows in his forehead above white eyebrows and pale blue eyes. Even his skin was pale which was at odds here where the sun was relentless. He was barely taller than her and it was impossible to see his build beneath the heavy, shapeless robe he wore, but his face was lean.

Reuben turned to leave. 'We'll be there at ten.'

After offering a small smile to the odd man on the steps, Liz quickly followed her team mate. They were almost back at the grave when she glanced back.

He was gone.

'I'm going to need an hour or so.' Meg's camera was away and she had set up a laptop on her table alongside a metal box with several narrow drawers. 'Any chance of putting some shade over this?'

'I'll find something.' Reuben jogged in the direction of the BearCat.

'What can I do?'

Pete was hovering. He did that when he was at a loose end and today wasn't the time for it. Meg had enough to manage and glanced at Liz.

'Do you want to check the church? I have no idea if Piper went inside.'

'Be right back.'

The minute he was out of earshot, Meg grinned. 'Finally alone. Jeff wants me to tell you he will hold the fort. And that although he really wanted to come for a road trip, he knows you need his eyes and ears to keep the hub safe.'

'Safe from what?'

'Anything really. He muttered something about doing research on cloning so there could be one of you there and one here.'

Liz burst into laughter.

'I'm pretty certain it was a joke. But he is a bit concerned his position might vanish if you're not around.' Meg opened one of the drawers. 'And me.'

'It has been pretty unsettling recently but Jeff has a contract with the powers-that-be which has another four months to run and Felix isn't about to mess with it. Jeff is an outstanding asset. Like you are.'

'Aw... you say that to all the incredibly talented, uniquely gifted, unbelievably special members of the team.'

'I do. Even Pete.'

Meg sniggered.

'Even Pete what?'

How on earth did you reappear so fast? And without me seeing you?

Passing him a handful of small tools, Meg answered. 'Even Pete gets the chance to assist Meg today.'

'Sure.'

'We're going to peel back the layers of the grave, dude. What more could you want?'

With a groan beneath his breath, Pete rolled his eyes.

12

Leaving Pete and Meg intent on the grave, Liz and Reuben walked the perimeter of the grounds, starting near the gate and going left. They hugged the fence line where possible, stopping now and then to take photos or make notes.

'This all looks so old.' Reuben used his foot to move a piece of barbed wire which was on the ground. 'Rusted through. Broken.'

'I guess there wasn't much money coming into a tiny town church. The land was probably dirt cheap to buy but the congregation being small wouldn't have generated much income, I imagine.'

Reuben opened the app on his phone and scrolled. 'Candace sent through some demographics of the town a bit earlier. Now and back at the time of both other suspicious deaths. Ah, here we go. There's a summary and then a lot of stats broken down so I'll stick to the latter for now. Current population is one-fifty and is a downturn of 5% over last year. In fact, for the past twenty years the town has been losing residents.'

'No growth at all?'

'Not outside a couple of newer businesses in town such as the café and the wine bar. Now, I'm going back to 1981.' He scrolled more.

'The time of the first death.'

'Quite a difference. The population from its closest census was more than triple that of today. In addition were transient workers for the wheat farms, railway of the time, and a couple of sheep stations. Candace estimates that at some times of the year, seasonal employment would have brought numbers up by another hundred or so.'

Liz frowned. 'My maths isn't mathing. Is there a round figure?'

He grinned. 'Closer to six hundred than five.'

They began walking again and he put the phone away.

'Transient workers would mean some illegal employment practices, no doubt,' Liz said. 'Backpackers without work visas. Cash jobs. No records kept. Which I know is going off tangent for my question about how much money might have been coming into the church but now I'm curious to find out if the investigations into both prior deaths coincided with one of the increases in population. Perhaps that affected how well the police could do their job.'

'The big stations and farms might not cooperate. Not want to come under scrutiny from the ATO.'

Liz nodded. 'Back then, keeping the Tax Office out of things was easier than now. And no Workcover to comply with.'

The open ground turned to shrubs and trees which encroached onto the property as they went. Hugging the fence line became impossible so they kept as close as they could. After reaching the second corner, they stopped and looked back. From here the church was a silhouette against the sky and the graveyard was barely visible. Meg and Pete were only shadows in the distance.

'There's the old residence.' Reuben pointed. 'Would have liked a chat today with its owner.'

Again on the move, Liz glanced in the direction of the sun as it followed a slow arc toward the horizon. 'Agree. If we weren't still so early in gathering intel I'd have pressed for it but Meg has enough on her plate and I've been keen to check the perimeter. Especially after doing the drive around the area earlier.'

She'd sent through her brief on that but so much played on her mind. The two gates in the dead-end road. Such a contrast yet something drew her to the one which didn't warn of imminent death for trespassing. It was almost too perfect compared to everything else she'd seen so far.

Part way along this boundary was a break in the fence.

'Reckon it was cut, but ages ago.' Reuben carefully inspected the ends, which had been rolled back and tucked behind wire in one of the posts. 'And that's almost like a path on the other side.'

They peered into thick bushland where a gap between shrubs was wide enough for one person to walk.

'Looks like it goes for a while. Shall we follow it?' Reuben sounded hopeful.

'Tomorrow. We need to finish this and go help Meg. And I've been thinking about the seasonal workers. What if the killer was here for the work both times? Except it wouldn't fit for the latest death.'

'Or, what if the killer lives here and used those times as opportunities?'

He made sense. He usually did, having a logical brain which was also able to connect more abstract ideas and information.

'I might give Kath a call while we finish walking. See about getting a room for us in the station. I'm keen to put that white-board to use.'

The team returned to the motel as dusk approached after meeting the helicopter on a sports ground on the other side of town. Meg had collected dozens of samples from the grave site and surrounds then moved to the church. While Liz helped her, mostly by holding equipment and handing over evidence bags, Pete and Reuben taped the entire building off, added bolts on both doors, and set up tiny surveillance cameras. If there was a squatter, they'd struggle to get inside tonight and hopefully show themselves.

Or the curious Mr Piper might make an appearance.

Liz was beginning to enjoy the investigation. The team around her were settling into their usual roles despite the different environment and each worked seamlessly with the others. Hopefully, in time, the merger between the sister opera-tions would bring even greater balance of skills but for now keeping this investigation tight was imperative.

'My room's big enough,' Meg said. 'If we use that for now then I won't need to lug my gear around as much.'

The phone call to Kath hadn't been productive. The station had one interview room and two cells in addition to the small working space. Pete was trying to track down a room to rent in town with decent security but none of them expected a good outcome, so for now it was a case of using a motel room.

'For now,' Liz said. 'I'll speak with Gordy in the morning in case there's a spare unit here or he might know of somewhere suitable. Anything we need to secure gets locked in the BearCat.'

'I'm sleeping with my laptop.'

'Why am I not surprised? Okay, let's get the whiteboard

and some chairs in there. Reuben can you make that happen and bring two more desks, please? Mine's fine to get if you want it.'

It only took a few minutes to rearrange Meg's room to an operations centre. Her bed was pushed against a wall and two small desks placed end to end beside the whiteboard. There were four chairs and her own desk was covered with equipment. Reuben had pulled the curtains closed before they started.

'Where's Pete?'

'Here, Meg.' Pete let himself in and locked the door. 'I've got two possibilities for secure spaces to use but we can't see either until tomorrow.'

'Good work, mate.' Liz gestured to the chairs. 'Grab one and we'll get started.'

'What about dinner?'

Reuben chuckled. 'Didn't you have lunch, Pete?'

'I did. And I'm likely to fade away without another meal soon.' Pete took a seat. 'Takes a lot to maintain this body.'

Meg finished setting up one of her computers. 'I've still got a bit of messing around to do here and could use half an hour of me time to concentrate. Any chance the three of you can go and get takeaway and we can eat and go over stuff once you're back?'

Pete was immediately on his feet. 'What would you like?'

'Pick something. Or send me a pic of the menu. Leave the BearCat and keys, thanks.'

'One of us can stay and help,' Liz offered.

'Then it wouldn't be me time. Me and my lovely instruments of data analysis. I'll lock the BearCat in a minute and then I'll lock myself in. Scat.' She led the way outside. 'See, Ms BearCat is right here to protect me and I only need a couple more things from her.'

There was no reason to feel uneasy, yet Liz did. She gazed around. The road was quiet. They were the only occupants of the motel. The office was closed. 'We might take the hire car. Save a bit of time.' Nobody disagreed and she gave Pete the keys again.

As they drove out of the carpark, Meg was taking a box from the BearCat and waved.

'She's fine, Liz,' Reuben said. 'Plenty of lighting and no bushes for bad guys to hide behind.'

Liz wasn't about to tell anyone she'd had one of her feelings earlier. Coming out of her room, before Pete arrived, she was sure she was being watched but couldn't see anyone around. She still couldn't. Across the road was a rest area with a toilet block set a long way back, a small playground, and a few shade trees over a couple of park benches. It was as empty now as it was when she'd driven out to explore the area.

Stop jumping at shadows. The team is fine. You are fine.

'So three places to eat at night?' Pete had parked and they were on the footpath. 'Thai, pub, and a mysterious wine bar which might be confused about where it belongs.'

'Not everything has to be inner Melbourne.' Liz grinned. 'Tomorrow night we might go there.'

They paused outside. The singer from last night was behind the bar chatting to Gordy. He noticed Liz and raised the beer in his hand and she nodded back.

'Open until eleven every night but Sunday,' Pete read a notice in the window. 'Might be worth wandering back a bit later. Give me a chance to get to know some of the residents. Who's that?'

'Gordon Brain, who owns the motel.' Not wanting the man in question to think they were talking about him, she continued along the street and stopped outside a closed shop. 'Waiting on a background check but he's been helpful with the rooms and comes across as genuinely pleased the murder is being investigated outside of the local police. I get the impression he's a long-time local.'

Reuben nodded. 'I'll follow up on the background check when we're back at the motel.'

'We're being watched.' Pete leaned against the wall, hands in pockets. His eyes were in the direction of the pub, where half a dozen men sat around a tall table. All of them were looking back and none of them were talking. 'Reckon I should wave?'

'I think we should order food and go back. There's bound to be interest in us.'

All the more reason to start talking to shop owners and the closest residents of the church. Perhaps I should have asked for more people on the ground.

Except it would have meant bringing someone the team didn't know into the investigation. No, best to work through the dynamics of personalities and skill sets in the hub, or at least in a case closer to home than way out here.

13

Damn them.

The first grave is desecrated. Holes dug into the soil scatter the surface. I drop to my knees and use my bare hands to refill them until the ground is smooth again.

'I'm sorry,' I sit back on my heels and finally gaze at her sanctuary as the familiar pain rises. 'So very sorry. I was careless and got the wrong kind of attention. Bringing another one to repent and give his life should have been like the others.'

There's a noise in the trees and I get to my feet and turn around.

Just night birds.

How I wish I could lie down between the resting places. Release the blood from my body to join those I love so fiercely. I'm weary beyond words.

But it isn't finished. No thanks to those who would dare touch what isn't theirs.

I'd thought the female cop was who I had to watch. Her friends have complicated matters. One of her friends. My heart begins to thud again, like it did earlier when I saw her here with her fancy equipment and complete disregard for what she touched. She must be stopped, the one with glasses and multi-coloured hair and sense of entitlement.

For a moment or two I squeeze my eyes shut and count backwards from fifty until my chest stops hurting.

When I open them, I see a tiny light near the church. A tiny red light over the doors.

14

'I like our mini hub,' Meg said. 'Almost like home but smaller.'

Liz agreed. Computers and screens took every inch of two desks. The whiteboard leaned against a wall, balanced on the back of a chair, a packet of markers ready to use. And the four of them sat in a circle eating from the selection of food spread across a coffee table. Pete had gone over to the pub's liquor shop and collected two six-packs of beer and two bottles of wine, which joined the takeaway containers, mix of plates and glasses.

'There's a few things I've run through the BearCat's printer which I'll show you once I stuff my face for a bit.' Meg busily piled a few spoonfuls from each container into a bowl. 'I keep thinking about the grave. You know I'm practical but somehow it felt a bit... well like I was encroaching.'

'We had to drill some soil out though.' Pete was sitting back on his chair and hadn't reached for a plate yet. 'And we didn't get anywhere near a standard coffin depth.'

'I know, I know.' Bowl filled, Meg picked up a fork and

napkin. 'Finding out who is actually in the grave seems important.'

As they ate, talk turned to the new leader and the sister team members. Liz said little, more interested in listening. And eating, if she was honest. Thai twice in a row was perfectly fine and delicious and her appetite was unusually high. She'd gone for a run this morning at dawn, keeping to her usual routine from home but instead of working her way through Docklands and along the Yarra River, she'd pounded firm red dirt for a few kilometres out of town and back, stopping to watch the sun rise.

'He's friendly, our new boss. I have to give him that,' Meg said. 'Told me he has no real experience with my kind of work but wants to learn enough to understand the basics.'

'Meggie, nobody understands what you do,' Pete grinned. 'You could tell him you're conjuring spirits from the dead and Felix would be none the wiser.'

Everyone laughed and Liz finally began to relax.

They cleared away the remains of their meal as Meg collected her printouts, handing them around.

The top sheet was gibberish to Liz. Numbers. Symbols. Notations.

'Jeff has some early results from the angel pendant.'

Meg approached the whiteboard and chose a black marker.

'There's more to come, but for now he has provided some of the makeup of the materials in the pendant and the chain, as well as soil samples you collected around it. Isn't it interesting?'

She sounded so enthusiastic.

'Um... English, please?' Pete asked.

'Sure. The piece is made from high content pot silver, which is basically part silver and lots of mixed metals including brass and pewter, in this case. The chain is different being sterling silver. There was trace located in a couple of links and around the break in the clasp.'

'Human origin?'

'Yes. And inside the pendant is a—'

'Inside?'

'Yes, Pete. Although not standard for the unique shape, the back opens and there's the remains of a photograph. And a minute inscription which he hasn't yet been able to read. And more trace.'

Everyone sat forward.

'I have your interest! But don't get too excited yet. Jeff has a lot of work ahead because not only was it old and water damaged, but the images are really dark and small. I can say it appears to be a photograph of a woman and two children.'

'This is positive,' Liz said. 'Any indication the jewellery might be locally crafted?'

'Likely to be Australian made. Jeff says there's enough common compounds to fit, but warns that until he has more results, nothing is conclusive. He's waiting on the rest of the organic information, not only the human trace but soil and plants and so on. Anything which has come into contact and might be preserved.'

'Even after being buried for... well, however long?' Pete looked sceptical.

Meg levelled a gaze at him. 'By now you should know how clever Jeff is. Please turn to the next sheet of paper everyone.'

'You sound like my old school teacher.'

'Pete, if you keep this up I'll make you write lines.'

He pretended to zip his lips, eyes full of humour.

'This one is a map of the church grounds with a layout of everything including the house and gates. There are two. The one we've driven through and another at the back.'

'Yes, Liz and I saw that. Not really a gate though. More an opening from wire being cut.'

Meg shook her head. 'It used to have a gate and was used as

access to the road behind and eventually the water. The other end of the path is almost opposite another one which winds down to what is an unusual geographical find for this area. Not an overflow from the Murray River but somehow connected to underground water as well as a catchment for rain, when it happens. Carver Basin.'

Making a note to get a date when the gate was removed, Liz nodded. That matched up with her findings earlier in the day.

'On the next page is a plan of the graveyard.' Meg turned to the whiteboard and attached a larger sheet of paper with a magnet. 'I am missing my table from the hub but once we move to a dedicated space, I'll at least be able to set up a projector. Now, as you can see, there's a total of thirty seven graves. I've got a list of thirty five names. The two which are not on record are next to each other and I'll let you all guess where.'

'Two?' Reuben peered at his sheet of paper. 'Trying to remember what the other one was like. A tall headstone, I think.'

'Full marks, buddy. There's a four-foot high headstone which has no inscription. The church records which I've accessed don't even acknowledge its existence.'

'And the one where bodies keep appearing?' Pete had found his voice. 'There's nothing about its resident?'

'Pete...'

'Sorry, Liz. Nothing about the person buried in that grave?'

'Nope, not a whisper. I've put a request into a number of agencies including our own people because someone has to know something.' Meg pointed to one, then the other. 'I believe there's a connection but have no theories or evidence yet. Tomorrow I want to get samples from the other grave. And if all else fails...'

She looked at Liz.

'Exhumation?'

Except how do we get permission when we don't know who is buried?

'Maybe a last resort. We can fit a camera to one of the drones which might show whether there are even any human remains in them first.' Meg spoke as she wrote on the board. 'I've confirmed the land is still owned by the Catholic Church. I'm working with someone I know who is better than I at dealing with religion and has contacts I could never hope for. She'll provide a report once she's done her thing.' She stopped writing and tapped the end of the marker on the whiteboard. 'Erik Piper. He doesn't own his house. Rents it from the church and has lived there for ten years. I'm running a background check on him right now, along with Gordon Brain.'

Liz opened her notes. 'Piper is a poet according to Kath Connor. Unsure if that is a career or an interest. He is English. Well-spoken and probably well educated.'

'He's hiding something.' Reuben began filling up the glasses of those who'd chosen wine, which was everyone other than Pete. 'There's a defensiveness about him. And from reading the report from the local officer, he was more worried or upset about his routine being interrupted than the death of a person, virtually in his front garden.'

'Well we should have more information by morning. Any questions for me?' Meg set down the marker.

Liz joined Meg at the whiteboard. 'Grab a drink and a seat. You've been on your feet for hours.'

She waited for Meg to pick up a glass as she settled onto her chair, then Liz chose a blue marker.

'Tonight I'd like everyone to rest and we can talk more in the morning. First though I just want to jot down what you all see as our highest priorities and if you don't mind, I'll start.' Liz began at the very top of the board. 'I want to see photographs from the three crime scenes.' She turned back to look at the team. 'Kath has put in a request for all the files.'

'And so have I. They should be catalogued and available to me digitally but alas, no.' Meg shook her head. 'My program picked up the similarities between those old cases and this new one based purely on a couple of written reports and some newspaper articles, so I can't even help with images.'

'And we're still waiting for approval to view the body,' Reuben added.

Liz returned to writing the dot-point list.

'We need to know about the priest.'

Everyone looked at Pete.

'He was there for both earlier murders. He was ultimately responsible for the graveyard including the anonymous graves. At the very least, he is a witness. And perhaps he has information which matters now.'

Reuben reached across and patted Pete's back. 'Always knew there was a reason you're the favourite.'

'Hang on, there are no favourites!'

But the laughter from the other three drowned out Liz's protest and she found herself joining in.

While Liz and Meg were happy to stay in Meg's room and talk, Pete was restless. He tapped on Reuben's door.

'Unlocked.'

Pushing it open, he stuck his head in. 'Sure that's a good move?'

Reuben was closing his empty bag.

'I was expecting you.'

Me? Or Liz?

'Thought I'd take a walk. Mingle with the late-night locals.'

'Happy to join. Come in while I change.' He stepped into the bathroom.

Pete closed the door and perched on the end of the bed. Both chairs from the room were in Meg's. Unlike his own room which had clothes and shoes everywhere, Reuben's was tidy. There was a laptop bag on the floor but little else visible.

Peals of laughter made it through the wall from the room next door. Meg's.

'Sounds like they're catching up.'

Reuben reappeared wearing jeans. He slid his arms into a polo top and pulled it over abs which even Pete had to admire.

'Probably into the second bottle of wine.' Collecting his wallet, phone, and keys, Reuben wandered to the door. 'You coming?'

They headed toward the main street of the town, passing a handful of homes along the quiet road.

'Wouldn't think this was the way to the next town.' Pete gestured behind them. 'Reckon I've seen a dozen cars in the last few hours. Kinda nice, for a change.'

'Not missing your front-row seat on inner suburban life?'

'Nah. Country boy at heart. Don't get me wrong. I like where I live but would swap it in a heartbeat for a view of the sea or a wide expanse of rural landscape. Only downside here is the lack of waves.'

'Hm. I can almost visualise you driving a dusty patrol ute as you cover a thousand square kilometres on your own,' Reuben teased. 'Nobody to annoy and few to arrest. Only wheat and sheep to talk to. Oh, and the birds and snakes. Then on your downtime you'd have your jet ski speeding around the basin, stirring up the crocs and farmers.'

'No crocs here, mate.'

'I know.'

'But there are emus. I think. I could challenge them to a race in my patrol ute.'

The conversation touched the part of Pete he kept to himself, but in a chilled way. Reuben was easy to hang out with. As close to being a best friend – other than Liz – he'd had in years. Too long working undercover with drug lords and betting racketeers for company. Too much passed him by which others took for granted. Friendships. Job security. A family. Love.

'Where shall we start?'

They turned a corner.

Pete shelved his thoughts. 'Much as I want to check out the wine bar, I'm thinking the pub for tonight. More people. Easier for us to be in the background.'

They passed a dozen darkened shopfronts and one lit from within. Both stopped.

'Interesting,' Reuben said. 'Looks like a combination of old wares, books, and handmade goods.'

There was no sign of movement inside, just products with lights over the top. Pete took a few photos then stepped onto the road and took another image, this time of the whole building. 'Might be worth a chat about local jewellery makers.'

The pub was noisy from a loud football game being shown on a screen on one wall, smelled of beer and smoke, and had a dozen or so patrons. The bartender looked barely old enough to drink, let alone serve at a public hotel. He dropped coasters on the counter in front of them.

'What'll ya have, gents?'

Pete ordered beers for them both and handed over cash. A handful of coins came back with the glasses.

'Quiet night or about normal?' Reuben asked the bartender.

'Was busy but had a brawl in here earlier about the footie

game and the copper came and sent some of them home to sober up. Just the regular late-nighters here now. And you two.'

'I'm Pete and this is Reuben. You run the place?'

With a roll of his eyes, the bartender began collecting empty glasses. 'Not even if I wanted to. Dad's the publican and he'll only leave if someone wheels him out. Pop's worse. Still lives here at the pub after Dad wrested it away yonks ago.'

Exactly the kind of people I want to talk with. Old timers.

The bartender went to serve someone.

The beer was icy cold and hit the spot. Reuben only sipped at his, eyes roaming the public bar. Apart from a couple of men perched on stools to watch the game, the patrons were in pairs or small groups. Four at one table. Three standing around a tall one. Three couples. And in a corner, slumped in an oversized armchair, a man stared at Pete through bright eyes. He must have been eighty and wore a checked shirt and smart pants. His feet were bare. He nodded as if encouraging a conversation.

'Fancy a chat, mate?' Pete nudged Reuben, who looked in the same direction.

'Think I do.'

15

'Sit. Sit.'

The old man waved at empty chairs around a table and Reuben obediently collected two.

Pete extended a hand. 'Pete. And this is Reuben.'

'Albie Walsh. Publican.'

Settling close enough to hear over the television but not to intrude on personal space, Pete leaned a bit forward.

'So that's your grandson tending bar?'

'Matthew's a good boy. Did he tell you he's going to be a doctor? Back from Adelaide between semesters. Does his training and all that, then comes home and gives his dad a hand.'

'Must make you proud.'

'Very proud. First of our family to go to a university but I miss him when he's there. Me and his dad.'

This was good. Albie was on the ball. Keen to talk. Probably a bit lonely. It was just a case of keeping things nice. Not pushing.

The bartender – Matthew – appeared, sweeping up an

empty glass on the table beside the armchair. 'Hey, Pop, it's almost ten.'

'I'd like another, young man. One of those cocktails you make so well.'

'Bit late, isn't it?'

'Maybe my new friends would like one as well. What do you say?' Those bright eyes were amused as they glanced at Reuben then Pete. 'Matthew can make anything.'

'Nah, but thanks. The beer is good.'

Reuben nodded in agreement.

'Fine. But don't tell Dad.' Matthew stalked away, grabbing glasses off tables as he went.

Albie chuckled. *Don't tell Dad.* One of these days he'll wise up and work out I still own the joint and Colin works for me.'

Reuben had pulled out his phone and was discreetly tapping. Probably keeping track of names and observations.

'Been in the family a while, Albie?' Pete asked. 'Terrific little place you have.'

'It does well enough. Unlike the bigger towns, we have no competition. My father built the hotel when he was a young man. Him and my uncle. Partnership didn't last past a few years and when my parents passed on, it was in the will to me.' Albie shrugged. 'Not that I look it now but once I was a promising boxer. Just not good enough to make a proper living and maybe my parents knew it, so I moved home and learned the ropes.' He sighed. 'Miss being behind the bar but my bones aren't what they once were.'

Albie glanced at his feet and wriggled his toes.

'You'd have seen a lot over the years,' Pete said. 'Probably know everyone who ever lived here.'

The man's toes seemed more interesting to him so Pete sat back and took a few sips from his glass. Reuben was in observation mode, his eyes flicking around the pub, resting on faces, moving on. Behind the relaxed expression he'd no doubt be risk assessing. The ex-intelligence officer might not say a lot but would move quickly if there was the need which made him a valuable person to be with in a strange town. One with a recent murder.

Matthew returned with a creamy orange concoction, umbrella and glace cherries precariously on the rim.

'Here, Pops.' He placed it on the side table and looked at Pete. 'More beers or anything?'

A man could get comfortable in here, other than the loud television. He glanced at it and Matthew immediately pulled a remote from a pocket and turned it down.

'Thanks, mate. We're right though.'

'Oh, Pop. Where are your shoes?' Matthew's voice was resigned. 'Point me in the right direction?'

Albie raised his head, a bit puzzled. 'Told you earlier I'd left them in my room. Prefer bare feet on the carpet.'

'Except you're breaking your own rules about not allowing anyone in without proper footwear. No bare feet, no thongs, no crocs.'

'Does the sign really say no crocs? I need to fix that. Most comfortable shoes ever.' Albie noticed the drink and reached for it. 'You've got customers, Mattie.'

Matthew hurried off and Albie tested the drink, wrinkling his nose. 'Reckon he left out half the alcohol. And yes, I have seen a lot and pretty much know everyone in town. In the region.'

So you were listening. I bet not much gets past you.

'Heard the population's not what it used to be.'

'Heard right. We're good here. Pubs survive, mostly. Bit of a worry for the youngsters growing up with nothing to do or inherit. Few farms still battling on. Us oldies won't leave but we're seeing our grandkids go.'

Reuben got to his feet, beer in hand, and peered at a series of framed photographs on the wall near Albie.

'See mine there? Regional title at just sixteen years of age.' Albie waved a hand in the air. 'Take a look, Phil.'

Holding his tongue rather than correct the older man, Pete obeyed. The photograph was black and white and a bit grainy but good enough to identify a very young and somewhat scrawny Albie in a boxing ring.

'Bet you were quick.'

'Sure was. Fast but never quite strong enough. Not when some of them were doping up. I should have been around the previous century, not the middle of last one. On top of that my heart turned out not to be up to the stress of it all. Guess it kept me from conscription so I could keep the soul of this town operating.'

The photographs covered decades, mostly taken inside the pub and a few outside.

Something stood out to Pete.

'In the really old pics, mate? First Nations bartenders weren't common back then.'

If ever. Let alone allowed into the public bar.

With a grunt, Albie pushed himself to his feet. 'See that one? My dad is the man on the left. Migrated to Australia from Ireland. Fell in love with a local girl when he was working up here on a station. He was the kindest man you'd care to meet and wouldn't tolerate the nonsense about the real owners of this land being anything other than his equal. Broke the law sometimes to keep the pub a place where everyone belonged. Even the cops. Everyone is welcome.'

Reuben smiled at Albie. 'Good man indeed. And you've followed suit.'

'Tried. Failed too many times.' Albie's hand went to the back of the armchair to support himself but he lifted his chin as he stared at Pete. 'Reckon you'll be wanting to talk to me about the killings.'

Dawn was taking its time appearing thanks to a low cover of cloud. The air was already steamy and storms were predicted in the afternoon.

Running in shorts and crop top, Liz followed the same route as yesterday. Along the straight road from the motel, all the way to Brown Horse Road. There, she stopped for a moment to drink from the bottle in the running bag around her waist. Sweat trickled between her shoulder-blades and she was half-tempted to turn back. Last night, after the men had gone to the town, she and Meg had had a good attempt at downing the second bottle of wine before being distracted with a phone call. She didn't have a headache but was already dehydrated and running was only making it worse.

Trouble was, it kept the demons at bay.

Another runner approached through the gloom. Reuben. He pulled up near her, grinning as he reached for his own bottle.

'How far did you go?' Liz gazed in the direction he'd come from, only able to make out the shapes of trees and the distant lights on a house.

He checked his watch. 'I've run just under eight k. Almost went up this side road but thought I'd keep to the main drag for my first outing. Are you going back to the motel?'

'I am.'

They fell into a walk, finishing their water as the sun finally made a feeble appearance.

'Spoke to Candace last night,' Liz said. 'She wants to come up.'

'Why?'

'I think she's planning ahead for when we get more crime scene photos, particularly the old ones. She says she's got a theory based on the couple she's seen and descriptions. Our upcoming interview with Piper interests her. And she said you'd sent through a brief about someone you met last night.' Liz glanced at Reuben. 'She copied it to me. Albie Walsh.'

He nodded. 'Interesting man. He's agreed to talk to us as long as Kath Connor is present and as long as he doesn't have to go to the station.'

'We can make that happen. How on earth did you come across him? Surely if he's in his eighties he's not tending bar?' The brief had been... brief. An outline of a conversation. A couple of old photographs in frames. The unsolicited offer of information.

'Grandson was bartending. Matthew. Old family pub going back to the early part of last century. You need to see it, Liz. There's a history which nobody notices these days. And these are good people. Those two, because I haven't met Albie's son, who is the current publican.'

'Not there last night?'

'Apparently not. Albie claims he still owns the pub and Colin works for him.'

'And the grandson?'

'Back between semesters from Adelaide where he's doing a medical degree.'

'Wonder when he came back?'

Reuben shot her a look, eyebrows raised. 'He doesn't feel like a killer, Liz.'

'And you're probably right. But what if Albie was involved in the first couple of deaths? He was a boxer, yes? Or his son...

Colin? And then it becomes generational. A rite of passage even.'

Liz enjoyed theories but she rarely shared them until they had legs. Well, that wasn't entirely true because she'd had many a brainstorming session with her old mentor, Vince Carter. He always took her seriously. Trusted her instincts. Encouraged her to dig beneath the obvious and then take a step back to revisit the facts.

I could use Vince right now.

'There's merit to that.'

'There is? I mean, sure is.' She smiled. 'I'm really just talking aloud.'

'If we don't hypothesise, we get caught up with only what is cold, hard evidence and policing is more than that. It's like here.' Reuben slowly gestured around them. 'We knew the trees were there but in darkness, or half-light, they might present as something else. Or nothing else. Logic works alongside our intuition and experience.'

The longer she worked with Reuben, the more Liz discovered. He was something of an enigma. An ex-Intelligence officer who could handle almost every kind of weapon and had a special interest in drones and surveillance. Seriously good in close combat and as tactical as they came. Yet he was vegan. A man who cared deeply for the world and other humans and would always go the extra mile for someone who needed it. She'd yet to come across anyone – other than bad guys – who didn't warm to him.

'And will she?'

'Will she what?'

His half-smile told Liz she'd missed something.

'Candace. Will she be coming here?'

'Let's get through the morning first. If she does, I'd like to make the trip worthwhile and ensure any new samples from Meg go back in the helicopter.'

The motel was in sight, the BearCat and hire car the only vehicles in front of the rooms.

'Is that someone in the trees? Across in the park area?' Reuben stared in that direction. 'Can't see any cars but thought that someone—'

'A man. Looks like Gordy.'

It was Gordy, who walked quickly past the toilet block out of the treed area.

They met him as he reached their side of the road. He raised a hand, like he'd raised his beer the previous evening. Around his neck was a camera strap attached to a decent camera with a large lens.

'Early to be out and you two don't like you've been photographing rare birds,' he said, sizing up Reuben. 'I'm Gordon Brain. Own the motel.'

Reuben shook his hand. 'Detective Reuben Barnes'

'I'm glad to run into you, mate,' Liz said. 'Hoping to make a time for a quick chat. Nothing formal but I'd value your take on recent events.'

Gordy nodded but one hand began playing with the strap around his neck. 'Yeah, sure. I can do early. Like, in an hour if you want. Before I open the office.'

'Perfect.'

'Um, yeah just tap on the office door and we can have a coffee in the back room. Got a machine.'

Liz grinned. 'Now that sounds good. We'll be there.'

They parted ways and at Liz's door, Reuben looked over her shoulder. 'He's watching us.'

'You sure?'

'Surveillance is my middle name.'

'What *is* your middle name?'

'You've not seen my personnel file?'

'Probably. Let me guess. Bruce.'

'Nope, although I have an uncle called Bruce.'

'Quentin.'

'Reuben Quentin Barnes? Regal, but no.'

'Is he still watching?'

Reuben's eyes barely flickered away from her face. 'He's gone.'

'Bob.'

'Sorry, what?'

'Reuben Bob Barnes' How she kept herself from laughing was a mystery.

'Sure. Bob is my middle name.'

'Suits you.'

'Thanks. I'm going to have a shower.'

Liz waited until he'd gone to his own door to put the key in hers. They turned them at the same time. Inside she realised she was smiling. '*Bob*. Now I have to check your file.'

16

'Gordon Brain has no police record and very little other information to be found.' Meg handed Liz a single sheet of paper. 'Born in Tasmania in 1966. No firearms registered to him. No next of kin. No Medicare card. Purchased the motel about fifteen years ago from a Hector Swift. No sign of a bank loan for it. Are you taking Reuben to speak with Gordy or could I borrow him for an hour?'

'I can take Pete. What are you doing?'

They were in Meg's room which was still set up from the previous night. She pointed at the whiteboard. 'I want to update that and talk to Reuben about setting some more cameras around the church. We got a hit last night.'

'From the cameras?'

Meg answered by opening a tab to a media player. 'I'll put the times and comments on the app shortly and the whiteboard. It is too distant to identify the person but there's someone at that grave.' She pressed play.

At first Liz couldn't work out what she was looking at. It

seemed like all was quiet. But a movement close to the ground, repeating for a while, eventually became the shape of a human. They appeared to be on their knees.

'I think they're smoothing the surface,' Meg said. 'We left it roughed up and full of holes. I want to get back out there.'

'Yes, we'll all go after I speak with Gordy. You can't zoom in?'

The person had gone under the police tape and straightened and was looking at the church.

'Do you think they saw the camera?'

'So many questions. I zoomed in and yes. See how quickly they turn now? And then into the darkness they go and no more human to view.' Meg turned to look up at Liz. 'This is why I need to borrow Reuben. Those cameras were only there to watch the church in case your alleged squatter returned, not so much the graveyard.'

'There's no alleged. I saw someone try to enter the church then run away and we found evidence of squatting.'

'Ah, but nothing to connect the two.'

'Yet.' Liz grinned. 'We just need to find whoever ran off. But the person I saw was like a skinny teenager and our graveside visitor looks larger. Anything for me on Erik Piper?'

'Oh there's more on him than Mr Brain. Nothing printed yet but I'll have a little dossier for you before you visit him. I've traced him back to his arrival in Australia in 2004 and he's got all the right paperwork.'

'Can I add something else to your workload?'

Meg held up her hand in a 'stop' fashion. 'Not a word. Is it Albie Walsh?'

'Mmm... mm... mmm.'

'Okay, fine, speak now.'

'Albie, Colin, and Matthew Walsh. Something isn't sitting right.'

'Ah, the world-famous Liz instincts have kicked in. Leave it with me. Actually, you'd better skedaddle if you want to find Pete and do that interview.'

'I can ask some hard questions, boss. Practice my interrogation skills.'

'You can sit quietly and observe,' Liz said. 'If you have a proper question then go right ahead.'

'You really are turning into the fun-police.'

Am I? Maybe I need to lighten up.

'Sorry.'

Pete gave her a weird look. 'I was messing around, so don't say sorry.'

'I don't mean to come over as... well, bossy.'

'You are the boss.'

'Not really. Felix is the boss. Ben was the boss. And Candace is technically in charge if they aren't around.'

They were only a few metres from the office and Pete stopped, face serious. 'Lizzie, the team sees you as our leader. Felix is admin as much as anything. Candace steps in by duty but she's best used in the investigations. You are in active service and have the respect of every member of Operation Nobody. There's nothing we won't do if you ask.'

Tightness radiated across her chest as she fought the prickling sensation behind her eyes. The fight inside – a struggle accepting she'd done the best she could at the mansion that night while blaming herself for the death of a good police officer – was sometimes overwhelming. Logic told her she'd been in an impossible situation which was not of her making and completely outside anyone's expectations. The deep, roiling emotions in her gut said otherwise despite counselling and being cleared of wrongdoing. It was a conflict like no other in her life.

'Thank you, Pete. I'm admitting now, but only to you, that I'm nervous about how the new members of the team will feel. There's a lot at stake to make it work.'

'Agree. We're all a bit nervous but I trust Ben Rossi to have worked with Fletcher to recruit the best people possible. Short of having another mole, I think we're fine and there's nothing to indicate anyone is left of your father's nasty little group.'

That part was all true. Over the past few weeks there'd been updates about more arrests both in Australia and Europe as the net closed in on the criminals behind assassinations, art fraud, and kidnapping thanks to the work initially done by Operation Nobody and then other major agencies. It was a relief knowing the vile organisation was all but gone.

'You two coming in? Coffee is about ready.'

Gordy's head was stuck out of the office doorway and the word coffee was enough to get Liz's moving again.

They followed him into the office, where all the lights were off and the curtains drawn.

'Lock the door, please.' He went through to the room behind the counter. 'Come in and grab a seat.'

The back room was larger than Liz had expected with a kitchenette, multiple armchairs, and a small pool table. A sliding door led to a small, enclosed yard with pots filled with different flowering bushes and a birdbath.

'Black? Lattes? Can do pretty much anything with this beauty.' Gordy seemed genuinely proud of a coffee machine big enough for a small café. 'I got milk, oat milk, and soy milk.'

'Just black for me, thanks,' Liz said.

'Cappuccino? Moo milk?' Pete sounded hopeful.

'Coming right up.'

While Gordy attended to his task, they chose seats which

more or less faced what had to be the other man's regular choice going by an upturned, open book on one arm and a pair of slippers at its side. His feet were bare and he wore shorts and a tank top, exposing sun-damaged, crepey skin on both arms and legs. Perhaps he was a bit older than Liz first thought.

The coffee was good and Liz was happy to take a few sips while Pete introduced himself and the men chatted about the weather for a minute or two.

'You want to talk to me?' He suddenly looked at Liz. 'This isn't official?'

'Just a chat. Figured you probably see and hear a lot of what goes on around here.'

He chuckled. 'I do at that. Right down to who is bonking who and shouldn't be but you see, they trust me when they rent a room for a few hours. Most women are good to go just 'cos they get to have an afternoon with cheap wine and the attention of some fella they like at the time.'

'When I came in to ask directions to the church, you wanted to know if I was here to investigate what you called the murders.'

'Did I? Odd thing to say.' He stared at his coffee then drank some and wiped a hand across his lips. 'Remember asking if you were a cop.'

'You did that as well. Must have been a shock when news broke about the body in the graveyard?'

'Lots of bodies in the graveyard. Just kidding. Saw Kath go flying past with her sirens on. Later there were more cop cars. Eventually found out about some poor person who'd died. Natural causes, I heard.'

'Where did you hear that?' Pete asked.

'Dunno. Someone at the wine bar or pub. Have they worked out who the dead dude is?'

'Still under investigation. You hadn't seen anyone fitting his description?'

'What, dead on top of a grave? That's all I know.'

The slightly humorous deflections were interesting. Liz tried another approach. 'Going back to the other day, you mentioned multiple murders. Did you know the victims from the 80s?'

Something passed across his face but was gone before Liz could identify it.

'You're not trying to trick me, lady detective? For one thing I wasn't even in the area back then. Only bought the motel fifteen years back. Other thing is I heard the others were never named.'

Oh, you are either very clever or genuinely innocent.

'I'm pretty straightforward, Gordy. If you've only lived here for a few years then of course you wouldn't have any first-hand knowledge of the previous deaths... I'd assumed you were a local man. The thing is that my team and I are on the back foot here. There's not a great deal of information available so we're working off some old reports and trying to piece together a picture by talking to long-time residents.'

Liz returned to her coffee, eyes on Gordy. His forehead creased while he finished his own drink and then balanced the cup on the arm of the chair.

'Bad for business. Dead bodies and nobody knowing nothing. You've seen how empty the motel was so I'm mighty glad to have you and your people here. Other businesses probably feel the same but most people won't talk much to strangers. They'll be friendly and take your money but good luck getting anyone to share what they know. If anything.'

'We won't take any more of your time but I have to say I enjoyed your coffee.' Liz stood and Pete copied. 'We'll wash our cups and be on our way.'

'Nah, just put them on the sink. I have to open soon so just leave the door unlocked.'

He picked up his paperback and settled back in his armchair.

17

The grave looked like someone had taken to it with a broom. All the drilling holes were filled and fresh dirt from the sides now mingled with the sparse grass.

I am sorry, whoever you are. It isn't nice to disturb where you rest.

More than anything, Meg wanted to discover who was buried here. Or rule out a body. She'd come across crimes where graves were empty or else had the wrong person in a coffin and this case was so bizarre, nothing would surprise her.

Reuben was going to send a drone up with a camera which should be able to see through a couple of metres of dirt. The outcome would dictate their next steps. But first he had the meeting with the poet and he'd come prepared. Pete had helped with Erik Piper's demand of morning tea, disappearing to the café in town and returning with a box of fresh scones complete with tubs of cream and strawberry jam. After all, Piper *was* English.

Liz and Reuben disappeared past the church and Meg got back to work.

'What do you need me to do?' Pete asked.

'I want to look at the next grave now I've taken new samples from this one to see if I can find whoever was here last night.'

'So more drilling?'

'Yes, but first let's look at the headstone. We might move the table closer.'

Between them, Meg and Pete carried her table the few metres to beside the grave in question. She'd already set up a laptop on it and began adding other equipment. Beneath the table she placed a case which kept its contents at a controlled temperature and humidity to preserve stored samples.

'Have you come up with a name yet for your magic trace machine?' Pete gestured to a device which Meg was unpacking. 'Is there anything it can't do?'

She smiled to herself. This little invention was proving invaluable and at some point she knew she should patent it or whatever people did to protect something they'd made. 'No name yet. And it doesn't make coffee, which is a bit disappointing.'

What it did do was look at a surface and analyse layers, including blood and other trace and fingerprints. Meg was still testing its limitations and making adjustments to its software and hardware. Her wish was to develop it into a device police could readily carry to assist with crime scenes. While it would not replace the other forensics testing, if it could shortcut the process of actually finding trace to test, then it would speed up an investigation, often in the most critical first few hours after a crime. This went beyond a blue light.

'No signal.' Pete was holding his phone above his head, squinting at it.

'You know that won't help?'

'Maybe I should climb the steeple.'

They both turned to look at the church.

'Tall enough to be a phone tower, almost. I might need to talk to Jeff while I work so can you dig up a satellite phone please?'

'Anything else from the BearCat?'

'Bottled water thanks. And the shelter for over the grave. Too hot and sticky to be in the sun any more than necessary.'

While Pete was gone, Meg took a closer look at the headstone.

It was about four feet tall, rounded on top and firmly entrenched in the hard ground. No inscription was obvious... as with the grave where the body had been placed. That on its own was enough to be of interest because when they'd arrived an hour ago, she'd taken a quick walk around the graveyard. Every other headstone was clearly inscribed.

Meg went back to her table as Pete returned.

'One satellite phone, fully charged,' he announced. 'One shade tent. One esky with bottled water and snacks.'

'Snacks?'

'Of course. Healthy stuff. With lots of sugar for energy.' He grinned.

'And you know that's not how it works.'

'But they taste good.'

'You are incorrigible.'

'I know.'

'Shall we erect the cover first because I want your opinion on the headstone.'

'Have it up in a jiffy and my opinion shall follow swiftly.'

Great.

Although Liz was confident in her ability to run successful interviews, she was happy to have Reuben with her for this one.

Something about the poet was unsettling and she couldn't put her finger on it yet. It might be as simple as Erik Piper's strange first impression the other day, watching her from the church and then vanishing into the dusk.

'Still three minutes until ten.'

Reuben carried morning tea in its white cardboard box, courtesy of Pete. Liz had a feeling her old partner had used the excuse to visit Ruby again.

'We'll take a breath then.'

They were twenty metres from the old priests' residence.

'Not really what I expected.' Liz gestured to the small patch of vivid green lawn surrounding a low stone building. There was a small pond overlooked by one wicker chair beneath a tree. 'Are those angel statues?'

'Let's wander to the front door while we look.'

Around the pond were half a dozen small statues, perhaps half a metre tall, made from grey stone. They were too far away to make out the details but each had wings... some outstretched and others cocooning the figures.

The front door was solid timber, so faded it almost matched the mix of stone constructing the house. There was no welcome mat but also no spider webs or signs of neglect.

'Exactly ten, Liz.'

She tapped on the door and stepped back just as it was opened.

Were you standing on the other side waiting?

'Come inside, please.'

Erik Piper held the door open. He wore a different robe, this one in a deep burgundy fabric with a pattern sewn into the ends of each sleeve in white cotton.

'Shoes off, sir?' Reuben asked.

'I would appreciate that.'

Liz quickly removed hers, placing them neatly to one side

of the doorway then taking the box from Reuben so he could follow suit.

'We brought morning tea.' She summoned what she hoped was a friendly smile.

'Excellent. You'll see the kitchen as you walk through so please leave the box on the counter then continue to the sitting room.'

The floor was cool beneath her thin socks. Large slabs of flat stone were pieced together like a jigsaw. The house wasn't big, just a few rooms which were all too dark for her liking, and sparsely furnished. One door was closed and the kitchen was little more than one counter with a sink, a wood stove, and a small refrigerator.

Placing the box down, Liz did as directed and walked to the last room. The walls in here were lined with bookcases filled to capacity, yet neatly arranged. A two-seater sofa faced one armchair and a heavy timber coffee table was set between them.

Reuben was almost right behind, followed by Erik, who waved at the sofa. 'Sit. I'd open the curtains but the heat will get in.'

So they sat in semi-darkness with only a side lamp to offer some illumination. Faces were shadowed. Small noises echoed.

Like a séance.

'Thank you for seeing us, Mr Piper,' Liz said. 'The past few days must have been difficult... intrusive.'

She'd thought a lot about how to start and got an immediate hit. Her words resonated.

'Intrusive. Irritating. Ruining my peace and creative flow.'

Reuben gazed around. 'What a fabulous collection you have, sir. I have to admit I did a search on your work and have ordered three of your books.'

Erik straightened in his seat. 'You have? How delightful to hear.'

The men began a sincere and in-depth conversation about poetry and Liz internally shook her head.

Who are you?

Once again, Reuben surprised Liz.

The men spoke for a few minutes and at one point Erik even smiled, nodding his head vigorously.

'You will let me know once you've read my books? We could have a telephone conversation about them.'

'I would like that.' Reuben glanced at Liz then back at Erik. 'We'd really appreciate your take on recent events around the church and graveyard. I imagine it is usually a quiet place?'

Erik puffed his cheeks out, a finger tapping on the arm of his chair. Then he slowly exhaled. 'My routine has become undone of late. I'm accustomed to visitors to the graveyard at odd times but none are noisy. None do more than bring flowers or tend to a grave or sit for a while with their loved one. I know each of them by sight, most by name, and should our paths cross we do little more than nod and pass.'

'Would you mind if I write down their names and their usual routine? It would help to speak to any who might have seen something unusual,' Liz said.

'Record me if you want. Faster than writing it all down.'

Reuben quickly set up his phone to record.

There were only a dozen or so names but Erik was specific about their habits, or most of them, finishing with two who were irregular visitors but would stay longer than anyone else.

'I understand you were alone when you discovered the body. You mentioned to Kath that the last person you'd seen at the graveyard was Mrs Georgio on her regular visit.'

'Yes, the previous day, late in the afternoon. Once she left, the blanket fell again.'

'Blanket?'

Turning to Liz, Erik gave her look of pity. 'Of peace. Some might use the word bubble to describe the sense of comfortable isolation. The world is not a nice place, which I expect you understand all too well.'

His words and the manner they were delivered felt uncomfortable. As though he knew Liz's history or could see into her soul. She shook it off. Now wasn't the time to take personally the words of a witness.

'Would you mind talking us through finding the deceased?' Reuben still held his phone, perhaps more casually, but still recording. 'Are you an early riser?'

'I am a fitful sleeper and my best work is done between midnight and dawn. On this occasion I had slept from nine the previous night until four in the morning. I made a pot of tea and read for half an hour and then went out to the pond to watch dawn change the colours on the water. It is a serene place where I meditate.' He shuffled in his seat and his eyes dropped to his hands. 'Time stands still yet swirls around us.'

How many joints do you smoke a day?

The house didn't smell of marijuana but Liz remembered how the aroma lingered near the church seconds after Erik had vanished on the first night she was here. Did he only smoke during his meditation or otherwise when outside?

'What alerted you to go to the graveyard?'

Erik shrugged. 'I normally walk the perimeter of both the church and the graves twice a day. It was only when I reached the front of the church that something felt... off. There were no cars nor could I see anyone there for an early visit. By then it was broad daylight. I waited for a minute or two, then when I stepped away from the building I saw him.'

The last two words sounded shaky and Erik covered his mouth with a hand.

'Take your time.' Liz spoke softly.

But Erik dropped his hand. 'No. No, I can finish this. It took a moment for my eyes to work out what I was seeing because from behind and at a distance, the man might merely have been praying. He seemed to be kneeling with his head lowered. I'll show you.'

With a surprisingly fast motion, Erik left his chair and sank to the floor.

'His feet were tucked beneath his buttocks like so.' Pulling the fabric of his tunic tight, Erik rested his bottom on the back of his heels. 'And his head was down.' He dropped his head, almost to his chest.

'That is very specific.'

'I have a very specific mind, Detective Moorland. As I approached, the oddest thing occurred. What I thought was someone deep in prayer began to tilt forward and believing he might be ill, I hurried to offer assistance. I spoke to him and even touched his shoulder but then I noticed he wasn't breathing.'

'Do you recall the position of his body when you reached him?'

'You may take a photo of me if you wish. Here, I'll hold this while you do.'

Through her phone's camera view, he did appear to be in a position one might use to pray, particularly inside a church.

'Thank you.'

'Now, I'll demonstrate how he was once I got to him.'

With a couple of groans, Erik lowered his torso to the ground while keeping everything from the waist down in the same stance. His arms flopped to either side, hands flat on the ground and his face to one side. Liz took several photos from different angles.

'I've got them, thank you again.'

Reuben got up and offered a hand to Erik, who grasped it. Once back in his armchair, he wiped his brow.

'Should I get you some water, sir?'

'You are impeccably polite, young man. Erik is fine and I don't require anything right now. I do want to spend some time writing though, so perhaps you could ask the rest of your questions?'

Liz had so many she barely knew where to begin but if he was about to kick them out, then she had to think fast.

'We do appreciate your time and won't keep you long. Once you realised the man wasn't breathing, what did you do?'

'I considered CPR but his face had the look and colour of death and his hands were quite cold. There was no life to be saved. I phoned Kath to report what I'd found.'

Wording her question carefully, Liz gently prompted. 'What you've demonstrated to us is immensely helpful, Erik. I do have a question about his arms and hands... being to his sides with the palms down. That is how you recall them?'

'It is.'

'Between the time of ascertaining that the person was deceased and the time Kath arrived, were you in sight of the grave and body at all times?'

'No. I never said I was. My phone was in the house, so I had to return for it and I dialled Kath as I walked back.'

For a second, Liz's eyes met Reuben's and then she smiled at Erik.

'We won't keep you any longer. But if we have follow up questions, may we intrude again?'

'As long as you keep bringing me morning tea.'

18

Liz waited until the church was between them and Erik Piper before coming to a sudden stop and opening her phone to the photos she'd taken.

'Look at this one, Reuben. Hands facing down and away from the body. Not clasping each other beneath himself!'

'The killer was still present.'

'Killer or accomplice or some nutter who thought it funny to alter a crime scene.'

'Unless Erik is mistaken.'

'Or involved. For all we know there were multiple people responsible.'

They started walking again and Liz shoved the phone in a pocket. 'Would you follow up on the cold case records please? Just get someone at the hub to do it but stay on it for me.'

'Happy to.'

'I'll call Kath Connor shortly and get her out here. We need a lot more information than we're being fed.'

Meg and Pete were setting up a new police boundary but

this was around the next grave over. Reuben hurried to take over from Meg, who gestured for Liz to come around the back of the tall headstone.

'We found something. A lot of somethings.' Meg stared solemnly at Liz. 'What's wrong.'

'Tell me what you found.'

'No, tell me what the bush poet had to say that has got you riled up. I'm good at reading faces and yours is kinda angry.'

'More frustrated. He has been helpful explaining how he found the deceased but between doing so and returning from collecting his phone to call the police, it appears the body was tampered with. We'll debrief soon.'

Meg looked around, her eyes on the distant tree line and then on the church. 'Something is wrong here. Really wrong, Liz.'

I feel that too. There's a ritual element and I need Candace here.

As though nothing had occurred, Meg pointed to the back of the headstone. 'We found trace.'

'What?'

'What did we find or what-the-heck?'

'Both.'

'Both is right. We moved over here as having a grave with no named occupant is a red flag. Now, it may be as simple as a burial without actual approval from the Catholic Church but agreed upon by a resident priest. Way out here there might be more leniency than a city church. If the priest was asked to bury someone not Catholic, or who'd broken a rule or whatever, pressure from the family or community might be enough. But they'd be under no obligation to do more than provide a resting place.'

'I believe there's only one other graveyard – actually I think it is considered a cemetery which is for non-denominational as well as some religious burials – but it only came into being in the mid-1970s.' Liz vaguely recalled it being on the other side of the town.

'Adding weight to my supposition. Main point being I wanted to take a look here. Just in case. I need Reuben to do his drone voodoo soon.'

Liz turned to where the men were almost finished pegging out tape. 'Reuben, leave that for Pete and get the drone up. Pete, help him once you're done.'

Meg's elbow poked Liz. 'I like it when you tell them what to do.'

Instead of laughing like she wanted to, Liz forced a serious face. 'Everyone needs a hobby.'

'And mine is the same as my day job. Find the evidence. Locate the bad guys. Prove it was them. Drink a lot.'

'Talk to me about the trace.'

'Blood splatter.' Meg squatted and used her hand-held device on the stone. 'I've taken soil samples as well as dozens from here. We absolutely need Jeff to get them pronto. What I'm seeing though isn't recent and it is too early to even hazard a guess other than more than a year. See this pattern... splatter almost at the top of the headstone then what might be drips? Some poor person was either shot or stabbed very close to the stone. I think shot.'

'Yet none of the bodies in our case showed signs of blood loss. At least from what we've learned so far.' Liz gazed at Reuben, who was walking toward the BearCat, phone against his ear. 'I asked him to get someone at the hub to chase up those cold case files.'

'We're being messed around with, aren't we? Files which don't appear. Even photographs which aren't forthcoming.'

'When I spoke with Sergeant Barnaby Hobson, he wasn't very accommodating. He did agree to give me access to everyone who came into contact with the body, and to the body itself as well as all forensic evidence collected.'

'Jeff called a few minutes ago about this very issue,' Meg said. 'He has a friend who has a friend who knows someone with a degree of authority up here concerning the coronial side of things. Jeff's made a request this person take a look at the body.'

'Okay, that's a positive step. If they consider the death suspicious then we'll get the body to Melbourne.'

'With finding the blood splatter here, I want to see if there's a trail.'

'Is that even possible? Between the elements and people's shoes and however many years it might have been here?'

'I don't know. And I'm now heading to the church steps.' Meg's face dropped. 'The blood and trace we found inside the building might not have anything to do with this except... I think it does. As far as we know, neither of the bodies found here last century were cut in any way.'

'So a fourth victim?'

A witness, killed to keep quiet? A ritual murder gone wrong? Or something completely unrelated?

'Go and do your thing, Meg. I'm going to make some calls while Reuben flies around.'

Kath Connor sounded strained during a brief phone call but promised to get to the graveyard as soon as she could. There were raised voices in the background and Liz quickly let her get back to whatever was happening.

She'd wandered from the graveyard and church and stopped in the shade of a gum. Reuben had his drone box open on the ground and was setting up the screen and controls he used. Last time she'd been around a drone was the night she'd killed her father. A drone had been shot down while Reuben desperately worked to find a shooter in the old mansion.

Pete was at the back of the BearCat, rummaging around. Meg had moved to the steps of the church.

Liz dialled Candace while checking the trunk of the tree was visually free of spider webs or other creatures which might bite. It looked okay so she leaned her back against it. It might not be touching earth, but the next best thing for now. The phone rang several times and just when Liz expected it to go to voicemail, Candace answered.

'Sorry, Liz. I was in the other office and needed a minute to find my phone.'

'All good. Should I ring back?'

'No. I'm just closing my door so we can talk.'

Since when do you close your office door?

Ben Rossi had always had an open-door policy, even back in his Missing Persons days. It flowed onto the hub and Candace – who had the only other office – followed his lead.

'I was going to call a bit later,' Candace began. 'There's been a few meetings this morning and a lot of hypothesising about this new case. If you haven't noticed, we're getting push-back from the powers-that-be in the region.'

'Oh, I noticed. With the team here, we're gathering information faster than we can sort through it but we're flying in the dark to a large degree.'

'What do you need from me? I know Jeff is doing a lot behind the scenes. Felix has requested a meeting with the board but that might take a day or two to happen.'

In the distance was a buzzing. A familiar sound which in the past was almost a comfort. Drones up, under experienced guidance, meant eyes on places those on the ground couldn't fathom. Liz's chest tightened and she closed her eyes. Last time... the smell of death. Of betrayal. Hamish's blood hot against her arms as she held him. Too late to save.

'Liz? Lizzie?'

'Yeah.'

Candace's tone change. Her voice softened. 'I can hear a drone.'

'Yeah.'

'Tell me three things you can see. Green things.'

They'd done this before. Ad nauseum. Liz opened her eyes.

'Leaves of the gum tree I'm under. A tuft of grass. Meg's top is bright green.'

'Tell me about the tree. Can you touch the bark?'

Liz's hand moved to the trunk. 'Yes. I'm leaning against it. The tree is old and solid and smells of eucalyptus.'

The drone hovered above the graveyard. The tightness in her chest eased as the panic faded. Grounding was a simple yet powerful tool. A way to hone in on the present and resist being dragged into the past.

'Thank you.'

'My pleasure. What do you need from the hub to help other than what is already going on?'

'I just interviewed Erik Piper, the person who found the body and lives in the old priest accommodation. He demonstrated how the body was positioned but there was a short time when it was unattended and it was moved. Assuming he is remembering correctly and being honest.'

'Moved how?'

Liz quickly explained what she knew from the local police and reports of the deceased with the account from the poet.

'I'll send you the photos I took of Erik.'

The drone appeared stationary, directly over the grave where the bodies had been found. Reuben was sitting on the ground as he preferred when flying it and Pete was working with Meg near the church steps.

'This has the feel of something ritualistic,' Candace said. 'Without an autopsy we don't know if the deceased died while kneeling or was moved after death but if Mr Piper is correct, then there was outside involvement in how the body was presented.'

'And there's more. Meg found blood splatter on the back of the next headstone over and is presently taking samples from the church steps.'

Candace drew in an audible breath.

'Meg needs a helicopter up here today, Candace. She'll have a lot of samples for Jeff.'

'I can arrange one.'

'And can you arrange to be on it?'

'Oh good grief, I thought you'd never ask. I've had a bag packed in case.'

Liz chuckled.

'No really, there's one here in a spare room. What time would you like the chopper?'

Pete moved the pop-up shelter to where Reuben sat, bringing much-appreciated shade. He never thought ahead about personal comfort. Too many years working in difficult terrain and that included the air-conditioned rooms of the country's worst-kept-secret Intelligence organisation.

'Thanks, mate.'

'Can't have you roasting. Anything I can help with?'

'Just taking a lot of GPR images right now. Once I move the drone across to the other site, getting some measurements on the ground would be useful.'

'Can do. Right for me to help Meg a bit longer?'

He glanced up at Pete. 'Go. I'm just hovering. Literally.'

'I'm the general dogsbody today. Shout if you need me.'

Pete was one of the hardest working cops Reuben had ever met. Most people didn't see that. He'd heard the detective called lazy and ineffective but nothing was further from the truth. Pete had a way of moving between jobs and multitasking effortlessly. He always had something going on. Always an angle. Like with the café. In just a day he'd built a rapport with one of the staff and the time would come when it would pay dividends.

'Going okay?'

Reuben had seen Liz jump when the drone elevated and he knew why. He'd had his own grim thoughts until getting the little bird up took his focus away from the past.

'Almost finished mapping this and like Meg, I'd like to come back after dark and run more tests.'

'We can do that. I've asked Candace to join us.'

'I think that's a good move, Liz. She'll see things we miss. And will be good in interviews.'

Reuben had everything he could get from the first grave and brought the drone back to land. With patchy internet here, he was relying on the on-board recording to provide a seamless stream of information stored on a tiny card which he'd now swap out for a fresh one.

'This is going to take about another hour, Liz. I think Meg's schedule looks similar.'

'And then we'll get some lunch and go over everything before Candace arrives.'

Liz looked strained and Reuben wanted to tell her everything was okay, except it wasn't. None of the team who'd been at the mansion that awful night were okay but Liz had borne the brunt of it. Sometimes, especially when he couldn't sleep at night, he'd go over the events dissecting what he might have done differently. And there was nothing.

All that mattered was the terrible criminal was dead and an insidious network of killers and thieves dismantled. Everything else would come back to together sooner or later. Operation Nobody counted on that.

19

There were rare times – and this was one of them – Meg wished she'd followed her other dream of becoming an archaeologist. Or an anthropologist. Even the fall back as a professional dancer held an unusual appeal... even if she'd never taken a dancing lesson in her life.

It wasn't the job. She loved her career and the interesting paths it took her down.

Nor was it the team, who she adored.

But this case was infuriating and her annoyance landed squarely on the people who should have made her work easier – the local police.

She was back in her room and had locked herself in, drawn the curtains, and sat cross-legged on her bed for a few minutes practicing deep breathing. Just for a while, the phone which was her lifeline was turned off.

Eyes closed, Meg did all the usual things to relax her brain but nothing worked. She needed information which appeared to be withheld by someone who either was incompetent or had a vested interest. It wasn't the fault of Kath Connor, who'd arrived at the graveyard as they'd been packing the vehicle. She'd had a conversation with Liz before being introduced to Meg and Reuben and was genuinely at a loss and being as badly treated as the team.

Why is it taking so long to find these files? And why aren't they available digitally?

Even if the cold cases had been boxed and put away, somebody had to know where.

With a sigh, Meg's eyes opened and she got to her feet. Her computers were all working hard searching for old news reports or any mention of the deaths here in the 1980s and there was little more she could do other than wait for a hit and to find out when the helicopter would arrive. All of the samples were tagged and ready for transport. Grabbing her phone and keys, and at the last minute shoving a sunhat on her head, Meg let herself out. If breathing wasn't working, then walking might.

Outside the heat was almost stifling. There was a storm heading in but not expected until evening, which was good for the team as the helicopter could land and leave without delay.

Meg gazed around. The BearCat wasn't here as Liz and Pete had gone to the local police station to talk with Kath. She had no idea where Reuben was but didn't really want company until she'd sorted out her thoughts. People relied on her to be level-headed and always have answers. It was tiring.

She crossed the road, drawn to the trees in the rest area.

They were an interesting mix of gums and some imported trees, creating a shady expanse over a small playground and benches for families to sit and eat. The toilet block proclaimed it included showers and there was a large tank against one of the walls.

She walked past all of that, following a narrow track into denser bushland. It was good to be away from people. Nobody was in the rest area, so short of running into a local, the place was hers. Here there were more trees, more bushes, and utter quiet. Not even birdsong nor rustling of branches. The air was still.

Meg stopped and took off her hat to wipe her forehead.

Behind her... or was it somewhere deeper in the undergrowth... a twig snapped.

Just some small animal. A rat. Possum? No, they're nocturnal.

Exactly how far had she walked?

She looked up. The sky was visible but only through the canopy above. And it was darker now. Not from cloud cover but the ecosystem of bushland.

'Okay. Might go back.'

Nothing scared her. Well, very little and it was usually tied up with poor results from a new model she'd written or making an online order after a few too many drinks.

How could this be scary? There were trees and bushes and pretty much nothing else.

Meg turned back.

She'd walked enough. She wasn't like Liz or Reuben who loved running. It seemed like a dreadful waste of time and energy although they seemed to like it. But there was a certain peace which came with being at one with nature.

A few metres on, there was another noise. Another *snap* but not like a twig or branch. It was immediately followed by a low and sinister growl and sounded human enough to make her want to laugh.

'Who is there?'

She didn't expect a response and didn't get one. If she'd been annoyed earlier, this nonsense only served to amplify it and hands on hips, she addressed the bushes.

'Just show yourself. What are you, ten?'

Another weird growling sound. She reached for her phone

and turned it on. What if she'd found some rare endangered species?

Or a teenager who needs a good talking to.

Her phone lit up and messages and notifications poured in. She quickly hit mute and began recording.

'I think you are nothing but a silly little kid trying to be grown up.'

There was something... footsteps moving away.

'Hang on, don't run off now.'

'Who on earth are you talking to?'

The phone flew out of Meg's hand as she jumped. Reuben scooped it up and handed it back.

'Not nice sneaking up on me. There's someone in the bushes making stupid growling noises.'

Reuben's hand shot to his holster. 'Where.'

'It'll just be some bored kid.'

'Meg, we're in a town with a recent alleged murder and a peppered history. You are alone in an isolated area with your phone turned off and no advice to your team members of your destination.'

'That sounds judgemental.'

'It isn't. Okay, it is, but what do I tell Liz if something happens to you and I was only in the next room over?'

The pained expression on his face was enough to make Meg take things down a notch. Independent and capable she might be, but he had a point. Several.

'I'd love some coffee. Something decent.'

A slow smile relaxed his face and Reuben nodded. 'Me too.'

'Shall we check out this café where Pete keeps disappearing to?'

. . .

Kath Connor carried two cups of coffee to the desk where Liz and Pete sat. 'I've asked again, which is the third time. Sergeant Hobson wasn't available to take my call, which isn't unusual so I spoke to Constable Joy Reed who's been at that station forever and knows everything.' She set the cups down and returned to collect her own. 'Joy should be running the place but reckons she's happy with her job.'

'What did she have to say?' Pete asked.

'She's careful about her words when she's working.' Kath finally sat opposite. 'Promised she'd follow up again about the cold case files as well as personally overseeing sending the DNA samples to your person in Melbourne.'

Maybe we need to talk to this constable.

Liz picked up her coffee and sipped. It was passable but not in the league of Gordy's or the café. What was it about police stations and coffee?

Pete hadn't touched his. 'If she's careful how she speaks at work, are you implying she's more... outspoken away from it?'

There was a rare smile from Kath. 'Joy visits my auntie a bit. They yabber on about anything and everything but once Auntie Dee settles down for a nap, Joy and I sometimes talk about work and stuff.' The smile was gone as quick as it came. 'Gonna trust you not to tell the sergeant what I have to say. Yeah?'

'We're not here to interfere with local hierarchy and are well aware some working relationships are more complex than others,' Liz said. 'As far as the majority of the department is concerned, we don't exist. And I'd love to know what you have to say, Kath. You've been nothing other than helpful and honest.'

'Well, I appreciate you saying it. I'm a bit frustrated because I like my job. Took a lot to go to academy and I still pinch myself I'm working in my own community. Know not to rock the boat but all this cat and mouse stuff is making our town look bad.'

'And you love your town.'

'Born here. Raised here. Only me and Auntie and my kid left of my family these days but that's enough.' Kath's expression portrayed her pride even more than her words.

'You're too young to remember the deaths in the 1980s,' Liz said. 'Did you hear stories or rumours growing up?'

Kath rolled her eyes. 'Oh, yes. At least, all us kids were taught to stay clear of the graveyard unless we were with an adult. And never be alone on the track to the basin. Best to be in small groups even in daylight.'

Pete leaned forward. 'Why that track? You mean the one through the gate of the boundary fence of the church grounds?'

'Nah. The one from the other road. Those two men's bodies were bad enough but it went back further to Janie Swift going missing back in 1971. Only a kid, maybe fourteen or fifteen. She used to cut through there and people say she must have been grabbed and probably drowned but nobody ever would dredge for her body.'

Swift... oh, the motel.

A funny feeling in her stomach wasn't fear or anxiety but excitement. Liz had no idea how, not yet, but a puzzle piece was landing in her lap.

'Any idea who was responsible?' Pete had his notepad out. '1971, Janie Swift?'

'Yes, that's right. Seasonal workers used to flood into the region for months at a time. Some were regulars but most came for a few weeks then left with their pay check and never looked back. Poor girl was never found nor has a body ever turned up which might be hers.'

'Didn't just leave town?'

'Anything's possible, Pete. I only know what I was told.'

He nodded and put the notepad down to pick up the cup.

Liz had so many new questions but circled back first. 'Going back to Joy... you said you sometimes talk shop. What about?'

'Sergeant Hobson, mostly. And his boys club, as she calls it.'

'Other cops?'

'Nah. The CEO of the hospital. And the mayor.'

'Of this town?' Liz asked.

'No, of Sanston. Play golf and eat out together. On several committees like the traders association and some land development group. Hobson grew up here, only two streets from my family but our paths never crossed, not that I recall, until I got the posting. He's more than twenty years older than me and should be retired but keeps hanging on.'

The landline began to ring. 'Sorry, just a minute.'

While Kath answered, Liz leaned closer to Pete. 'The motel used to be owned by a Hector Swift.'

His eyes narrowed but whatever he was thinking, Pete kept to himself.

They'd both emptied their cups by the time Kath hung up with an apology.

'Sorry, I'm going to have to go. One of the stations north has found a truck trying to pinch some livestock and they've detained the driver.'

'Need help?'

'Have someone coming from Sanston so I'll just stay until they arrive and make sure it's not an honest mistake. I mean, it isn't but procedure and all that.' She checked her watch. 'Should be back by four to sit in on the interview with old man Walsh but I'll call if there's a delay.'

Liz and Pete followed Kath out and waited as she locked up.

'We won't slow you down but thanks for talking to us. I'd

like to know more about Janie Swift though.' Liz found sunglasses and slid them on.

'I can get Joy to ring you.'

'Please do. Pete and Reuben will meet you at the pub at four unless you get held up.'

Kath waved and headed to her patrol car. In the distance, deep clouds slowly rolled toward them and a hot breeze picked up. Something was changing. Liz felt it in her bones. Whatever the next few days held, she had to keep her team safe because there was more going on in this small town than so-called accidental deaths. Much more.

20

The team gathered in Meg's room mid-afternoon. Liz had written a quick checklist and wasted no time diving into it.

'Pete, updates about a room? So that Meg can have her privacy back?'

'There's one left which might do and I'm meeting the owner about six.'

'Okay, let us know. Pete and I had a chat with Kath Connor and among some other interesting information, she mentioned what might be another cold case. This one is older and doesn't fit the MO of those we're looking at. I've added what I know – which isn't much – to our app. Basically, a teen named Janie Swift disappeared in 1971. Kath remembers talk that people assumed she was killed, possibly drowned in the basin. No body was ever found. Or she was a runaway, although she had strong ties to the town.'

Meg was nodding. 'I've begun running a search for her. Very early results are newspaper articles, including front page of the largest in the region *and* a mention in all the major Melbourne papers, about her. She was fifteen.'

'A baby,' Reuben said. 'Missing and forgotten.'

'Is she forgotten? Or is there a tie-in to these other deaths?' Liz asked. 'I want to know everything about Janie and her family. Who she was, where she went to school, who did she hang out with. And the investigation... there may still be people around who were local police at the time. Members of any search parties. Journalists who covered the story.'

Everyone was busy writing notes.

'Last point about Janie. What is her relationship to Hector Swift, who until fifteen years ago owned this motel. Let's put him up the list.'

'Boss, is this case now ours as well?' Pete asked.

'Not yet. Let's get more information and see if any dots connect.'

Her phone alarm beeped and she glanced at it.

'Just under one hour until the helicopter lands. Meg, do you want me to take your samples to the pilot so you can keep working?'

'Don't drop them.'

'I won't.'

'Okay then.'

Pete chuckled and Meg looked at him over the top of her glasses.

Liz ignored them and continued.

'Once Candace is here I want to take her out to the church and graveyard. I also want us to work on a plan for tomorrow, as we'll have another experienced team member here and hopefully a lot more information. Kath Connor has sent me the contact number for a constable in the Sanston station who has strong ties to the community and a long history in the force. Constable Joy Reed is currently doing her best to secure the cold case files and I know Reuben has someone back at the hub applying pressure on the senior officer.'

'The somewhat strange Sergeant Hobson?' Pete asked. 'Is his name on our list to look into?'

It was an uncomfortable thought, investigating another police officer.

It used to be.

Since the catastrophic events of the night at the mansion, Liz's feelings on this touchy subject had changed.

'Yes. Discreetly, Pete.'

His face lit up. 'That's me. Discreet Pete.'

'I mean it.'

Now, he feigned wounded feelings and everyone laughed.

Reuben lifted a hand to speak once they'd settled again. 'May I go off on a slight tangent?'

'Of course.'

'Couple of things. Last night Pete and I came across a shop in the town which sells a range of locally crafted goods, books, art and some second-hand products. I'd like to go there before our meeting with Albie Walsh, assuming they're open. Have a look and quiet word about jewellery makers.'

'I was going to ask about that after we went for our coffee earlier,' Meg said. 'It looked like such a haphazard mix of items that there may be little gems tucked away. Gems, as in, something of interest rather than gemstones. Although, they probably have gemstones as well.'

'Go for it.'

'The other thing concerns Erik Piper.' Reuben tapped on his phone a few times. 'Liz heard me tell him that I've ordered some of his books, which are in hardcover. But I've also downloaded all of his works which are available as eBooks and am working my way through them.' He turned the phone to show a book cover. 'This one is interesting. *The Tears of Certain Angels* is the title.'

He had angels around his pond.

'I've only had time to look at the first few poems but would appreciate some wisdom from Candace because there's a lot in them which feels… odd.'

'Odd?'

'Might be the way I'm taking them but there's a sense that he's writing about something deeply personal.'

'Do you have an example?' Meg asked.

'Sure.' Reuben cleared his throat. 'Hopefully I'll do it justice.'

> *'Watchful is the one*
> *Tasked this role so long*
> *Weary, yet keeping rest at bay*
> *Holding the truth*
> *Protecting she*
> *Who lies so deep*
> *Until the angels weep.'*

The hair rose on Liz's arms.

'I have goosebumps,' Pete said.

'Me too.' Meg turned in her chair to open a screen. 'Send me the title of the book and that poem please, Reuben.'

'Until the angels weep… I'd like to take a closer look at that pond of Mr Piper's and his collection of angels.'

Except he only moved to Australia ten years ago.

'Meg?'

'Can't turn around but I'm listening, Liz.' Meg's fingers were flying over one of her keyboards.

'Do we know for certain Erik Piper has no prior life in Australia?'

'I'll find out. Go and get Candace because we need her more than ever.'

. . .

Liz arrived just as the helicopter was in sight, flying low around the outskirts of the town to land at the sportsground. Not only was there a cricket pitch and footie goalposts, but a full basketball court and two tennis courts across the narrow road which circled the main field. Like so many regional towns, sport was a vital part of the community and often funded by the very people who used it, alongside some government and state sports association assistance.

Metal signs were screwed into the fence along more than half the perimeter, showcasing sponsors which were mostly local businesses. Liz wandered along them, taking photos. They included the pub and other eateries from the town, a legal firm, several shops, and the motel. The latter had a number of small holes in it and on closer inspection, Liz was certain they were from bullets. None of the other signage was affected. She took close-ups and sent them in a message to Reuben.

In a sponsorship sign. Bullet holes?

The helicopter closed in, aiming for the empty carpark, rather than the grassed area. Liz left the sportsground to collect the box of samples from her hire car parked on the grass verge.

As the chopper hovered and lowered, the air was disturbed, picking up dust and dirt from the tarmac and lifting Liz's short hair. She covered the top of her eyes with a hand until it landed and the rotors slowed with the cutting of the engine. The pilot would want to stretch their legs and possibly have a comfort stop but had already advised of a quick turnaround thanks to the incoming storm.

Seeing Candace climb out almost brought Liz to tears... the

kind one gets at airports or huge train stations, watching loved ones arrive or depart.

'Well I'm not certain I'll do that again in a hurry, but the view was captivating!' Candace drew Liz to her in a quick hug and a quiet word. 'I'm very happy to be here.'

'Happy to have you here. As are the team.'

'Hi Liz, we've only met remotely. I'm Helen.'

The woman from the zoom call the other day appeared around the front of the helicopter, hand outstretched.

'Really good to meet you in real life. And thanks for bringing Candace up.'

'Pleasure.' Helen looked at Candace, who faintly smiled.

'I have a box of samples for Jeff. Meg's asked they be secured but you know what you're doing.'

'I'll look after them. Can you point me in the direction of a loo?'

After directing Helen to the toilet block on the other side of the sportsground, Liz placed the box of samples on the ground, in the shade of the helicopter.

'She's very talented,' Candace said. 'I think she'll be a terrific asset to Operation Nobody but she might need to lighten up a bit.'

Liz almost burst into laughter. She'd never heard Candace speak that way. Somehow she maintained some control. 'Lighten up?'

'Yes. She refused to allow me to take the controls although I explained I am qualified to fly most light aircraft.'

'You are?'

'Of course. It was important when I travelled around the world because it was a self-propelled journey, for want of a better description. I'm sure I've mentioned Iceland.'

Deciding her own life was dull, Liz helped with the luggage. There was Candace's personal suitcase and a second bag which probably held her laptop and other devices, as well as a box-like case on wheels.

'Jeff sent this one for Meg.'

'Do you need a comfort stop?'

'Good grief, am I seven?'

Now Liz did laugh.

'Actually, yes. I'll be right back.'

Candace and Helen crossed paths, stopping for a quick chat and a hug. In all the time Liz had known the doctor, she'd rarely seen her touch another person. Perhaps at the end of one of her fabulous dinner parties she'd do air kisses, and on occasion she'd squeeze Liz's hand to offer comfort during stressful times, but she wasn't an openly affectionate person. It was a change of character. New. And something Liz would watch because since the arrival of Felix Fletcher, she'd felt Candace wasn't quite herself, although she couldn't pinpoint how.

By the time Liz had packed the car and was nosing out of the grounds, the helicopter was lifting into the air. A couple of kids on bicycles leaned over the fence, mouths open.

'I hope we're not upsetting everyone with all the helicopter comings and goings,' Liz said.

'What is the general feel from the residents?' Candace adjusted her seat belt and turned more in Liz's direction. 'I know what has been put on the comms but I'm interested in your take on this.'

And you'll ask us all in time.

Building a picture from many parts was a skill which the doctor excelled in and was done using a number of techniques, including whiteboards, tables covered in notes, and conversations.

'On the surface, people are friendly enough. I'm excluding law enforcement for the moment. The only person who's been a bit harder to read is Erik Piper and thanks to Reuben's attention to detail, it looks as though he may have reason to protect himself. Will come back to him in a minute. My interactions have mostly been with the motel owner, Gordon Brain, and some of the staff at the Thai restaurant and the café. Pete, on the other hand, is making it his business to talk to anyone who will have a chat.'

'And the police?'

'Kath Connor is a gem. She's honest and direct and frustrated by the lack of help with the recent death. I did a brief about Sergeant Barnaby Hobson.'

'Yes, I've read it. But you left out your real opinion.'

Liz grinned. 'In that case, I found him difficult to deal with. He has an air of superiority and uses it to keep Kath under his thumb. There's more going on with him than meets the eye because he's close to several major players in Sanston, including the mayor. On its own it means nothing, but add in the reluctance to facilitate what we've asked for on several occasions, and the fact he grew up in this town and is old enough to be well aware of the two earlier deaths... maybe even that of Janie Swift...'

They were on the road to the motel and Liz waved to Reuben and Pete who passed the opposite way in the BearCat.

'On the way to interview Albie Walsh at the pub.'

'Shouldn't you go?' Candace asked.

'Not at this stage. Albie has made a connection with those two, so let's see what they come up with.'

There wasn't a reply and when Liz glanced across, Candace was smiling at her.

'What?'

'Nice seeing you comfortably in command. It suits you.'

Liz flicked the indicator on and slowed. 'I admit there are times I'd much rather quit my job and lose myself in the outback or the mountains somewhere, but then I hear your voice in my head and remember to breathe.'

'Good woman. Proud of you, Lizzie.'

She parked outside her room, which was next to the one Gordy had provided for Candace. He'd almost rubbed his hands in glee hearing another guest was coming.

'Welcome to our somewhat humble abode. Part accommodation and part remote headquarters. I have checked your room and it is clean. In fact, Meg ran a blue light over it and all is well.'

'In a motel? Were you both drinking?'

'I find that question offensive, even if true.'

Having Candace here was good. Liz felt her load was a bit lighter. Even though Meg and Reuben and Pete were doing their jobs beyond well, the doctor added other elements. Between them all, they'd get to the truth.

As Meg emerged from her room with a huge smile and hurried to greet Candace, Liz glanced in the rear-vision mirror. For once her eyes were clear and unworried. About time.

21

Another disruption. The youngsters might find helicopters interesting but I see it differently.

Hovering where they don't belong. Snooping around private property. Probably taking photographs from the air.

What's worse... what breaks my heart anew is them stealing from the sacred ground. This never used to happen. No samples of so-called evidence ever made it to anyone who cared enough to investigate. I don't understand why now. What changed?

This is personal business and they are strangers.

And now there is yet another one of them.

Another woman.

Older.

More refined than the others.

Easier to deal with if it comes to that.

Or she might be in charge and decide there's nothing to see here.

My senses say otherwise but I'll give it a little time. Watch more.

As long as they stay away from the sacred ground.

22

It took Candace next to no time to freshen up and let herself into Meg's room. Liz was cleaning the whiteboard.

'Is that for me?'

'One side only,' Meg said firmly. 'But that side is all yours and the rest of us will share.'

'Generous.'

Meg waved her arm at the room. 'We've been learning to share. Chairs, space, oxygen. Perhaps the hub has spoilt us too much.'

Liz put down the cleaner. 'A mini version of your table would be nice.'

Back in the hub, a glass-topped table hid a clever computer system which allowed users to work in 3D or any number of other options. For a big job such as this, it would prove invaluable.

'I taught Phoebe how to use it so there's no reason we can't do a call and she can drive while we look on.'

'She's taken a couple of days off. But some of the new team members are there learning the ropes and Fletcher could probably follow instructions well enough.' Candace shrugged. 'Scrap that. He'd need them written down line by line with simple words in crayon.'

Sorry... what did you say?

Meg clearly had the same response as she also stared at Candace in surprise, who fanned her face with a hand.

'Aloud. I did say that aloud. Anyway, where shall we start? Earlier you mentioned Reuben's attention to detail.'

The silence dragged. Liz's original feeling that something wasn't right between Candace and Felix was back. There was history there, but what kind?

Candace pulled up a chair. 'Reuben?'

'He's been reading Erik Piper's books, one of which is titled *The Tears of Certain Angels*. One of the poems is interesting, to say the least, mentioning something buried deep. But you need to read it yourself so I don't accidentally influence your thinking.'

'Nobody influences my work. No need to be concerned. Is Mr Piper your main suspect?'

Liz grabbed her own chair. 'I hadn't thought of him as a solid suspect and there's evidence he couldn't have been involved in the previous deaths.'

'Doesn't stop him copying them, though'

One of Meg's computers dinged. 'That's from Jeff. Oh. You both need to look at this.'

There was a report about the angel pendant. Lots of numbers and symbols beyond Liz's comprehension but then a written statement, which was long.

'Shall I summarise?'

'Thanks, Meg.'

'The results of the human trace located on the clasp of the pendant have a familial match to the DNA of a woman only known as Maude. Her DNA was collected during some trials back in 1970.' Meg glanced up, her face drawn. 'This is horrible stuff. DNA testing as we know it was unheard of in Australia until the 1980s but there was a short-lived experiment taking samples as a trial which was used in just five small towns around the country. This town appears to be one which should mean that somewhere, there's DNA of anyone from that time.'

Meg read a few more lines and her shoulders dropped.

'What's wrong?' Candace asked.

'As I suspected. Ethnicity was the goal of the experiment. Maude's came back as a mix of, hang on... paraphrasing here... one parent probably of English descent and the other part Irish and part Chinese.'

Meg was still reading fast, the page scrolling until she backed up a bit. 'Right, so there is a trail to follow. If you approve, Liz, I'll prioritise this. There's a ton of DNA info which we can cross-reference to find who Maude is or was, as well as anyone else who was here back then.' She glanced up. 'Sorry, that wasn't much of an explanation.'

'We got the drift,' Liz said. 'Potentially there are samples of a lot of people and some of them might be related to Maude.'

'Near enough. So, do I have the go ahead?'

'Of course you do. Jeff might be busy but keep him in the loop and ask for any additional help if you need it. I might take Candace out to the graveyard.'

Candace was on her feet and heading for the door. 'Good idea. Give Meg some peace and quiet.'

'Meg can work with company, you know.'

But Meg waved them away, her eyes back on the screen as they closed and locked the door behind themselves.

. . .

Pete and Reuben finished speaking to the owner of the gift shop, coming away with contact details for a number of local artisans.

With a glance at his watch, Pete nodded in the direction of the pub. 'Better get going. Five to four.'

'No sign of Kath yet.'

They walked briskly toward the corner.

'Hoping we'll get something helpful from Albie.' Pete had a long list of questions in his head but one was burning. Why was the man so willing to raise the old murders with two police he'd just met? Over the years, he'd taken a couple of death-bed confessions and although this wasn't quite the same, there was an element about Albie's blunt *reckon you'll be wanting to talk to me about the killings* which gave the same vibe. This was an unexpected and welcome opportunity to listen to someone who'd been around at that time. Probably more than just been around.

At the corner they looked for the patrol car. Nothing.

'She ain't coming.'

A middle-aged man stood in the doorway of the pub. He wore a top with the pub's logo and a scowl.

Reuben stepped forward, hand outstretched. 'Colin Walsh? I'm Reuben and this is Pete.'

No hand was offered in return.

'Dad's resting.'

'Have you heard from Leading Senior Constable Connor?' Pete asked. He'd already checked for recent messages and there was nothing.

'She's always on time. Said four. Its four.'

Pete grinned. 'Might be held up. Traffic.'

Colin snorted. 'We're not in Melbourne.'

'Dunno. Got caught behind a combine harvester once. Can't hurry them along nor overtake.'

The other man's eyes narrowed.

'I'll give her a quick buzz.' Reuben stepped away, tapping his phone.

A couple of patrons wandered in, Colin making room with a grunt. He wasn't the friendliest person Pete had ever met and it was a stark difference from his son and his father. That made him interesting. Was he the one the responsibilities all fell on? Or was there a sinister undertone?

'Must be proud of your son. Matthew? A doctor, eh?'

The smallest of smiles touched Colin's lips. 'Good boy. Works hard. Not a bad bone in *his* body.'

Is that an emphasis I hear? Who does have a bad bone, my man?

'Nice having him back for a bit?'

'Yeah. He's popular behind the bar.' Colin actually laughed. 'More with the girls. Even the older women, although they know better than to try it on.'

'Don't understand.'

'Cougars.' Colin held up both hands and made a motion like a cat with its claws out. 'Got some spinsters here. Few more divorced. And widows. Too many older women looking for a way out of the town. But not with my kid and I've told more than one to stick to their own age.'

'You married?'

'Not now. Never again.'

Reuben was back. 'Kath's half an hour away.'

Colin turned to go inside. 'Told you.'

'We're happy to wait for her. And Albie might feel up to a chat in half an hour.'

'He won't. And I've got patrons.'

The man was gone.

Moving a few metres away, Pete and Reuben stopped to look back at the pub. It wasn't busy yet but the smell of beer and cigarettes wafted out. Not that anyone should be smoking in there, but who was going to stop them? Kath didn't seem the kind to rock the boat unless she had no choice.

'What now?' Reuben asked.

'Fancy a drive? And then a beer later. Once Albie's had a chance to rest.' Not about to give up so easily, Pete was already planning how to circumvent "Gatekeeper Colin".

Back in the BearCat, Pete took the wheel and headed toward Brown Horse Road.

'I ran past here this morning. Going to check out this gate Liz found?'

Pete grinned at Reuben. 'Love me a person who broadcasts their bad intentions.'

'I'll see if there's anything updated on the address.'

While Reuben checked the app, Pete cruised along the narrow, mostly straight stretch with bushland in the direction of the church and open fields the other side. Something made him wind down the window, the humid air blowing his hair around.

'Can't see anything other than a satellite image. I'll send it to the screen once we stop.'

Unlike most info screens in modern cars, this one was extra-large and had far more options than the usual maps, music, and phone calls. It was a computer in itself with full search capabilities and monitored everything the vehicle's multiple cameras saw.

Pete slowed to a crawl as they entered the dead end road. The property in question was obvious with its big signage, barbed wire, and homemade excuse for a gate. He nosed the BearCat close to the gate. 'Reckon we could drive through it.'

'Prefer you don't.' Reuben cast an image to the screen. 'This is better. I'll just enlarge the text first as I'd not spotted it on the phone.'

'Time for an eye check?'

'Just had one. Right, the property is owned by one Betty Carver, aged sixty-seven and—'

'A woman? Does she live here or just own it?'

'Mate, let me finish. She inherited the place from her parents and is the sole resident. Fourth generation living here. Never married. No children. No work history yet.'

'A woman.'

'Why are you surprised?'

'Nothing surprises me, but the signage and whole air of 'keep out or else' reeks of male ego. Guess I need to step outside the norm a bit more.'

Reuben reset the screen to show the property. The land was long rather than wide and ran between the front fence and the distant waterway. On the other side of the gate was a track leading to a house after a few hundred metres. 'Big house. And other buildings.' He pointed to a long shed then what appeared to be two cottages. 'This was probably a going concern in the past. Must be a thousand acres and they've got several dams and a creek running off the larger body so water wasn't an issue.'

'Is that a camera?' Pete pointed to a small box which was attached below a 44 gallon drum-turned mail box. 'Let's check it out.' He grabbed a card from the centre console before climbing out.

Up close, it was definitely a camera blinking at them.

Pete held the card close to it for a few seconds. 'Do you think there's audio?'

Reuben nodded.

Pulling the card back, Pete bent down to address the camera. 'Afternoon. Detective Pete McNamara and Detective Reuben Barnes. We are requesting a short visit to ask some questions. You are not a suspect or under any threat from us.

Our team is visiting the town in relation to a number of queries and we'd appreciate your assistance.'

Both men stepped back to stand near the BearCat, eyes on the gate.

Nothing changed.

'Do we look intimidating?' Pete looked Reuben up and down. 'I mean, you're a tall, muscular dude but wearing a polo top and shorts makes you blend in, if anything.'

Neither wore holsters or other kit.

'Should I go flash my badge?'

'Maybe leave a card. Might not be home. Or would prefer to talk to Liz.'

Pete wrote on his card then 'posted it' in the mail box. He leaned down to address the camera. 'You can reach me at the number on the card. If you'd prefer to speak to a female officer, we can arrange that but we do need to schedule a brief interview.'

A light blue sedan approached along the road and the gate next door slowly swung open.

'Isn't that Gordon Brain's car?' Reuben asked. 'Saw him park it at the motel.'

The car turned into the next driveway and stopped, idling as the driver wound down the passenger window.

'Gents. Think you're wasting your time there.'

Pete and Reuben leaned down to talk to him through the window. The interior was spotlessly clean yet an unpleasant odour – a mix of chemicals – lingered. There was a mop and bucket in the backseat.

'This is your place?'

'Sure is. I'd invite you to the house but I'm only here to grab my laptop. Forgot it this morning.'

'And Betty Carver?'

'Silly old bat. Probably not the right thing to say these days, eh? Woke crap and all that?' Gordy rolled his eyes. 'She hates people. Lives alone in that big old house. Doesn't give most of us the time of day like one of them sovereign citizen types. Probably won't shoot you on sight but one can't be too careful.'

His eyes moved from Pete to Reuben then back to Pete and although his mouth smiled at his own poor taste joke, his expression was frigid. He was working hard to cover up something and all of Pete's spidey senses went on high alert.

'Gotta get going, boys.'

After they stepped back, he disappeared along his driveway, the gate closing behind him.

'Just made my top two suspect list,' Pete said.

'With Erik Piper?'

'Yep. Want to go write some names on the whiteboard?'

23

The church was now a familiar shape dominating the landscape by its sheer size. While Candace went for a wander, Liz checked the police tape around the church was intact, and the locks on the doors in place. There were now several cameras strategically covering more of the area, thanks to Reuben, but Meg's last mention of activity was a slow moving mob of kangaroos overnight.

She leaned against a wall, making a few notes to remind herself to follow up when they returned to the motel. Who controlled the church and grounds... or was at least responsible for their upkeep? Was there any intel about the priest who'd been in residence at the time of the earlier deaths? And who was buried in the two unmarked graves?

With a heavy sigh, Liz wandered toward Candace, who was squatting a few metres from the second grave.

'This one is important to the killer. Or at least, the person responsible for the body or bodies being put on top of the next grave.' Attention on the headstone, Candace slowly straightened. 'My brain is sorting what feels like a million snippets of information, yet at the centre of the maelstrom is a certainty.'

'Certainty?'

That didn't sound like the doctor, who was careful with fact-checking and historically disliked being pressured for an early opinion.

'Tell me what you see here, Liz. Not the police tape. Not the disturbances from Meg's work. Look at this and then the other.'

'I've looked so often.'

'But have you seen?' Candace finally met Liz's eyes. 'Think like a killer. Or a victim.'

A shiver rushed up Liz's spine. There was old blood on the back of the headstone. A trail of it leading to the church. More inside, along with other bodily fluids.

Can I think like a killer? What kind of killer, though? Someone like Dad, who was ruthless and self-serving? Or a person out for revenge?

The switch in her mind was immediate. Vengeance was a different motivator than anything else. It could simmer for years. Decades.

'Revenge is a dish best served cold.' The words came out softly.

'Go with that.'

Liz walked behind the headstone, gazing at it and then the church beyond. 'A tiny town isn't where you expect multiple unexplained deaths, let alone three which have too many common denominators to be random. At present their only connection is where they were found after death.'

'The inefficiency of past investigations has let those victims down.'

'Yes, or deliberate acts to cover or misdirect.'

Candace joined Liz. 'I agree there may be outside influence

at play. Does it mean a killer is protecting themselves, or someone else? Are there multiple killers responsible across the years?' She gestured to the church. 'This may well be another connection or even the catalyst.'

'Because of the trace we found inside?'

'Meg believes the blood on this headstone belonged to a person who was shot. If they were wounded and sought refuge in the church or were carried in, then at least one other person was involved. Was the shooting an accident or murder? Answer that and perhaps it will lead to the mystery of the dead men.' Candace ran fingers through her hair.

'These are the only graves with unmarked headstones. The local police officer, who grew up here, doesn't know who they belong to. Reuben had the drone up this morning but the data needs analysing before we can do more than speculate whether there are coffins. For all we know, both might be empty. Prepared for funerals which ended up being done elsewhere, like at the public cemetery.'

'Or, whoever was shot may rest in one of the graves.'

Which would mean exhumation was becoming more likely.

Speculating wasn't helpful. Liz needed facts.

'I'd like to come back in the morning. I'm keen to reread some of the briefs,' Candace said. 'And have a drink.'

'Oh, I am so sorry. There's water in the car but I should have made sure you had a bottle in this humidity.'

'Not that kind of drink.' Candace chuckled. 'But water will do fine for now.'

Liz left Candace with Meg and Reuben and tapped on Pete's motel room door.

'Not locked.'

'Should be.' Liz let herself in. 'I believe you met Albie's son.'

Pete was near a wall, walking his fingers up the bricks as high as he could, then down again. It was nothing Liz hadn't seen him do as one of his ongoing exercises since he'd been knocked off his motorcycle but it still made her feel sorry. Or sad. At least she'd moved past believing she was responsible for her father's actions.

'Good old Colin. They say traits skip a generation and the friendliness of Albie jumped right over Colin and landed on the grandson. Aargh.' He dropped the arm and shook it. 'Overdid push ups this morning.'

'Can I help?'

He was rotating his shoulder. 'Not unless you're hiding a remedial massage degree somewhere?'

'Sit. No degree but I did a year of physio before going to academy.'

Pete's expression almost made her burst into laughter but he pulled out his only straight backed chair and sat on it sideways to give her access to his shoulder.

'I didn't know that, Liz. Top off?'

'Probably best.'

He pulled the top over his head with a low grunt.

You're in real pain, mate. Just won't admit it because you think I'll send you home.

She started looking through the cupboards of the small kitchenette. 'Seen any oil?'

'Sure. I keep gallons of that special shiny stuff the body-builders use in competitions.'

'Cooking oil will do.'

'In the bathroom there's some bio-oil.'

Liz closed the cupboard door. 'That's even better.'

There was half a bottle on the vanity and she unscrewed the lid on her way back. 'Using it on the scars?'

He nodded. 'Phoebe put me onto it while I was still in hospital. Told me she used it on the sites of some operations she had ages ago. Kinda weird at first, rubbing oil over a new scar. Felt a bit ick. Never did a thing for the old ones and it shows. See where I got stabbed?' Pete pointed to his side. 'Ten stitches. External that is but heaps inside as well. Looks like crap still after all these years.'

'Nothing to stop you using this on them now. Who stabbed you?'

Liz poured a circle of the thick oil onto one palm.

'Nasty ringleader of a drug cartel. Gotta love undercover policing.' He laughed shortly. 'He's rotting away in Barwon Prison these days.'

'I'll work on your shoulder then down the arm. Okay?'

With a cheesy grin, Pete nodded.

'Maybe I should ask Reuben to do this.' Liz stepped back, oil now on both her hands. 'More appropriate.'

'You do remember he's a highly trained killer, right? He knows how to do lethal stuff with his bare hands and I'm not game enough to find out if massage is one of them. And as amazed as I am about your physio training, I'm not about to suspend my disbelief of some coincidence that he has similar capabilities.'

'It wouldn't surprise me.'

'Yeah, me neither, actually. If you want I can video us.'

'*Detective!*'

'No. Oh, shit. You know what I mean. To protect you from some stupid workplace complaint about a senior officer manhandling – sorry, womanhandling—'

'Mishandling will do.'

Feeling sorry for Pete, Liz started working on his shoulder, trying not to laugh aloud. He was such a stirrer himself but didn't read her well when she was returning the banter. Too many years of having a reputation for being serious didn't help.

His shoulder muscles were knotted and she took her time digging her fingers and thumbs in and around the painful areas, careful not to apply too much pressure to begin with. She could feel him tense at first and then rapidly relax and at one point his eyes were closed. They opened when she squirted more oil onto her hands.

'I thought you always wanted to be a cop?'

'I did. Anna was against it.'

'Your sister?'

'You have to remember she'd taken me in once Mum died and she was terrified of losing me in a risky profession, and of authority. I never understood until she told me what our father was really like.'

'Ouch.'

'Sorry.'

Drawing in a long breath to lower the tension which had made it into her fingers, Liz worked her way up and down Pete's upper arm. There was a long scar and she paid extra attention there, gently massaging oil into the slightly raised skin.

'My school results would have got me into medicine and Anna thought that was a good path but I could never see myself as a doctor. I loved running and sport and thought physio was worth a shot. But my heart has always belonged to the idea of catching and incarcerating bad guys.'

'I get that. But I appreciate that year of training.'

'Feels better?'

'Much. Thanks, Lizzie.'

She went to the bathroom to wash her hands and when she returned Pete had his shirt on and was opening his laptop.

'You wanted to talk about Colin?' Pete asked.

'And Albie. What's the plan?'

'We all go out for dinner and then head to the pub. Reuben and I agree that having mass matters. With you and Candace and Meg all observing as well, you might see something we miss. We both believe there's more to that family than meets the eye.'

He opened a tab to a map. Liz looked over his shoulder as he zoomed to the two properties she'd earmarked for further investigation.

'So we went for a drive. Saw on the app that the owner of the place with the trespasser warnings is a Betty Carver. We've left a card in her mailbox and I talked to her camera for a bit to ask for a few minutes for a chat.'

'Yes, I saw her name pop up. Interesting.'

'If you want interesting... do you know who her neighbour is? Gordon Brain.'

'What.'

'He fronted up to get something from his house and was pretty uncomplimentary about Ms Carver. Basically told us we're wasting our time. She's unfriendly and reclusive.'

'What is it about reclusive people here? Erik Piper. Betty Carver. Unfriendly senior police.'

'Add Colin Walsh. And I did a search and despite Albie claiming to own it, Colin does, and is the registered publican. How did it go with Candace?'

Liz dropped onto the end of the bed and Pete turned in his chair.

'We need to look closely at that second grave.'

'Because?'

'Someone was shot or stabbed or whatever close to that second headstone. Meg says shot. We don't yet know who or when, let alone why. We also don't know if the person was wounded or killed. I'm going to grasp at straws here.' Liz took a moment, getting her thoughts in order and aware she had Pete's undivided attention. 'Whoever that victim was? They mattered to someone. What if that someone has been administering their brand of justice ever since?'

He gave it a moment then nodded. 'It would make sense given the placement of the bodies. Even the recent one, which we know was interfered with between Piper finding it and returning with his phone. But there's decades between the first two and the last, so would the timing even fit?'

'Possibly not. Any news on a room for us?'

Pete frowned. 'Nothing suitable. I had a look at the most promising one and there was no way to make it secure. Best suggestion is talk to Gordy about another room.'

'Okay. I'll go and do that now.'

'And I'll go next door and see if those slackers have solved the case yet.'

<h1 style="text-align:center">24</h1>

The wine bar was larger than it looked from outside. Liz had phoned to make a reservation and was assured that as long as they were there by six, there'd be room without a booking. It was exactly six now and beyond the piano were half a dozen tables, none occupied.

'Take your pick and I'll bring menus in a min.' The woman Liz had seen the first night was behind the bar, her bright red hair swept up into a messy bun. 'None of that silly QR code ordering nonsense here. We believe in old-fashioned customer service.'

Candace chose a rectangle table and took the seat at the narrow end facing the door. Meg and Liz flanked her and the men took the next two seats. From here they could all see the street and the bar, where a couple of middle-aged men were chatting, each with a vivid green cocktail.

'You could drop this place into most inner-city suburbs and it would be a hot spot,' Pete said. 'Nice vibe. Eclectic and a bit eccentric.'

There was already a jug of iced water on the table and

Reuben poured for each of them. He'd been quiet when Liz returned to Meg's room after speaking with Gordy. Reuben *and* Candace. This wasn't the place to debrief as such, but Liz knew them well enough to sense there was a lot of thinking going on. Having this many of the team here took a weight off her shoulders and she had new confidence in their investigation.

'Here you go, my lovelies. And I'm Mandy.' Menus were placed in front of them. 'We're a bit of a fusion eatery here, we are. Love our sharing plates, we do. And the food is a real mix thanks to the owner being a chef with a Spanish dad and a First Nations mum. Don't be afraid to ask me about the ingredients because not everyone has come across some but let me say they are all delicious.'

Reuben smiled. 'Hi Mandy. Am I going to be a pain for your chef because I'm vegan?'

'Not in the least. We cook to people's preferences so I'll let him know. Would you all like to start with a glass of wine? I can highly recommend the very dry white or the full-bodied red which are listed at the top of the drinks menu.'

'A bottle of each, thanks Mandy,' Liz said.

'Lovely. I'll get those and be back to take the food orders.'

Meg hadn't taken her eyes off the menu since taking one. 'I'm so hungry. They do mostly small plates which are for sharing. Anyone want to share the spicy peach cheeks with gingered ricotta?'

'Share? I'm having one all for myself,' Candace said.

By the time the wine arrived, Meg had collated a comprehensive list of dishes from the team and offered to text it to Mandy, who insisted she would remember everything without writing it down.

Other diners wandered in, some obviously regulars who went straight to a table and settled in. The two men at the bar had gone, replaced by half a dozen other customers. The street outside seemed quiet, with only the occasional car going by and few pedestrians.

'Weather is closing in,' Pete announced. He had his phone open to a weather app. 'Storms expected in the next two hours with substantial rainfall. So much for night-time testing. Is that going to mess with our crime scene?'

Meg shrugged. 'It's already rained since the last body was found. And the older trace has had years of environmental impact so I don't think a few hours of rain is going to change much. Some of the holes Pete and I dug today will fill and it might be worth re-sampling in the morning, in case there's anything new. I'd really like a glass of wine if anyone wants to nudge a bottle closer.'

Reuben had both in his hands, reading the backs of the labels and glanced up. 'Red or white?'

'Both.'

'So, two glasses?'

'Nah, just mix them together and right to the rim. Been a long day.'

Everyone laughed. Other than Liz. Earlier, Reuben had a quiet word with her about seeing Meg disappear into the bushland opposite the motel and finding her alone and reporting she'd heard odd noises close by. Meg had seen the footage of someone at the grave – someone who could be a killer – so why she'd deliberately isolated herself was a question burning in Liz's mind. But it would wait until they were alone.

Glasses all filled, the team tapped them together.

Candace put hers down and looked from one to the other. 'We need to talk and I know here is not ideal but before we go anywhere else tonight, I'd like to say a couple of things.'

As they all leaned toward her to better hear over the background noise, Reuben's arm brushed against Liz.

'Sorry,' he whispered, moving slightly away.

'It's okay,' she whispered back.

Why are we whispering?

'My focus has been on this case since the briefing before Liz flew up. Being here is reinforcing some early conclusions and firing off a whole lot of new thoughts. What appears straightforward on the surface is not even close to being simple beneath it.'

Meg nodded. 'Tonight will be busy later on as I'm expecting a deluge of results to arrive at once.'

'Happy to work late with you,' Candace said.

'And me.' Pete was the first to say it but they all chimed in.

'Now how do I get any work done with a room filled with humans? And furniture?' Although Meg smiled, she followed it with a large mouthful of wine.

'I managed to secure the last room in the motel,' Liz said. 'We can't use it tonight but tomorrow can move everything into it and set up a better mini-hub. Gordon is providing some extra chairs and a table and moving the bed out.'

'You could have led with that.' Meg sounded like she was grumbling but her shoulders relaxed.

'Before our food arrives... there's two things I really need you all to take on board. I'm not police. I'm not an investigator. But I understand human nature fairly well. This little town didn't have three, potentially four suspicious and unresolved deaths in the past fifty years or so without developing coping mechanisms. Apart from the handful of people who might be considered suspects, are the everyday locals. Some have grown up here and others being more recent arrivals.'

Liz's mind went to Gordy Brain. Fifteen years was new in the scheme of things for a town which had close on two centuries of colonisation behind it. Add that to the thousands of years the traditional custodians cared for Country and he was but a grain of sand in a bucket.

We all are.

'I'm asking you to be careful. Stay alert, even with the friendly folk. If anything, pay close attention to those who'd help you without a prompt.'

'Here we are with the first plates. What if we pop them down the middle of the table?'

Mandy and a young male server held trays of food. Liz had been so intent on listening to Candace she'd not noticed them approach. How much, if anything, had they overheard?

'I've got the ones safe for you, love.' Mandy placed two plates close to Reuben. 'You can also trust the finger lime parfait tartlets and the yam wedges.'

'Thank you. The meals look amazing.' Reuben offered a warm smile, and Mandy's face turned the colour of her hair.

'Rightio, well I'll let you all dig in before the next round comes.'

Once both Mandy and the server were gone, Pete gazed seriously at Reuben. 'Don't see it myself.'

'See what?'

'The attraction. One smile and you had the poor woman all flustered.'

'I did not.'

Meg held out her glass. 'Hate to agree with Pete, but he's right. So Reubs, *darl*, may I have some more vino?'

Shaking his head at them all, Reuben nevertheless half-filled her glass.

'I really need to learn to speak faster. Don't eat a thing until I'm finished!' Candace sounded like a school teacher and her face was set until Reuben offered to put more wine into her glass. 'Thanks, I know everyone is hungry and a bit stressed but I'll be quick.'

'We're listening,' Liz said.

'Be careful of overly friendly people. Don't drop your guard but pay attention to the little things. And secondly, unless there's no option, pair up when out and about. If you have to go somewhere alone then make sure at least two of us know where and have your app showing your location. And I know I sound like a worried mother but the reality is we are in a unique situation for our team and...'

'And?' Liz prompted.

'My belief is there's a high chance a killer is around and more so, either they or an accomplice is set on protecting those graves.' She picked up her glass. 'Humour me.'

'No, listen to Candace. Each of us is used to danger, even Meg. But we're not in Melbourne. We don't have the luxury of accessing multiple backup options. We are each other's backup.' Liz felt better for saying that and looked at each team member. 'We all good?'

'All good, boss,' Meg said. 'Can we eat now?'

'I'm going to need another shower if this humidity doesn't ease up.'

Pete hadn't stopped complaining since they'd finished dinner and he was getting on Liz's nerves. The others had sped up a bit, having their own conversation but probably it was more about not wanting to hear another word about the state of the stock market, politics, or now, the weather.

'Do you and Reuben have a plan of action?'

'With Albie? No. Yes. If Colin still has him hidden then no.'

They'd reached the corner opposite the hotel and Liz stopped and faced Pete. The others were already using the one pedestrian crossing in the town.

'Spill. What's bugging you?'

He started to speak, probably to deny anything was wrong, but then he dropped the façade.

'Candace is right. I've thought about what she said earlier… not to drop our guard. To be careful of people who seem very friendly. And I've been out and about trying to make people like me in order to get them comfortable enough to talk without it seeming like an interrogation. What if I've already messed up?'

Oh… this is about one person. About Ruby.

'Seriously, dude? Since when do you second-guess your instincts? One of your strongest talents in the job is reeling people in. Getting them to trust you – whether a gangster or a terrified drug addict – that's a talent. Out of everyone, you are the last person dropping their guard so keep doing what you are.'

'You sure?' He glanced in Reuben's direction. 'He's got the lot, Liz. Reads people well. Hugely talented with tech and weapons. And… and decent. Doubt if he's had to shoot up just to keep a drug lord from suspecting they have a cop in their midst.'

'God, Pete. That should never have happened to you and sometimes I wish I *had* walked away from the force last year.'

His hand squeezed her shoulder. 'My fault you didn't.'

'I know.' But she smiled. 'Your endless complaining is rubbing off on me so let's catch up with the others and find Albie Walsh. As far as Reuben goes? I don't know what the team would do without either of you.'

'The team, or you?'

Liz stepped onto the road and he scrambled to keep pace.

'Are you angling for me to pick you as my favourite?'

'Yes.'

'You are. Happy?'

His grin was almost too good to wipe off but she had to.

'Favourite partner I've known the longest.'

'Wait. That's a consolation prize.'

'Participation, dude.'

'No, hang on a sec... that means I'm more important than Vince Carter.'

She threw her hands up as if he'd won, which made the other three give her weird looks as she joined them.

Moving right along...

'How are we handling this?' The question was for the group in general.

'Pete needs the chance to speak with Albie if we can make it happen,' Reuben said. 'If Colin is around we might need to distract him.'

'Shall I go with you, Pete?' Candace offered. 'Or should Liz?'

'You go,' Liz said. 'I'm keen to speak with Colin.' Her phone started to ring, a number she didn't recognise. 'I'll catch up.'

'We'll be watching out of the window. Remember, nobody is allowed to be alone.' Meg smirked.

Stepping a few metres away, Liz tapped 'accept'. 'Liz Moorland speaking.'

'This is Constable Joy Reed. I'm sorry to phone so late.'

'Not at all. I was hoping we'd be able to talk.'

'I'd have left it until morning but wanted you to know I've been able to secure some cold case files as well as photos and reports from the recent case.'

For a moment Liz closed her eyes in relief. Finally they were getting co-operation.

Joy continued. 'I've got three evidence boxes in front of me.'

Liz opened her eyes. 'I can collect them.'

'No need. Kath has to come over first thing for a regular

briefing and is happy to bring them back across. It will be late morning, if that's okay?'

It was better than nothing.

'I wonder... is it an imposition to ask you to send me the photos from the current case by text or email? Our profiler is here with us and it would be incredibly helpful to get hold of some images while we work tonight.'

'Already took photos. Had a feeling you might. I'll text them to you. Give me a few minutes.'

'Thank you so much, Joy. Kath told me you stand up for what's right and we need more police like you.'

The call ended, Liz was alone on the street. In the far distance, lightning silently flashed within heavy, slow-moving clouds.

25

Albie was nowhere to be seen and Colin glowered at Pete as he approached the bar, Liz at his side.

The pub was much quieter than last night. Probably the incoming storm had locals scurrying to be home out of potentially bad conditions when some would be under the influence. Only one group sat watching what looked like a recorded past grand final game of footie, while a couple of young women perched on stools at the end of the bar.

'If you're back looking to harass my dad then you can—'

'Came for a drink, mate. Three lagers, a glass of red, and a bottle of sparkling water. Long day for the team so we are here to relax.'

'Might be closing early. Storm and all.'

Liz leaned on the bar. 'Still a way off by the look of the sky. Bit of lightning but in the distance.'

Colin grunted but set to work filling the order.

Pete gazed around. The rest of the team had chosen a table in a corner with visibility to the main door, bar, and stairs.

Candace was slowly checking out the space and their eyes met and she nodded. A good spot to watch from.

'No Mattie tonight?' Pete asked.

'Out with his mates.' Colin put the beers onto a small tray in front of Pete. 'House red and sparkling wine?'

'Sparkling water,' Liz corrected. 'Red's for me. Do you have a recommendation? Something local you like?' She took out a credit card and held it up. 'We need a bit of spoiling.'

He added the bottle of water with a glass and Pete carried the tray to the others. Liz would keep Colin talking and give him a chance to find Albie. After putting the drinks down he took a seat between Candace and Reuben. 'Should I shoot up the stairs?'

'No need.' Reuben looked toward a pair of bare feet slowly descending.

The feet grew legs then stopped and Albie's face peered down. His arm gestured to come up and once he knew Pete had seen him, the feet turned and began to ascend again.

Liz had positioned herself so that Colin's back was turned to the group and he was showing her bottles of wine. Candace moved quickly to cover the distance to the stairs and Pete was close behind. Every one of the steps creaked.

Like a horror movie.

They reached a landing with a door to the left, the stairs continuing up, and a hallway to the right. Albie was nowhere to be seen.

'In here.'

Pete jumped as Albie opened the closest door from inside.

'No point standing there. Old grumble-bum downstairs will try to send you off again so come and sit in my room to talk.'

The room was sparsely furnished. Just a bed, one side table, a small wardrobe and an old armchair. But the walls were covered in photographs, almost all in black and white and two boxing belts were framed behind glass.

'Nice.' Pete stood in front of one. 'Tell me about it.'

For a couple of minutes, Albie's voice brightened as he recounted the titles he'd won. Then he seemed to notice Candace for the first time, standing quietly just inside the door.

'You ain't Kath.'

'I'm Candace and I'm a friend of Pete and Reuben. Do you mind me being here?'

'Depends. You gonna arrest me?'

'Not me. I'm not police so I don't arrest anyone but I'd love to hear why you think that might be an outcome of talking to us?'

'Sit on the armchair. And you sit on the bed.' Albie perched on a deep windowsill and looked from one to the other, until everyone was where he'd directed. 'Colin means well but he doesn't speak for me. Nor is he in any way involved in the events of all those years gone by.'

'Understood,' Pete said. 'We're here to listen.'

'You can write it down. Record or whatever.'

'I'd appreciate that, Albie. Is it okay if I record the conversation on my phone?'

Albie shrugged so Pete quickly set up the phone and said a few words about the time, place, and who was present.

'Last time we met, you said you thought we'd want to talk to you about the killings. Is that how you remember it?'

'Yup. Time this all came out before anyone else dies.'

Pete didn't want to move an inch, or even breathe. Was this a breakthrough coming?

Candace appeared to have no such issues. She was relaxed, her body language open and voice conversational. 'Where would you like to begin?'

'Long way back. My ma and pa died when I was just

twenty-five. I'd been helping out here after my uncle went his way a bit before, so I knew enough to get by. Stumbled around to make it work despite some of the customers and staff being conscripted and there were days of barely making a dollar. Course, some of the younger men, teenagers really, were raring to go. And get this, it was mostly the sons of the wealthy families. Vietnam War was everything and they'd be heroes.' Albie looked disgusted. 'Nothin' good ever came of killing each other now, did it?'

Candace made a sympathetic murmur without actually saying anything.

'Then in the summer of 1971 one of the sons comes home from finishing his studies at one of them big private schools in the city. All of eighteen years and thinks the sun shines out of his you-know-what. Accustomed to being a bigshot and now he's only got his younger brother and the like to look up to him. So he's bored and wants to prove how clever he is and bad things start happening around town.'

'Bad things?' Pete asked.

'Stuff getting pinched. Guns even, not that anyone would report them. Livestock found dead. Like, riddled with bullets. Couple of women complained about being watched through windows when alone but never saw who it was.'

'And this young man was behind it?' Candace asked.

'For sure. He and his brother and a couple of other kids wanted to have a crack at me after closing one night. Waited outside. Told me I was a coward who'd conned my way out of conscription.' Albie chuckled. 'Took a swing at me but I still knew how to box. Gave his backside a couple of good kicks on his way down the street for good measure.'

Which probably made you an enemy for life.

The laughter faded and Albie's face turned grim. 'Day later a girl went missing. Lived with her uncle and little brother after her mum died. And her mum had only died recently so there was talk she'd taken herself off to grieve for a couple of days. School got worried when she didn't show and the family hadn't seen her. A search happened. I was part of it. Had a tracker involved. Never found the poor kid and it was accepted she'd either left for a new life or drowned in the basin.'

'What was her name, Albie?' Pete knew the answer but wanted it on record.

'Janie Swift.'

'You knew her?'

'Everyone knew everyone. Her uncle was a good man and he never recovered. First his sister from cancer, then his niece. And I reckon he knew who'd done it but had his nephew to raise. Lasted it out until the little boy was eighteen then shot himself. Sad place, this town.'

Leaning forward a little, Candace offered a gentle smile. 'But you stayed.'

'Guess I did.'

'What do you believe happened to Janie?'

'He killed her. Jock. Him and his little group of thugs. She'd go up and down the track every day and visit the grave-yard after her mum passed and it wouldn't take much for them to grab her and do god-knows-what. So he had it coming. Him and his brother. And their mate Neville.'

Heavy footsteps were coming up the stairs.

'Are you saying Jock was one of the people found dead on the grave back in the 8os?'

'Someone waited a long time for revenge on those two. Just never thought there'd be a third and now I reckon there might be more coming.'

The door flung open and Colin stalked in, red-faced and furious. 'You two get out.'

'These are my guests, son.'

'They are police and have no right to be interviewing you without a lawyer. I said to leave. Both of you.'

Pete picked up the phone and stood. 'No worries, mate. We'll head off. It was just an informal chat at your dad's invitation.' He walked to the door and Colin stepped aside.

Candace rose but instead of following, she extended her hand to shake Albie's, leaning in to speak quietly. He replied and then looked at Pete and winked.

'You are certain he said Carver. Jock Carver.' Pete's head was spinning with the new information.

Candace nodded. 'He did. I wish we'd had just a few more minutes with him although I imagine the next step is a formal interview.'

The team were almost back at the motel. Liz felt bad for not being able to keep Colin from noticing the absences because when he had, he'd clenched his fists and stalked off. Meg had told him they were at the bathroom which had slowed him for a few seconds but then he'd been up the stairs as if the place was on fire. During the whole thing, messages started arriving on her phone from Joy.

Meg unlocked her door. 'Give me two minutes then come in so we can debrief.'

It was a bit longer before they all piled into her room. At least tomorrow she'd have this back as a motel room rather than workplace. Liz helped get the chairs into place around the table, while Meg checked her computers.

'Before we get into the stuff with Albie... my phone call earlier was from Joy Reed, the constable Kath mentioned. She's got boxes of old material from the first two deaths which Kath will bring to us late tomorrow morning.'

'Oh thank goodness!' Meg muttered.

'And she has photos and reports from the recent crime scene.'

Meg's head shot around. 'We should go and get those now.'

Liz held up her phone. 'I have ten messages all with multiple images and I'm about to send them to our group. Just us here, for now.'

'I'll set up the projector.' Reuben got to work. 'Pete, can you move the whiteboard? Should be good to view on the wall.'

'What can I do?'

'Sit, Candace. I have a feeling your skills are about to come into play again.'

'There's forensic results in a report from Jeff,' Meg announced. 'What are we doing first?'

'I think we check what Joy has sent. It won't take long then we can talk reports and then Pete and Candace share what came of the chat with Albie.'

There were no objections and once the projector was running, Meg sent the images to it as a type of slideshow. Reuben sat with the projector and Pete turned off the overhead lights. For a moment there was a peculiar sense of anticipation in the room. And then the first image appeared.

Liz's stomach turned.

'I think that's one of the last taken so let me sort these.' Meg sat with her tablet.

The photograph was a close-up of a male face, left cheek flat on the ground. Lips were almost white but an outline of blue-grey was at odds with dried remains of vomit on the chin. His eyes were open and vacant and his eyelids oddly stiffened. Rigor mortis was underway.

'Okay, this is probably closer to the chronological order. I'd say the first few are from Kath's phone.'

The first image was taken from a distance and showed the entire grave, including the headstone. To the waist, the body was almost flat on the ground, elbows against to his sides, hands beneath the torso. His knees were pulled in with his buttocks sitting on his heels. Almost in a position of submission or supplication.

Another half dozen or so photos were taken from different angles. There was also one focused above the body in the direction of the church.

'Is that Erik Piper on the steps?' Liz stood and went closer to the wall. 'Yes, I recognise the robe. Can anyone see what's in his hand?'

Meg zoomed the image in and it became grainy. 'I can run it through a filter to clean it up.'

'A phone. I think so.' That was Reuben. 'We know he returned to his house to get it to phone Kath and she told him to stay at a distance. I wonder if he took photographs of his own?'

I should have considered that.

'Start a list for me, Reuben and put that question at the top, please.'

Seeing the police photos compared to how Erik had described initially finding the deceased was making her brain work overtime. She told herself to think in the background and returned to her seat.

The next round of photos were clearly from a police photographer. There was a typical look about them Liz had seen hundreds of times. Nothing new jumped out at her other than to reinforce the feeling that the body had been tampered with between Erik finding it and his return from collecting his phone.

'Perhaps Erik is lying,' Pete said. 'He might well have arranged the body to suit some weird poetic thing. Or been high.'

'Or the killer might have been lurking to make sure someone found the body. They'd already placed it in a particular position but according to Erik, it fell forward. In the heat, depending on when the death occurred, rigor might well have been accelerated and putting the body back in the same position impossible.' Meg found the first image. 'Placing the hands together as if in prayer might have been doable and with Erik possibly about to reappear, time was an issue.'

Most of the remaining images were variations on the first, other than a few of footprints, random distance shots, and one with several police helping move the body onto a stretcher with the morgue staff from the hospital.

'I'll go through these again on my screen,' Meg said. 'I wonder if it's too late to ask Joy to send some photos of the first and second cases? Even just a couple of any photos of the bodies at the scene.'

'Assuming any were taken.' Pete shook his head. 'The incompetence is doing my head in.'

Liz glanced at her watch. 'I'll send a message and ask. Even if she's gone home, she could take some in the morning before Kath arrives which gives us a small head start.'

'While you do that, I'll set up the whiteboard because after the report I'm about to read, we're going to need it.'

26

The expected storm completely missed the town but Liz had struggled to get to sleep after the team finally called it a night after one. Too tired to go for a run, she sat, cross-legged, on the bed, meditating after her shower. But her mind still refused to settle and when someone tapped on the door, she gave up completely.

'Got coffee,' Candace called. 'Instant but strong.'

The aroma wafted in when Liz opened the door. 'Strong sounds perfect, thank you.' She took the offered cup and closed the door behind Candace. 'Grab the chair if you like.'

Candace did so and gazed around. 'What is it about country motels? Go almost anywhere in Australia and you'll find the same thing, well, with a few minor differences. White brick walls seem particularly on-brand. Air-con room which works if you smack it hard enough. Toaster and kettle hidden in a cupboard with their cords wrapped around them. A dreary shower curtain which attaches itself to your legs.'

That made Liz laugh aloud as Candace continued.

'Although I've stayed in worse. Imagine we all have.'

'Where's the best place you've ever stayed?'

After taking a small sip from her cup, Candace gazed off in the distance. 'Without a doubt it was a cave hundreds of metres beneath the ground, accessed through an extinct volcano. We hoped it would stay extinct for the duration.'

'What a life you've led. You only ever hint at adventures but I feel you've seen more of the world – in more unusual ways – than I could even imagine.'

Eyes back on Liz, Candace tilted her head slightly.

'I have done and seen some amazing things and we really need to find time, away from work, to talk more. Life is one big adventure and we all should embrace it more. *You* should embrace it more. After this case, Lizzie, do something outrageous.' Candace drank more coffee.

'Is that a challenge? Outrageous isn't in my wheelhouse and you know that better than anyone.'

'Nonsense. Life is there to be lived, darling. Even the big mistakes.'

Sounds like you know about mistakes but I'm a bit afraid to ask in case it involves jumping off a platform in the stratosphere.

The coffee was gone too soon. At least it woke Liz up a bit. 'We should go get breakfast soon. All of us.'

'I'd like to talk first. Away from the rest of the team.' Candace played with the coffee cup, slowly rotating it between her fingers. 'At dinner I felt a bit like a school principal telling the children to be safe. Not something I'd normally do, not that way. The truth is I'm a bit unsettled with the change of leadership and merging of the two groups, each of which has existing relationships. Coming up here is a welcome opportunity to get back to what I do best.'

'Profiling. Investigating.'

Candace nodded. 'At the hub I've been doing a lot of the admin side since Ben said he was leaving and I'm happy to do whatever's necessary for however long, except...' She took a quick breath. 'My role is not admin support. Fletch needed a reminder of that to hurry him into appointing someone and now he'll have to manage without running to me every five minutes to ask how something works.'

'Felix?'

'Yes. Old habits and all that. He suggested I'd be more helpful to him staying at the hub and that anything this investigation needed from me could be handled remotely.'

'Wait on, does he not understand how heavily we rely on your expertise? And that proximity matters in this instance because we need you involved in interviews as well as at the crime scene. I'm happy to call him and outline exactly how important you are to us now, and have been in every investigation.' Liz's voice was rising a bit. 'Sorry. I'm annoyed.'

'So was I. Then I very quietly told him I could either fulfil my obligation to this case as requested by you, the team leader, or he would have my resignation.'

Liz gasped. 'No. Oh, Candace.'

With a shrug, Candace got to her feet and collected Liz's empty coffee cup. 'I was serious but I also knew he'd quickly reassess the situation. Which he did. But there's no need for you to call him because he knows my worth. He was just doing what he always does. Micro-managing with a side of control thrown in. Well, what he used to do because I don't play that game anymore.'

She headed for the door. 'Shall I round everyone up for breakfast?'

It took Liz only a couple of seconds to beat Candace to the door. 'Not until you explain what you're not saying.'

'About?'

'Um... all of this. Calling Felix, Fletch. Talking about him as though you've worked together in the past. Is that it?'

Candace reached for the handle and offered a wry smile. 'We can work well together most of the time. It was being married that ruined our relationship.'

The team gathered in the new room after everyone helped move the equipment. Other than Meg's main computer, which she kept in her room, the rest was quickly set up. As well as a larger table and more chairs, there was a large-screen television which Meg was preparing to use in place of the projector. The whiteboard was the current focus and Liz stood beside it, holding a long ruler in place of a pointer.

'We promise to behave, miss.'

Pete had made a few wisecracks already and Liz was almost at the point of smacking the back of his hand just to shut him up. She resisted the urge. Barely.

'Meg, I understand there's a few more results in?'

'There are but I think it would help us to go over the existing list of outstanding items and cross off anything we can first. Make some space for new stuff.'

Last night the team had worked through Jeff's report. It made sense to revisit it after having had sleep, a decent breakfast, and better coffee at the café. Liz picked up a red whiteboard marker and looked around.

'Where do I start?'

'Do you want to close off false leads? Or highlight unknowns?' Meg asked.

'Or both.' Reuben glanced up from his tablet. 'I've got a running list of what might be considered a red herring.'

'Go ahead.'

'The person Liz chased at the church? We've had no sighting of them on the cameras.'

'Just got an email that the trace from the old sleeping bag, clothes and so on in the storage room are identified as belonging to a petty thief who is currently serving a jail sentence. That gives them a good alibi so they were probably just squatting there and whoever opened the church door was likely a local being curious,' Meg said. 'I'd cross that off, Liz. Also, my contacts have confirmed that Erik Piper did arrive in Australia just over ten years ago. While that doesn't exclude him from the most recent death investigation, it does from the prior ones.'

Liz shook her head. 'I'm going to leave Erik there. We all know people can change their identity or slip through the cracks.'

'Meant to say, Liz. I did look at that metal sign at the sports-ground and while the holes might be from a bullet, the disturbed area is rusted enough to indicate it happened ages ago,' Reuben said.

That she did cross off. 'Anything else we know for certain is no longer in consideration?'

Heads shook so she found a whiteboard eraser and removed the words in question. Deselecting was every bit as important as homing in on clues.

'Meg, what is new since last night?'

Candace lifted her hand. 'Can I be a pain and ask we go back over some of the information because I want to be certain I'm not factoring the wrong things in... or out for that matter.'

'Go right ahead,' Meg said. 'I do have more to share but I'm still fiddling with the connection to that antiquated excuse for a screen on the wall. And no, Pete, I don't need your help but thanks.'

'Hey, I didn't say a word.'

'Okay, okay. Seeing as you want to volunteer, how about you jump up here and I'll take a seat.' Liz held the ruler out. 'I'd like your take on all of this, anyway.'

Pete screwed his face up but took the ruler, tapping it into his palm a few times as he took a long look at the whiteboard. Last night they'd sorted this side into halves, one with existing points to follow up, and the other only for relevant results from tests and new information. Liz had seen him ready to offer his services to someone who had the most knowledge of tech of all of them. He obviously needed to do something so now he could and she really was curious about his perspective.

He tapped the end of the ruler on the first item. 'I like this one. We have an address for the priest who lived at the church from 1970 to 1984. He is eighty-eight years old, apparently in good health, and lives alone in the next town west which is not a long drive and one I'm happy to volunteer for.' His eyes met Liz's. 'With Candace, maybe?'

After the glimpse he'd recently given her into his early years, Liz's first thought was to say no. But why? He was an excellent choice... as long as he kept his history out of it.

We might all be guilty of bringing our pasts into our job.

'Happy for you to both visit him.'

Pete slightly nodded. He might have expected resistance. 'Right, so next on the list is from the chat last night with Albie Walsh. He gave us the name of Jock Carver as a person of interest in the disappearance of Janie Swift. Now, living next door to Gordon Brain is a woman by the name of Betty Carver who – according to Gordy – hates people and leans toward the sovereign citizen philosophy. Her age is sixty-seven which potentially makes her the younger sister of Jock.'

'Do we know where Jock is now?' Candace asked.

'Not yet, but I'm doing a search.' Meg finished whatever she was doing and turned in her chair. 'I've fed all the information from Albie into my database as well as that of Betty. The Carvers appear to have been early settlers here and Carver Basin is partly on their land.'

'Reuben, you and I might take another look at her place this morning. I'll speak to Felix about getting a warrant if she digs her heels in.'

'I have a question Meg,' Reuben asked. 'The data from the drone?'

She raised her eyes to the ceiling. 'Still waiting. It went to Jeff's own lab as they do a lot of work for private surveillance companies and probably government ones and have a better chance of extracting anything as deep as we'd expect a coffin. Well, that is, we could see a coffin shape in the second. And the first grave was clear until about a metre down then the signal kind of bounced back. Very strange.'

'Theories?' Candace leaned forward.

'Possibly pockets of air or something as simple as the camera dealing with light at the wrong second. Or a slab of concrete or a big rock is in there. Even though this camera is the newest tech for checking the ground, there's still only so much it can do. I know you'd talked about redoing the imaging after dark so we could do that tonight if there's no definitive answer beforehand.' But Meg looked thoughtful and swung her chair back to her keyboard. 'I'm going to ask Jeff to check the age of the soil samples we took.'

Was it possible something... some*one*, was in that first grave? Buried then covered with whatever was blocking the view of the camera. Liz's gut told her they had to revisit the site. And the church. And that pond belonging to Erik Piper with its strange angel statues and—

'Liz?'

Everyone was looking at her.

'Sorry, just thinking.'

The television was on and an image paused. Meg gestured at it. 'I have some video taken by Jeff's friend of a friend but before I play, please be warned the subject is the body in the current investigation and it isn't in great shape. Will was able to access it to view but not take samples or even touch the body. There's a written report which I'll read as we watch but if anyone finds it too much, just look away.'

The video began with a wide view of a male corpse on their back on a steel pull-out table.

'I'm so cranky right now,' Meg said. 'Me, not what Will said. Here's the report from him.' She began reading as the camera closed in on the head. 'Deceased male, body in poor condition post death presumably being affected by extreme heat, long exposure to direct sunlight, and incorrect handling. Age approximately late sixties to middle seventies. Current state is post rigor mortis and some idiot has manipulated the limbs to straighten them. Oh, that is what he said, not me.' Meg added.

Jeff's friend of a friend sounded like someone Liz wanted to meet.

The video closed in on the face, neck, and shoulders.

'There are signs of linear bruising which, with the thumb marks on the neck, indicate manual strangulation. Without being permitted to touch, I cannot ascertain if the hyoid is broken.'

For a minute or two the rest of the body was panned across.

'No unusual marks other than the neck and an injection site here.' It zoomed in on the vein inside one arm. 'I believe this was made within the hours prior to death and there is no other indication of habitual injection sites.'

Pete raised a hand and Meg paused the video. He'd returned to his chair at some point while Liz had been thinking. 'Not an addict. Not a diabetic. A drug to sedate him? Make him easy to get to the grave before he was strangled?'

And someone doesn't want us to find this out. Someone who can control normal police processes. Barnaby Hobson?

'Sounds plausible. I'll keep going.' Meg touched the remote

again and looked at her tablet. 'My recommendation is this be referred to the Coroners Court as a suspicious death and a proper examination take place including a tox screen, although it may be too late to show a full profile.'

The video turned onto the face of the speaker, a man in his forties with thick glasses and a goatie. His voice was finally heard. 'I was able to view the victim's clothing, boots, wallet, and some jewellery. I was not allowed to film it nor handle it. The wallet appeared to be water-damaged but perhaps I am guessing. Sorry I was unable to report more but I'm confident that a proper examination will declare the death suspicious.'

'Water damaged?' Reuben looked at Liz. 'The basin?'

'Rumoured to be where a teenager may have been drowned? Which has an old track leading to it from the church grounds via the road where Betty Carver lives?' Liz stood. 'I'd like a closer look at the Carver property.'

27

'You might as well hear it from me, Pete, because sooner or later Fletch will spill his guts to the team or make a comment to me which makes no sense to anyone. I've told Liz. Just this morning, actually.'

Pete was driving Liz's hire car to visit the priest and Candace had barely said a word until they'd passed the welcome sign in the next town.

'Hear what?'

'We were once married. A long time ago.'

'Sorry? You and Felix?'

'Well, yes. Who did you think I meant?'

'And now you're not married?'

'Not for over twenty years.'

He glanced across. She smiled.

'Wow. Didn't expect that. Was the divorce friendly?'

'Not even close but we've managed to find a way to remain civil enough. This isn't the first time we've worked together but it is proving the most challenging.'

No wonder you've been distracted. Working with an ex? No

thanks.

'Shall we remove his locker? Only give him lukewarm coffee? Stop the wheels on his office chair from turning? Get Meg to change his biometrics and lock him out?'

Candace burst out laughing.

'I have more ideas.'

'I'm sure you do and if it gets to a point of needing help, I will ask. Promise.'

Felix Fletcher had annoyed Pete since the day he arrived. There wasn't much logic to his reaction other than the man being yet another bureaucrat who'd probably waste too much time with paperwork. Ben Rossi was never like that. He'd been a decent cop and a fair-minded human. Not only could he manage the higher-ups but was always quick to be out in the field with his team. And as much as Pete understood Ben's reasons for leaving, he hadn't quite forgiven him yet.

'We all miss Ben.'

'What are you, psychic?'

'Maybe. Look, I don't mean to rain on Fletch's parade. He's a good operator and brings excellent skills to the job.'

'We'll see. I think this is the road.' Pete turned a corner and slowed to navigate a narrow residential street. 'Need number seventy-two.'

'Just passed forty-eight.'

The houses were all small and relatively new. Probably some kind of estate suiting older residents without being an aged care community.

'Sixty-four.'

Pete found a parking spot and turned off the engine.

'Seeing as we're doing show and tell, doc... can I share?'

Candace shuffled so she could see him face to face. 'Go on.'

'Not saying I need any therapy. Just that... Liz and I were in the church at one point. A conversation came up and since then I've been going over some things. From being a kid.'

Her face remained neutral but Pete could see the compassion in her eyes.

'Go on.'

'Nothing about me. But kids I knew were... by our priest. You know what I'm saying?'

'I think so. Are you worried about speaking with *this* priest?'

'No. Maybe. I mean, I've interviewed plenty of them in the past but knowing a young girl might have died there is bugging me.'

'You volunteered us to do this.' Her lips rose a little in the corners. 'You'll be professional, particularly given his advanced age. I saw you with Albie and while I know these men are quite different, the way you treated him was with respect. If nothing else, hold onto that.'

'Yeah. Yeah, I can do that.'

Before leaving the motel he and Meg had quickly touched on the evidence concerning the church and he'd focus on the facts. As they climbed out, he glanced at Candace, half-wishing he'd said nothing. Bad enough he'd let too much slip with Liz the other day.

Number seventy-two was a small house with a concrete garden. There were pots with sticks instead of live plants, and a bird bath with barely any water. It felt sad.

'Bit different from where he must have once lived. Where Erik Piper is now,' Candace said. 'Easy to maintain, I imagine.'

Pete tapped on the screen door. The front door was open and after a minute, sounds of footsteps trudged toward them.

'Who is it? I can't see very well.'

'My name is Detective Pete McNamara and I'm with Doctor Candace Carroll. Father Bryant?'

There was a cackle-like laugh and the screen door slowly opened. 'Nobody calls me Father these days. Long time since I heard it. Mr Bryant will do. Did I call the police? Or a doctor?'

Standing inside was a small figure, a man barely over five feet in height, wisps of white hair, and leaning on a walker. He peered at Pete and then Candace.

'We hoped to have a chat with you. May we come in?'

'Better show me a badge or something. Can't see a physician's bag or a uniform.'

'Easily done.' Pete held out his ID. 'Doctor Carroll isn't a police officer but a consultant who works with our team.'

'Close the screen door on your way in.' Mr Bryant took some time to turn the walker and shuffle back along a short hallway. 'I can offer some water.'

'Lovely, thank you.' Candace pulled the screen shut and lowered her voice. 'He's frail.'

In other words, go easy on him.

Pete didn't know how to answer, so didn't, leading the way to what turned out to be a tiny kitchen. There was barely room for the three of them and only two chairs at a small table. He backed into a corner while Mr Bryant poured water into three glasses from a jug, holding it tightly with both hands. Candace thanked him with a big smile and handed a glass to Pete before collecting the other two and placing them on the table.

As Mr Bryant settled onto a chair, Candace sat. 'How long have you lived here? It looks quite new.'

'Two years, near enough. It was this or a nursing home and I'm accustomed to my own company. Just wish I could walk further than the shops around the corner. And sometimes I miss my old home.'

'Near the church?' Pete asked.

'I've lived elsewhere since then but now you mention it... yes. All that open space. Big old trees. The wildlife. Something special about the red dirt even if it did make it hard to keep my white attire clean.' Again, the cackle. And a sudden, sharp look at Pete's face. 'This about the poor men who passed away in the graveyard?'

You can see just fine. What else are you pretending about?

'What do you remember about it? Did you find the bodies?'

'Me? No. Why would you think such a thing?'

Candace leaned a little forward. 'Perhaps we are misinformed but our understanding is that you were the priest in residence from 1970 to 1984.'

Hands curled around his glass, the old man bit his lip.

'There's not a great deal of good information available but now that another man has died in similar circumstance, we really could use your help.'

'Nothing to help with. The men died while praying. Might sound unusual but it happens. People become overwhelmed with grief, regret. The heart fails.' His eyes were now on Candace. 'Twice is unusual in the same spot. I'll give you that. But I didn't find them. No. No, I was away both times.'

'Do you know who did find them?'

'It was a very long time ago, detective.'

'Certainly was. And going back even further to 1971? A teenager went missing. Janie Swift was her name. What can you tell us about her?'

'Who?'

Pete's resolve to play good cop was being tested. The priest, ex-priest, whatever he called himself, was playing some stupid game with them. 'Do you still follow your faith?'

Candace shot Pete a warning look.

'Of course. Not a priest now but as staunch a Catholic as I ever was.'

'I was Catholic,' Pete said. 'Lived with faith. Followed the rituals and rules. And was *completely* honest. Mum said God was always watching.'

Mr Bryant drew a long breath through his nostrils.

'In 1971 you'd been the priest there for only a year and it must have been a shock. We've spoken to Albie Walsh who clearly remembers helping search for the poor girl. Did you also join the search parties?'

The old man's hands were shaking as he picked up his glass. 'I remember now. Everyone looked for her. I held extra masses. Prayed with her family.'

Candace beat Pete to speak. 'How thoughtful of you to do that. Be there to offer comfort at such a worrying time. Her family must have been distraught.'

Mr Bryant nodded vigorously. 'Very.'

'Her mum and dad. They'd be beside themselves.'

The glass was placed down and Mr Bryant stared into it after a single nod of his head. No answer was forthcoming and Candace glanced at Pete as if asking what to do.

'Sir?' Pete began. 'When I was chatting to Albie, he mentioned Janie only had her little brother and uncle. Her mum had recently died. Our investigative team includes a very clever person who understands forensics and she found signs of blood and other bodily fluids. Some on a headstone right next to the grave where three men have turned up dead. Now, neither of those headstones have a name on them. Can you shed any light on why? Or who the graves belong to?'

Still no answer but the man's face was losing its colour.

'I was inside the church a couple of times and found more blood and bodily fluids. We also found a pendant on one of the graves which had DNA belonging to a woman named Maude.' Pete needed the truth.

Mr Bryant's head shot up. 'Maude? How would you know about her?'

'What do *you* know about her?'

Eyes glistening, a tear escaped and slid down the man's cheek. He leaned back in his seat and gazed at Candace, his chest heaving. 'Maude Swift. Janie's mother. God took her and then her oldest child.'

Pete hadn't expect that.

'Took her?' Candace spoke quietly.

'Maude had cancer.'

'And Janie?'

The head dropped again.

'Who took Janie, Father?'

The old man's mouth opened then closed and he shook his head.

'You don't know? Or you won't tell us?' Pete's questions came out more harshly than he intended but he was beyond caring. 'Is this what your faith tells you to do? Protect killers? Is it what *God* would want?'

Abruptly pushing himself to his feet, Mr Bryant glared at Pete. 'Do not elevate yourself to such heights as to know the thoughts of the Almighty. Sometimes helping another is more important than worrying at the time about human consequences. My choices will be judged by Him and Him alone. I want you both to leave.'

Stomach churning, Pete forced himself to brush past the man and head for the door. He wanted to be here alone. Make the priest confess what he'd done to Janie because why else would he be so evasive? He pushed open and held the screen door, barely hearing Candace speaking. She went by and he let the door close but Mr Bryant pushed it open again.

'Young man. You said you were a Catholic. Why are you not still one?'

Pete made it partway along the short path before turning.

'Because of priests like you.'

'Like me? Oh. Oh, you mean… but no. Not me, my son. I would never have harmed another. Not even the bad ones.'

The roaring in Pete's ears drowned out any more words and then he was running. Onto the footpath then to the car. And in the gutter beyond it, he dropped to his knees and vomited.

Normally, Meg preferred to work alone. Although she was an excellent multi-tasker, including answering questions and solving people's personal problems while doing a multitude of other jobs, there were times when having a quiet space and no competing needs made things a bit easier. But right now she was unsettled. Again.

'No walking in the bushland today,' she muttered. 'They're all okay.'

Since Liz and Reuben had driven off she'd kept a screen open tracking them. Right now they were parked on the road where Gordon Brain and Betty Carver lived. While Gordon seemed nice enough and had been happy to answer questions, Betty was an unknown quantity.

For the third time in an hour, Meg walked to the whiteboard.

Both of their names were above dot points.

Gordon (Gordy) Brain

- Purchased motel fifteen years ago from Hector Swift
- Small digital footprint and no red flags – no legal or financial issues
- Appears well liked locally
- Lives next door to Betty Carver

Betty Carver

- Only known resident on family land with strong
  warnings to stay out
- Likely a close relative of Jock Carver, named by
  Albie Walsh as troublemaker and person he
  believes killed Janie Swift
- No response to attempts to contact
- Lives next door to Gordon Brain

'So why am I so bothered?' Talking aloud helped her think. 'The only connection is where they live and that has to be purely accidental. Or is it?'

Back at her desk, Meg pulled up records she'd accessed earlier. They were local council land records going back almost one hundred years and included changes in boundaries, any covenants, and title deeds. She located the Carver property first having already gathered information about the age of the title. This time she read right through the succession from the original Carver four generations back, passed down to Betty. The only deviation was in 1972. Ten acres was divided off and sold. It might as well have been gifted as only ten dollars exchanged hands. A dollar for every acre?

'Another relative? Rewarding a loyal employee? Or something corrupt?'

Meg found the title for the newer parcel of land. The deed began with a person called Lenny Field. She made a note to look at who he was in the scheme of things.

The next owner was noted as 'family inheritance' and was not what Meg expected. 'Hector Swift. 1978. What the heck?' The current owner was Gordon Brain, sold to him in 2011.

She turned to look at the whiteboard. Hector Swift had owned the motel and sold it to Gordy around fifteen years ago. And now it appeared he'd also sold his house and land to him at the same time. A two for one deal? Buy the business, need a home. Could it be so simple? If Hector Swift intended to retire, he might have wanted to cut ties with the town. But how many people at any time were looking for a business and a home in a tiny, remote town?

Instead of returning to her keyboard, Meg picked up her phone. Something was terribly wrong and Liz needed to know before she poked around too much in that street.

28

I can't watch them all at the same time.

Two cars. Five people. All in different directions.

Do I follow the first one who came? Except the man she's with right now is clearly a soldier. Powerful. Looks smart.

And she's too observant and bossy.

Or the shameful excuse for a law enforcement officer? Long hair. Unfit. No respect for his position or himself. Can't bear carelessness and he reeks of it. Doesn't care for himself. Or his privilege as a police officer. Probably doesn't even care for the people he works with. I'd like to go a round or two with him.

Not today.

He's with the new one and she's still an unknown quantity.

Instead, I take a risk. My natural caution needs to be suppressed because if I'm to rid the town of these intruders then I have to discover their intent. I find the smallest gap between the curtains and use my phone to record the little I can see from my car. Not ideal. Ten minutes and I have some footage. I'll leave now and look at it later.

Knowledge is power. Power over evil.

29

Reuben stood on a boulder, one of several alongside the Carver property. Using binoculars, he surveyed the land beyond an adjoining barbed wire fence.

'Anything?' Liz was a few metres away attempting to get phone coverage. The bars fluctuated between one and none. A message had arrived from Meg asking her to call and if she couldn't get a signal soon, she'd trek back to the BearCat and grab the satellite phone.

'The house looks empty. I can see through several windows and there's no sign of furniture nor any lights or movement.'

Liz climbed up and he handed her the binoculars.

After several minutes at the front gate making another attempt to raise anyone through the speaker, they'd walked along the road in the direction away from Gordy's driveway. More than two hundred metres on there was a break in the fence and Liz made the decision to go through it. From the overhead map of the property it was unclear if this was part of the Carver land. Easy enough to apologise and retreat if challenged. Once they reached the boulders, they'd taken advantage of the height to look for signs of habitation.

Adjusting the focus, Liz looked in the same direction Reuben had, finding a large and old weatherboard homestead. 'See what you mean. Even the plants in the pots on the verandah look dead. I wonder how long since she's been home?'

'Perhaps she occupies the other side of the house. Or one of the cottages. Might be less to manage.'

Liz handed back the binoculars. 'I'll ask Felix to start the process to get a warrant. Actually, what about flying a drone over in the interim?'

'Happy to. I can come here while it's still light then move to the graveyard for a closer look at those graves. Unless you want it done earlier?'

Still on the boulder, they turned to look down to the basin, whose water glistened between trees about half a kilometre away. 'Later is good. I'd like to walk there, Reuben.'

He jumped down and held his hand out for Liz, who pretended not to see it and pointed toward the house again. 'We know there's two cottages plus multiple other buildings. I just have a feeling there are answers on the property.' Her phoned beeped. 'About time.' She tapped on a message from Meg. 'Whoops, there's three. All asking me to call and the last says she will walk here if there's no response in ten minutes. And that was sent eight minutes ago.'

Liz climbed down and dialled then put the call on speaker. 'We'll do the water later. Kath is due in the next hour or so.' They headed for the road.

Meg answered. 'Well, about time!'

'There's poor coverage here. Are you alright?'

'Of course I am. I'm not the ones facing potential death and who-knows-what-else.'

'We're safe, Meg,' Reuben said. 'Just taking a look at the Carver place over the fence.'

'Well I know that. But do you know what you are up against?'

At the moment a worried team member and rough terrain.

Meg continued. 'Did you know that the Carver property had a piece subdivided? Ten acres in 1972. And it is where Gordon Brain lives after buying it at the same time as he bought the motel. And that the seller of both was Hector Swift?'

Liz glanced at Reuben, who'd raised his eyebrows.

'Are you coming back?'

'Yes. We'll be there in about ten minutes.'

There was a slight beep on the line indicating an incoming call and Kath's name was highlighted.

'Answer the call and I'll put the kettle on.' Meg rang off.

Tapping 'accept' on the screen, Liz kept the speaker on. 'Hi Kath.'

There wasn't a reply, just vague background noises.

'Kath, its Liz.'

'Pocket dial?' Reuben suggested.

'I'm... here.'

Both Liz and Reuben abruptly stopped walking. Kath sounded dreadful.

'We're listening, Kath. Reuben and I.'

'Car... crashed. Hurt.'

'Where? Can you pin your location to me?'

Reuben opened his own phone and dialled.

'Yeah. But the files. Damnit. The files.'

A location popped up on Liz's phone. 'Got you. We'll call for more help and it looks like we're only a few minutes out. Are you safe?'

'Yeah.'

'We're coming, Kath. I'll call you straight back.'

She and Reuben sprinted back to the BearCat. He was barely out of breath, barking information to Meg as they ran. Liz sent the pin to the rest of the team then she called Pete. One of their own was hurt. But what had Kath meant about the files?

First sight of the accident scene took Liz's mind back to the crash which killed the daughter and son-in-law of Vince Carter. Kath's patrol car had hit a large tree, its bonnet forced in on itself. Shattered glass and a tyre littered the road.

Reuben angled the BearCat across the road for traffic management and Liz was out and running in a second. Beyond the wreck, Kath was on the ground against a fence post, partly upright. Liz hadn't been able to raise her in the twelve-minute dash from the Carver property.

She dropped to her knees beside Kath. The officer was in a drowsy state and bleeding from a jagged cut across her forehead. Her left arm hung awkwardly.

'We're here, Kath. There's an ambulance on the way and police. Can you look at me?'

It was clearly an effort but Kath raised her eyes.

'Arm? Head injury? Anything else I need to look at?'

Kath groaned as she adjusted her body. 'Ouch.'

'I know. Paramedics will come and fix the ouch. Probably a nice green whistle to suck filled with happy drugs.'

There were sirens in the distance and Kath's eyes widened. 'Get what's left. Take them. I was knocked out... woke up and someone... stole some.'

A chill went through Liz.

The hire car had arrived and both Pete and Candace were running toward them.

'Get what's left. Before anyone else.'

'I'm staying with you.'

'No. Go and get them. I was forced off the road, Liz. For the files.'

Candace arrived, a first aid kit in hand, and immediately started evaluating Kath's condition.

'Go, Liz,' Kath said. 'Hurry.' She kind of sighed and her eyes closed.

'Keep talking to me, Kath.' Candace glanced at Liz. 'The boxes are going to be collected right now but I need you to keep your eyes open.'

Liz waved for Pete to meet her at the wreck. He'd taken point the other side of the crash site but there was no traffic. Apart from multiple sirens which were closing in. He was only seconds behind.

'We need to locate the boxes of files and anything else about this case.'

Without asking a question, Pete reached through a shattered window and withdrew a box. 'Here.'

Grabbing it from him, Liz raised the lid and her heart sank. Only a couple of large envelopes.

He located the second box and without opening it, gazed at Liz. 'Can you manage both?'

'Of course. Why?'

'Get them to the BearCat. I want to have a better look.'

Carrying the boxes on top of each other, Liz rushed to the BearCat and locked them in before running back to the wreck. Pete had hauled a back door open and was on his stomach inching across. An ambulance came around the long curve of road and when Candace stood, waving both arms, it slowed and headed toward her.

'Anything?'

'Gimme a min.'

The broken window was the passenger side of the front and almost certainly where whoever had touched the boxes gained access. Pete had crawled behind the driver's seat and had a flashlight on. His spare arm was squeezed between the bottom of the seat and the floor.

'Gotcha.'

He wriggled backwards, Liz making space for him to get out and shielding him from sight as a patrol car stopped behind the ambulance. His face was red with effort but he grinned as he stuffed another of the envelopes down his top.

'You are a legend, mate,' Liz said. 'Add it to the boxes and make sure everything is out of view.'

'Guarding it with my life.'

He'd gone before she could say that was a bit extreme.

'Detective Moorland!'

Sergeant Barnaby Hobson was the last person she'd expected to arrive so quickly. Even if Kath had called the crash in first, the drive from Sanston was at least thirty minutes.

He stalked in Liz's direction and she met him not far from Kath, who had a paramedic checking her vitals. Candace was close to her, quietly offering reassurance.

'What are you doing here?' The sergeant crossed his arms.

Tempted to ask him why he was talking to her before checking on his officer, Liz managed to tone down her annoyance.

'Kath seems to have a broken arm, a bad head cut, is drowsy, and probably in shock.'

'Are you a doctor as well?'

'I'm happy to wait if you want to speak with her.'

He finally looked at his injured officer and something in his face changed. His expression softened and his shoulders dropped a little. This was the first time Liz had seen him show more than bluff and bravado. His eyes moved to the wreck and he paled. 'She walked out of that?' But then he hardened again. 'What the hell made her lose control of the unit? Now we're down a vehicle and an officer.'

'Doubt she did it to annoy you.'

Hobson shot her a nasty look. 'Why are you here? Why is your whole team here?'

'They're not. But the one who isn't here is our intelligence expert. She sees emergency calls come through.'

Not a lie. Meg would have found out at some point.

There was no chance Liz was telling this man, or anyone outside Operation Nobody, about Kath's desperate phone call. He was a suspect. Same as half the town.

'How did *you* get here so fast?' Pete wandered into the conversation. He was happy with himself and knowing Pete, ready for a bit of what he'd call fun. 'Took me eighteen minutes and I was only just up the road'

'I was on my way back to Sanston after visiting family in Branonville. Turned around when the call came in.'

'Still have family here?'

Pete had that look about him of wishing he was in an interrogation room. Liz had seen it often enough to know he was about to upset the senior officer. He was welcome to go right ahead and do his thing.

'Still?'

'Grew up here from what I hear. You'd know everyone.' It wasn't a question. 'Whatever happened to Hector Swift?'

Drawing in an audible breath and stepping back, Hobson's neck and face went a peculiar shade of purple.

'See, we heard he sold his motel and his house to Gordy, who's a nice fellow and looks after us well. Maybe Hector decided to retire to the Maldives after a successful life running the town's only motel. Bit odd that there's no trace of him now. Not anywhere.'

That was news to Liz. Unless Pete was fishing.

Hobson had gathered himself and almost sneered at Pete. 'Have you personally looked in the Maldives? Worth a trip, don't you agree?'

Pete's smile was a thing of beauty. This was him at his best. Pushing and prodding without coming across as anything other than a cop who was clutching at straws. Nobody could do this as well as he did because he'd home in on the slightest sign of weakness or a shift in body language and use it to his advantage.

'Have you been? Damned brilliant for a holiday but I wouldn't want to live there. And I can't imagine a man who worked hard all his life living there either. No, I see Hector Swift more the type who'd stay in the region. Lots of friends, I imagine. Maybe even some family.'

'None. No family at all. Or friends. He just retired and left town once he sold up. Nothing more sinister.'

More police vehicles arrived and traffic was gradually building on either side of the road.

'Make yourself useful and clear those cars, detective.'

Hobson tried to use his height to intimidate Pete, moving into his personal space. Pete grinned up at him. 'Sure thing, mate. We can keep chatting later. Alligator.' With a wink at Liz, Pete jogged toward Reuben's end of the road. Liz coughed to stop herself laughing.

'Get your officer in line, detective. I'm a senior police officer and will not be spoken to with such disrespect.'

'Sure. In the meantime, where *did* Hector Swift go? We're keen to have a conversation with him.'

'What on earth for?'

Liz took a moment to answer. Hector was a sore point for Hobson. If he was the killer or protecting the killer then was Hector yet another victim? Were more bodies to be discovered?

'We think he might have been involved in some serious criminal activity.'

The man blinked. He'd not expected that. But he shook his head dismissively. 'I have to check on Kath. Excuse me.'

Watching him stride away, Liz knew she'd found a major key to all of this. Her gut told her so and he'd have to do a lot to prove it wrong.

30

Through the small screen of Liz's phone, Felix Fletcher's expression was hard to read. She was in the BearCat alone after they all returned to the motel. The call was at her request and she had the impression – from his sharp tone and set face – that she'd caught him at a bad time.

'I appreciate you speaking with me on short notice,' she said. 'We've had some developments and updating you is quicker this way. I wouldn't have interrupted but there are police officers involved in this development.'

They'd not spoken since before Candace arrived in town, although Liz sent through briefings twice a day and he'd respond. She had no idea what he was really like and felt she had to work extra hard to keep communication lines open.

How she missed Ben.

'Sorry if I'm not myself. An old friend passed this morning. I need to tell Candace.'

Mentally kicking herself for jumping to conclusions, Liz softened her voice. 'My condolences on your loss. If there's anything I can do... would you like me to speak with Candace?'

'I should be the one. He was a friend to us both. It will help though if you keep an eye on her? She's the strongest person I know but even so, this will be a shock. And if she wants to come back I'll arrange transport.' Felix suddenly smiled. 'Except she won't. Work is always the answer to everything for Candy.'

Candy? Good grief, please don't get any more personal!

Perhaps Felix realised he might be over-sharing because he straightened and stared directly at Liz.

'What developments and what does it have to do with police? Which police?'

'I received a phone call late this morning from Leading Senior Constable Kath Connor. She was transporting boxes containing cold case files pertaining to the deaths in the eighties, as well as reports concerning the recent deceased. Her patrol car was run off the road – her words – and she was briefly unconscious.'

'Oh my god. Is she alright?'

'On her way to hospital with a number of injuries but not openly life threatening. When she came to, a person unknown had accessed the evidence boxes. Much of the contents appear to have been removed, although we are only just now auditing what is left.'

'Removed?'

'We know it's more than simply the result of the impact. The boxes were still closed. Yet an evidence envelope was located beneath a seat and although we're yet to open it, I wonder if the thief dropped it in their rush to disappear.'

Liz filled Felix in on the conversation with Hobson, including his statement about having been in town to visit family.

'Are you thinking he had opportunity?'

'Maybe. But not in his patrol car. Too risky.'

'What do you need from me, Liz?'

'Any chance we can access Hobson's complete employment history? Meg only has so much she can view without alerting anyone.'

'Done.'

'And we need a search warrant for the property owned by Betty Carver. Reuben is sending a formal request through in the next hour.'

'We'll secure it as fast as possible. If it is urgent... any due cause to enter?' Felix's expression brightened. 'Strange sounds. Someone in danger?'

'The buildings are all too far from any boundary to tell. I hope you don't mind me saying but for a minute you reminded me of Pete.'

'Have been compared to far worse cops than McNamara. I'm looking forward to getting us all together when this is done. Have a few drinks. Dinner. Must be tricky having a new person in Ben's job without a chance to properly meet.'

Candace stepped out of the motel room and tilted her head at Liz.

'Sir, I need to go. Thanks for your time and again, condolences on your loss.'

'Keep in touch, Liz.'

The connection cut, Liz climbed out and locked up.

'Everyone's ready.' Candace reached to open the door but her phone rang and she glanced at it. 'Just Fletch. I'll ring him back soon.' She swiped the call away. 'Were you speaking with him?'

Part of Liz was grateful Candace had rejected the call. It was important the team debrief to give Meg the best chance of doing her job. All of them really. But the other part was already sad for the doctor because soon enough she'd get bad news. Liz didn't like either parts of herself at that moment. She was selfish.

'Liz?'

'Um, yes. He'll arrange the search warrant once he gets the request from Reuben and is going to get us more on Hobson. Hopefully that will be soon.'

'I want to tell you all about Kath. What she told me. Poor darling.'

The door opened again, this time Meg, who raised her eyebrows. 'I see. Out here gossiping instead of inside, making a plan.'

'Sorry.'

'Fine. Come on then. Between what you all need to tell and all that I need to share, it's going to be a multiple coffee meeting.'

Although she'd already downed several cups of instant crappy coffee, Meg had another on her desk.

'Boss, I need to make an equipment request. Is that via you or who? It's an important addition.'

Liz glanced up from a conversation with Candace. 'Unless it's a weapon, isn't that your thing to do?'

'So it is. What if I need an assistant? I can order one of those at the same time?'

'I can take over the requisitions if that helps?' Pete offered. 'Might even have contacts, if you know what I mean.' He grinned.

'Trouble is, this might need to be fixed inside a BearCat, so does it make the equipment a weapon?'

Everyone was looking at her and Meg was tempted to come up with an elongated name of a non-existent thing. But at last she had their undivided attention which would move the process along. The process of finding killers.

She lifted her coffee mug. 'We cannot function on this. A

proper coffee machine is hereby approved for all trips away from the hub of longer than two hours.'

Reuben looked thoughtful. 'There is a small space I could fit one into. Not a big coffee machine. But nowadays there are some compact units which will do quite nicely. We'll need to confer on how to manage storage for cups, coffee, various milks and so on.'

Just as seriously, Meg continued the game. 'I'll create a little program which identifies how often we use every item in each BearCat compared to how often we drink coffee. Shouldn't be difficult to remove some lower scoring equipment.'

'Such as?' Liz asked.

'Have we ever used the bazooka?'

Pete's eyes lit up. 'What bazooka? We have one?'

'So now that we are in agreement, are we debriefing about Kath or shall I update with my latest?'

The team jostled into seats.

'Me? Right. I have some results from Jeff. Trace from the soil samples Pete helped me retrieve. There was mixed DNA, most of which needs a lot more time for identification or at least, adding to the database. However, he did match to records from someone who'd been arrested for disorderly conduct. One Jocelyn Carver.'

'Jocelyn?' Liz looked interested.

'More commonly known as Jock Carver.'

'In the soil? Which grave, Meg?'

'The first.' She couldn't keep a grin off her face. 'And the second. And even more... it is on another part of the chain from the angel pendant, mingled closely to that which has the familial match to Maude Swift.'

'The pendant? As if he'd handled it?' Candace asked.

'Exactly as if he'd handled it. There's a full report to go

through which I'll send to each tablet. We really need to identify the connection to Maude.'

'Janie Swift.' Pete was nodding. 'She's Maude's daughter. The sorry excuse for a priest told us God took Maude and then her oldest child.'

Why are you so angry? Your hands are clenching.

Candace had her eyes on Pete and after giving him a small smile took over the conversation. 'Yes, he did say that.' She gazed around the room. 'Maude died from cancer but he refused to answer questions about how Janie died. He didn't deny it was her he referred to as the oldest child, however he became defensive and stopped the conversation. The other thing is that Albie Walsh believed Jock Carver was responsible for Janie's death.'

'We need to do a formal interview with Mr Bryant.' Pete's voice was toneless and he abruptly stood and went to the window. His fingers played with the drawn curtain. 'I'll excuse myself from any further dealings with him. If possible.'

Liz half-stood then sat again but she was staring at Pete's back, her forehead creased. Yet her tone was matter-of-fact. 'Reuben? Would you please find a way to access the local police station for the purpose of a formal interview, then take Candace and request Mr Bryant accompany you both?'

'Will do. If he refuses?'

'Then interview him at home. We don't want to find ourselves accused of harassing an elderly man so I'm relying on you both to use your best judgement. Please record it.'

'We recorded ours, Pete and I.'

Candace was also looking at Pete.

Something had obviously happened during the earlier interview which freaked Pete out and he wasn't easily spooked so it had to be bad. Eventually he'd come and talk to her. Probably with his customary bottle of something expensive and a need to share.

Meg cleared her throat and everyone gave her their attention again. 'Please send the recording to me. Shall we look at these evidence boxes, for what they're worth?'

Pete mentally kicked himself. He hadn't dealt well with the priest. And he wasn't about to share his shameful episode near the hire car. Candace hadn't said a word, slipping in behind the wheel while he sorted himself out and handing him a packet of wet wipes and a bottle of water once he climbed in. Excluding himself from any further contact was best for the investigation.

And me.

He was all too aware of a sympathetic look from Candace and worried ones from Meg and Liz. Reuben was busy on his tablet, probably following Liz's request to find a way into the police station now Kath was out of commission.

The evidence boxes sat on a trestle table. As he was already on his feet, Pete might as well do the honours.

Liz took a minute or two to go over the scene they'd found at the crash site while he unpacked each box, laying the contents in front of them. There was precious little. A couple of files plus an envelope in the first and three envelopes in the second... one of which he'd found under the seat in the wreck.

'Kath told me what she remembered,' Candace said. 'She's convinced it was a deliberate act.'

Reuben looked up from his tablet. 'Go on.'

'She was partway around that long bend and a van came in the opposite direction. It crossed into her lane, not like it was out of control but with intent, just enough to force her to go onto the shoulder to avoid a collision. And that shoulder is narrow and gravel, which sent her into a spin.'

'They didn't stop,' Liz said.

'They did. Kath came too and as she scrambled out she fell onto the ground. She recalls someone running away and then heard a vehicle drive off.'

'Any description?' Meg was tapping fast on a keyboard. 'I'm requesting the hub find any fixed cameras within twenty kilometres of the crash site.'

'All she remembered was a white van. Like a courier has.'

'Good, thanks. I'll ask for a broadcast to go to all law enforcement, emergency services, petrol stations, courier companies, and so on within the region. We need access to the SD card in the patrol car for whatever footage it picked up.'

'I can drive out to the scene and collect it,' Pete said. 'Except, we probably can't just take it.'

Liz was nodding. 'Correct. But we might head back shortly anyway and take a look around. Meg, you can start things rolling for us to be copied in on whatever the cameras picked up?'

'Already requested.'

'Anything else from Kath, Candace?'

'No. I'd like to check on her later.'

'We will. Let's look at what's left of these files. According to Joy there were three boxes and now we have two.'

Pete lined them up. 'I've already taken photographs of each and noted which box they were from. Other than the one under the seat, that is.'

The first few envelopes offered little the team didn't already know about the older suspicious deaths. Inside two loose files was a handful of witness statements dated 1981 and 1984.

'Together in one file?' Liz glanced up. 'Someone was treating these as one case.'

A newer file contained the same photographs Joy had sent to Liz.

'What else did she say should be here, Liz?'

'Copies of police and other witness reports for a start. Unless they are in the envelope you located?'

Pete opened the last one. 'Feels much thicker than the others.' After clearing a space, he slowly slid the contents onto the table. 'Oh, man.'

At the very top was a large photograph of a deceased male on the ground.

'It's almost the same.' Candace gently picked it up. 'Look at his positioning. He might have died while praying and that is exactly what the killer wants us all to think. And is that... is that a chain in his fist?' She handed it to Liz. 'A fine silver chain with a pendant.'

Liz looked closely. 'Just like the one I found. Complete with an angel.'

31

The room was a hive of activity, each person engrossed in tasks Liz had set once they realised they'd made a breakthrough.

And not just one.

The pendant was an extraordinary find and Meg had custody of the photograph and several others which showed it. She'd scanned each into a program and was concentrating on improving the clarity to get decent images.

But there was more in this final envelope.

Two original police notebooks included observations from both of the 1980s deaths and Candace was reading through them and making notes. She'd already seen a brief report from a doctor and snorted at what she called 'bulldust' before putting it aside.

Pete was scouring through a local newspaper dated a few weeks after the death in 1981. The front cover a photograph of the church and a headline. *Grave death explained.*

The other find was a man's wallet inside an evidence bag. Reuben was taking photographs using Meg's main camera but it would be her job to remove it for fingerprinting. It appeared to be empty. Jeff's friend who'd seen the wallet found on the most recent body had sent through a written report and Liz read it to Reuben.

'Cheap black vinyl. Very worn with cracks along the crease and what seems to be water damage.'

Reuben put down the camera and lifted the evidence bag. 'I'd say vinyl. Old. And water damaged. This one was on the first body in 1981. So where are all the other belongings?'

'I can help with that,' Candace said. She closed the second notepad and looked at Liz. 'According to Constable John Fraser, all items of clothing belonging to the deceased were lost in a miscommunication. They were accidentally thrown away.'

Meg swung around, her face aghast. 'They were *what*? But how? I mean, who is so incompetent to not properly lodge evidence?'

Liz was just as perplexed. Systems existed for a reason and keeping a proper chain of evidence was fundamental to any investigation. Even ones considered accidental. 'We need to speak to this constable who is most likely retired. And find out whether Hobson was part of the investigation or in a position to influence how evidence was handled. He would have been young though, so probably not.' She gazed around the room. 'I'm about to phone Joy to ask exactly what was inside the missing box and what might be missing from the two we retrieved. Although I messaged her earlier about taking more photographs and I've not had a response. And she might now be dealing with the fallout from Kath's crash. But what we have is solid and I appreciate the work you are all putting in on this.'

'We're all keen to find the truth, Liz.' Pete held up the newspaper, which he'd folded back into its original shape. 'Not much of that in this because it reports that following an intensive investigation, police and the coroner found no evidence of foul play. Thing is that the body never went to the State Coroner's Office and from Candace's earlier reaction, whoever conducted the medical examination made things up along the way.'

Candace nodded vigorously. 'I've seen the half-dozen photos which Meg has and it is obvious that pressure was applied to the throat of the deceased yet the so-called doctor who signed the death certificate mentions nothing other than natural causes. Does anyone naturally strangle themselves on top of a grave in the middle of the outback? And there's another vital piece missing.' She glanced at the letter. 'One line mentions the deceased was never identified.'

'How can that happen? Liz crossed to the whiteboard and wrote in large letters.

WHO IS PROTECTING A KILLER?

She replaced the lid on the marker and faced the team. 'Accidentally lost evidence? Even if it is true, why would it be for two cases which happened three years apart? Each should have been separately lodged and housed. And how can not one but three bodies be so-far unidentified? The bodies are in a recognisable state. Fingerprints must have been taken even if DNA wasn't during the 1980s. Two men are buried somewhere without their families being notified of their deaths and a third is in a hospital morgue with nobody apparently looking for next of kin.'

Meg returned to her keyboard but the others looked at Liz. Expectant. Waiting for orders.

Hobson has to be behind a cover-up. But what if I'm wrong?

A familiar wave of panic rose from the pit of her stomach.

She'd completely missed having a corrupt law enforcement officer in their own team. Completely missed seeing what were – in hindsight – glaringly obvious clues about a woman Liz once considered a friend. A mole in their midst had fed classified information to a criminal network and ultimately led to the death of a valuable member of Operation Nobody. What if her suspicions about Hobson were an over-compensation from the dreadful events from that time?

'Pete? We'll go and take a look at the scene of the wreck. Reuben and Candace? Please speak to Mr Bryant. Meg?'

'I know, I know. Stay here and make sure none of you get into trouble.'

Liz hesitated again. Should Meg go with one of them rather than continually be in here alone?

'Hello, I'm perfectly fine but I do expect a decent coffee from whichever of you lot get back here first. I need to do a video call with Jeff anyway, thanks to all this new information.'

Reuben's expression was thoughtful. 'The pendant in the photographs? What if it is the one you found, Liz? We don't know if it dropped onto the grave when the body was moved and was accidentally pushed into the ground by careless feet.'

Meg picked up her phone. 'I'll ask Jeff what else he's found on it.'

'If it is the same chain and pendant... the DNA matched Janie's mother, Maude as well as Jock Carvers,' Liz said. 'Is he alive? Or is he the unidentified body from 1981?'

Once again, Liz was reminded of the crash scene where Vince Carter's daughter and son-in-law perished. She'd been there twice. First with Pete as an early responder. Then alone, trying to make sense of why a car would veer off a relatively straight, quiet country road with no other traffic. Speed wasn't involved. The initial findings by investigators was an accident. A lapse of judgement after a couple of glasses of wine over dinner.

'You changed everything, Lizzie.'

Pete was slowly walking around the tree, which was now devoid of the car which had hit it. There were no police markers or other sign of a proper investigation.

'What do you mean?'

'When Susie died. You didn't give up when everyone else did. Other than Carter, of course. And you found evidence which saved lives.'

She had. Something as insignificant as a half-smoked cigarette a fair distance from the scene. It had belonged to the killer who'd forced the car into a spin then stood there, watching as the driver and front passenger died. His mistake was leaving little Melanie, only eight at the time, alive. And now he was where he belonged. Six feet under.

'They've moved the patrol car too fast,' Pete said. 'Not nearly sufficient to properly process the scene which leads me to think there is someone pulling strings.' He stopped circling and crossed his arms. 'Do you think Hobson is the killer? Or the enabler?'

'That, my friend, is the question of the day. I'm hoping by the time we're all back at the motel that Meg will have a time-line of events. I know she was working on it early in the piece and we keep throwing more at her with higher priorities.'

'Yeah. In the space of a couple of days we've gone from a case with barely any substance to one which has me puzzled, for sure.'

'If we're going to do future remote investigations, we need to manage everything more efficiently. Meg might seem invincible but she isn't and I won't have her, have any of the team, overwhelmed to the point of exhaustion.'

Pete laughed shortly. 'As if the powers that be give a flying proverbial.'

'I think they do. At least, I know Ben got everything he asked for so Felix should as well.'

'Yeah, but will he ask?'

About to say he would, Liz stopped herself. He'd tried to guilt Candace into staying in Melbourne to make his own job easier. It was in the back of Liz's mind that he needed to earn her trust.

'Guess we'll find out. Thoughts on the scene.'

'She was run off the road. Even without what Kath told Candace, there's signs on the bitumen of braking.' Pete gestured a few metres up the road. 'And tracks on the opposite shoulder. Bigger than car tyres.'

'We'll take photos. With the car gone there's little point being here other than that.'

Pete collected a camera from the hire car while Liz walked down the middle of the road. She'd told Candace and Reuben to use the BearCat as it was an official vehicle if they needed to transport Mr Bryant. They'd been given permission to use the local police station thanks to Felix talking to someone at the main station. An officer was going to be there while Kath was out of action.

'I couldn't get hold of Joy.'

'What, no reply?' Pete began taking photographs.

'There's an out of office response. An auto one. I might try again while you do that.'

Liz rang Joy's number and this time it was answered promptly.

'Why are you harassing my officer, detective?'

The angry voice came through the phone loudly enough for Pete to turn, eyebrows raised. Liz put the call on speaker.

'Ah, Sergeant Hobson, I'd like to arrange a time to have an informal chat with you.'

Why are you answering Joy's phone?

'With officers down I hardly have time for a *chat*. Detective.'

'May I speak with Constable Reed please?'

'She's taken personal leave. You have phoned and messaged her on multiple occasions in the past twenty-four hours and I'm telling you now to stop. In addition, those evidence boxes are to be returned to this station immediately. Or to the officer who has just arrived to fill Kath's position until she recovers.'

'Where would you like to meet for an informal interview? Any evidence we don't require I will bring with me.'

'I told you I am not available to speak to you.'

'Let me know when that changes and I'll arrange to get those boxes to you.'

Hobson's tone hardened further. 'That sounds like blackmail.'

'Does it?'

Pete's mouth dropped open and he gave Liz a thumbs up.

'You... are playing a dangerous game. This conversation is terminated.' Hobson disconnected the call.

Liz's hands shook a little as she slid the phone away.

'Oh, boss. Firstly, you rock. And secondly... there's no way he's not involved.' Pete returned to taking photographs. 'Despite him initially agreeing to give you access to all the cold case evidence and that of the recent case, nothing happened until Joy made it happen and yet here he is demanding you return it.'

'Which is interesting. Why would he approve Kath collecting the boxes then want them back. Unless...'

'Unless he didn't know until it was almost too late. Hobson never intended for them to reach you.'

Taking out her phone again, Liz scrolled through her messages with Joy.

'I should have phoned her rather than messaging. Damnit. There's the photographs she'd taken and sent. And my later request she photograph and send any from 1981 and 1984. That was never answered but Hobson will have read the message. If Joy had got hold of the evidence boxes but bypassed Hobson, he might have had a shock discovering they were coming our way.'

'Makes you wonder what he has to hide.'

Pete packed up the camera and they climbed into the hire car as Liz's phone rang, Candace's name appearing on the screen.

'Hi Candace, I've put you on speaker and Pete's with me.'

'Same here, with Reuben. We're parked outside Mr Bryant's house but he isn't home. When I was here with Pete, Mr Bryant complained about not being able to walk further than the local shops so we thought we might do a drive around and see if we can easily spot him.'

'Probably hiding,' Pete muttered.

'Take a look. Chat to his neighbours if you can't find him.'

'Will do.'

Pete started the motor as the call ended. 'Where to?'

'Back to Meg. We'll get started on our next steps and once Reuben and Candace return, review what we already know and what we need to discover. I think some formal interviews are on the cards.'

As they left the scene, Liz gazed in the side mirror at the tree slowly disappearing from sight. Kath could have become a statistic. Another death on the roads. And all because someone – or multiple conspirators – were protecting a deadly secret.

The team sat around the trestle table with coffees and a collection of wraps from the café. For now the evidence boxes were locked in the BearCat after Meg had made digital recordings of everything possible. Candace was quiet. She'd gone straight to her room after returning with Reuben. He'd mentioned she'd had sad news and had asked for a few minutes alone. As much as Liz wanted to go to her, she respected the request but gave Candace a quick hug when she joined them.

'We drove around a few blocks near Mr Bryant's house without seeing him,' Reuben said. 'Stopped at the strip of shops, all five of them. Nobody had seen him since yesterday morning and according to the man who runs the bakery that is unusual. Normally buys a bread roll or two each morning.'

Meg peered inside her wrap then withdrew a long slice of cucumber. 'What about his neighbours?' She delicately lowered the cucumber onto the wrapping paper before taking a bite of her lunch.

'On one side the lady was so hard of hearing that we ended up pointing at Mr Bryant's house but all she kept saying was he wouldn't do mass. Man on the other side hadn't seen him for a couple of days but reckons they have plans to play chess at three today at Bryant's house. He has our contact details and promises to call if nobody is home then.'

Liz recounted her conversation with Hobson.

'We have no idea why Joy suddenly took personal leave? Except it was more likely a suspension if Hobson kept her phone.' Candace hadn't touched her food. 'By getting her out of the station he has one less person likely to question him. Let alone an officer who has shown herself to be honest and to do her job properly. If he's responsible for the van which ran Kath off the road, then he's attempted to murder one of our own.'

'And for what?' Liz couldn't sit any longer and went to the whiteboard. 'Why would a senior police officer, one who is past retirement age and has a decent pension waiting, risk his future? I know this is all supposition but after speaking with Hobson I'm deeply suspicious of him.'

'Feel free to rub everything off this side, Liz,' Meg said. 'I've got screenshots. This wrap is delicious now I've removed the dastardly cucumber.'

'I like cucumber.' Pete reached over and to prove his point, helped himself to the slice, popping it into his mouth with an exaggerated sound of pleasure.

Liz left the others to talk about the pros and cons of vegetables while she cleaned the whiteboard. It was difficult to look beyond Hobson right now but she had other suspects and it was becoming more likely that more than one person was involved in the cases. That done, she watched the team for a moment. Pete and Meg were squabbling, Reuben was on his tablet reading something, and Candace stared into space. Liz's heart went out to her. How awful to get bad news when so far from home.

As if she felt Liz's eyes on her, Candace focused and offered the tiniest of smiles.

Reuben lifted his head. 'I've been reading more of the poems from Erik Piper's book. *The Tears of Certain Angels*.'

'Anything of interest?'

'Some of these poems feel as though he has an interest in death beyond the fascination with angels.'

Now he had the full attention of the team. Liz sat again. 'Go on.'

'There are fifteen poems in this collection.' Reuben leaned back in his chair, eyes on the ceiling while he thought for a moment. 'Each has a reference to an angel but not your garden variety type. Some are dark. Really dark. The collection as a whole was published around nine years ago.'

'We've heard the one about the angel weeping,' Pete said. 'So is it just he has a thing about angels which is why he lives near a church and graveyard? Some morbid curiosity with the afterlife?'

'He certainly has enough angel statues around his pond,' Liz added. 'I think we need to look at all options and narrow this down. If I've stirred things up with Hobson and he *is* involved, time might be our enemy.' Back on her feet, she picked up a black marker and wrote a vertical list of names.

Sergeant Hobson

Erik Piper

Gordon Brain

Albie Walsh

Hector Swift

Unknown person/s

'Anyone else?'

'Betty Carver and for that matter, Jock Carver.' Meg had her tablet open. 'After a lot of digging I've put together a history of the Carvers which is worth a quick mention. There were three children born into the family. Jocelyn aka Jock in 1952, Skipton aka Skip in 1953, and Elizabeth aka Betty in 1959. Both Jock and Skip attended a private boys-only boarding school in Melbourne. Betty went to a local school and became a teacher for about five years before being institutionalised for more than fifteen years, on and off, for mental health issues. I can't access her medical record but I can tell you it happened in 1984.'

'Albie mentioned a brother. Have you found Jock and Skip?' Pete asked.

'I have not. There is a trail of sorts with both brothers moving to Perth to live with a distant relative. They were seventeen and eighteen and the year was 1971.'

'Janie Swift...' Liz crossed to the other side of the whiteboard.

JANIE SWIFT, DIED 1971
UNKNOWN MALE DIED 1981
UNKNOWN MALE DIED 1984
UNKNOWN MALE DIED 2026

'Where are they now, Meg?' Pete looked ready to jump out of his skin with excitement. 'Jock and Skip.'

'Unknown. I have located a newspaper clipping from 1981 which mentions Jock being captain of the local football team. So at some point, he at least, came home.'

'I'd like to have another talk with Albie Walsh, Liz.' Candace had her own tablet open and was looking at notes. 'Clarify some of the events he mentioned to us before Colin interrupted. Ah, here it is. To paraphrase... he had an altercation with a group of teens who called him out for not serving in the Vietnam War. Albie called Jock an evil thug and mentioned he led a small group of admirers, particularly his brother and a friend of the brother.'

'And he believed they were responsible for the disappearance of Janie. I'm with Candace,' Pete said. 'Get Albie away from his son and have a proper conversation.'

Liz wrote *Interview again* beside Albie's name, then tapped the board. 'Meg? Please chase up the brothers. Get whatever help you need from the hub. If they are the first and second deceased males, we have new connections. And possibly a motive for the killer.'

The room was silent. Heavy with the thoughts of these amazing people Liz called her team. For the first time in a long time, she was ready to face whatever was ahead.

'Get the hub to help, she said. Like they have any idea what to look for.' Meg was muttering under her breath as she sent a message to Phoebe.

The podcaster might be taking some time off but they'd chatted every day and Phoebe had made it clear she could call on her research team once there were enough facts. This might not all be facts – not yet – but Meg's workload was overflowing. Operation Nobody was too new in its revamped format to be her first call when it came to a deep dive although she would do as Liz asked and send through requests.

In the background the discussion continued. Meg's senses

were tingling because she was seeing patterns emerge. And she liked patterns.

'Can we discard anyone?' Liz asked. 'Talk to me.'

Reuben was first to speak. Out of everyone in this core group, he was slowest to put forward ideas unless he was close to certain. His words held weight.

'Logically, Erik Piper isn't in the frame for 1981 and 1984. He lived in England the entire time other than regular trips to Thailand. Stepped foot in Australia for the first time around ten years ago. It doesn't exclude him from the investigation into the recent death but if we do, it would be in the capacity of a copycat.'

'Yeah, he's a bit of a wildcard,' Pete added. 'My gut says he's more involved than just an onlooker but the evidence doesn't support my gut.'

'Less cucumber would help your gut.' Meg didn't bother turning around but smiled when Pete laughed.

'Okay, so we won't completely discard Erik but put him in the background for now.' Liz was writing on the whiteboard, the marker slightly squeaking. 'And Gordy?'

An email notification popped up from Jeff.

'Low-profile life. Been in Victoria for only fifteen years so probably not a contender for the 1980s deaths. Other than living next door to the Carver property, there's nothing about him to look at. Is there?' Candace asked. 'Unless his purchase of the two assets from Hector Swift are a factor.'

Meg read the email then forwarded it to everyone's tablets and turned around to look at them. 'Can I butt in? Jeff is a miracle worker when it comes to jewellery and fine arts and the contact details Reuben and Pete got from the local gift shop got a hit. He tracked down the son of the man who made the angel pendant.'

'Holy...' Pete grabbed his tablet.

'Yes, dearie. Angels are considered holy.' Meg rolled her eyes. 'His dad sold handmade jewellery from home for decades and kept immaculate records and the short version is that Maude Swift purchased two angel pendants in 1970. Each has an inscription. *Love and protect each other, darling daughter.* The second inscription was *Love and protect each other, darling son.*'

'One for Janie and the other for her little brother. We need to confirm he is Hector.' Liz looked at her watch. 'Almost three. Give it a few minutes, Reuben, then follow up with Mr Bryant's neighbour. He will know. Candace, are you up to going with Pete to see if Albie is around because he will also know.'

'Of course. We'll go now?'

'Soon. Has there been any further information on Lenny Field? The person who paid ten dollars for the ten acres sub-divided from the Carver property.'

Meg started a search using a program she'd written to gather references to names which was more efficient and more accurate than any browser, partly because she had access to some departments which the general public did not. 'Gotta admit I've not had a chance yet to do anything for him. Okay, so Leonard 'Lenny' Field was born in 1946 in Branonville. Had a brief stint in jail for injuring a police officer while resisting arrest during a protest across the South Australian border about land and water rights. Something of a hippy... bit of an activist. Then worked as a farmhand for the Carvers before owning that ten acres between 1972 and his death in 1978.'

Liz had walked over to Meg. 'Relatives?'

The rest of the team approached as Meg began a new search. She could feel the sense of anticipation from them.

'We've touched on revenge being a motive for the graveyard deaths and if the Carver brothers and others were responsible for Janie's disappearance... who would be her avenger?' Liz squatted beside Meg to better see. 'We know Maude is Janie's mum and probably Hector's as well.'

Information populated the screen and everyone closed in around Meg. 'Oi, let a girl breathe. I'll read aloud, okay?'

Murmurs of sorry accompanied a collective step back.

'We already know Maude Swift had her DNA taken as part of the trial and Lenny likely had his own DNA tested so I'm cross-referencing them. And there we have it folks.' Sometimes what she did surprised herself. 'Close match between Maude and Lenny. Enough to be half-siblings or similar. And I have more. Birth dates for Janie and for Hector, who is four years younger.'

Reuben's phone rang and he excused himself to answer.

'Lenny Field died in 1978, three years before our first mysterious body appeared. And Hector lived with him and was eighteen when he lost his uncle, according to Albie. But if Jock and Skip killed Janie, why would Lenny accept a parcel of land from their parents?' Liz was puzzling aloud. She did that a lot and Meg liked it.

'The equivalent of guilt money from the family. Possibly there was even cash involved to keep things quiet. Lenny needed to provide for his nephew. Keep him safe because that was the last of his family.' Candace's eyes glistened. 'What a choice to make. And then Hector inherited it.'

Liz got to her feet. 'And Hector didn't need to be safe. He needed revenge.'

'In which case... where the heck is Hector?' Pete gave himself a funny look at his word choices. 'I mean, we're now assuming he killed Jock and Skip then packed up and left town. Did he come back just to kill whoever morgue-man is?'

With a sudden smile, Liz tilted her head. 'Or are we asking the wrong question? Not where is Hector, but who he is. Did he even leave in the first place?'

33

Liz was behind the wheel of the BearCat with Reuben ending up a call with the hub. Mr Bryant was still missing and his neighbour was worried, telling them the ex-priest never went far from home.

'Once you hear back from the community care nurse please update me. Okay, thanks and hopefully he'll be located quickly.' After hanging up, Reuben turned in his seat to look at Liz. 'You heard it all. At least his neighbour is willing to talk to our team and help with info about Mr Bryant's visitors and helpers.'

'He might have had a scare, being approached by us,' Liz said. 'I should have arranged a formal interview from the beginning. Not given him time to overthink it. In hindsight, he must know a lot more than what he told Candace and Pete. With all the blood and trace inside the church he oversaw, did he cover up a murder? Even help bury a body?'

'How could he not have known something terrible happened?'

'Is that Gordy's car?'

They were on Brown Horse Road and it was the blue sedan coming toward them. As the vehicles passed Liz raised a hand in greeting but Gordon didn't respond. His attention was on something in the footwell of the passenger side.

'Should we stop him?' Reuben looked into the side mirror. 'He's erratic.'

Liz checked her mirror. 'He's still on the road so no. Without that search warrant for the Carver place yet, having another look is the best use of our time while Pete and Candace visit Albie. Actually, would you call the hub back please? See if there's an update on the warrant?'

The call was answered by Felix. Abruptly. 'Liz?'

'And Reuben is here as well.'

Why are you answering the central number?

'I was about to call you. Sergeant Hobson is stirring the pot big time. He's planning to file a complaint against you and Pete for harassment and interfering with an active investigation. At this point he's done no more than make threats but you need to back off, Liz.'

Not even slowing the BearCat, Liz shook her head. 'Sorry.'

'Don't apologise. Just steer clear of him.'

'Why?'

There was a silence and Liz almost sighed in frustration. Was he so easily swayed by an angry man who was hiding behind a badge? Reuben's expression was grim.

Liz wasn't in a backing down mood. 'Sir, Sergeant Hobson is a suspect.'

'I expected he was from the briefs. This action of his is a distraction and in my experience, it makes for a dangerous, possibly desperate person. Do your job but keep your distance from Hobson. I'm meeting with my bosses late today and he is one of the items on our agenda, along with pushing through a warrant to search his premises and the warrant for the Carver property. Just wish I could be up there to give you a hand.'

Slowing as they reached the turnoff, Liz finished the call with a brief, 'Thanks, boss. We'll wait to hear from you.'

There was nothing more to say. He had their backs.

'Thought for a minute he was telling us to overlook Hobson.' Reuben sounded relieved. 'Would have been awkward for us to go ahead and arrest him if it comes to that without the superintendent's support.'

'Just a little.' Liz grinned.

As they approached the two gates, Liz braked.

'Am I seeing things?'

'Gordy's gate is open.'

'He's left in a hurry. And he wasn't watching the road very well. Shall we take a closer look? A quick one.'

Liz turned the vehicle and parked beneath a tree opposite. If the gate was open there was no reason for them not to walk down to the house.

'I'll get a satellite phone and binoculars. Anything else?' Reuben headed for the back of the vehicle.

'Sidearms. Betty Carver might not take kindly to seeing strangers on her neighbour's land. I'll let Meg know what we're doing.'

Before she could do that, Pete rang.

'We're with Albie, Liz. He's confirmed Hector is Janie's younger brother and that he left town one day after saying goodbye to everyone and putting his motel and the property on the market. Said he was off to travel the world with Thailand as his first stop.'

'Thailand.' Why was that familiar? 'And he never returned?'

'Apparently not. Gordon Brain took up residence a year later. Properties were pretty much empty until he bought them.

He has a reputation for being pleasant if quiet. Likes a drink or dinner our but doesn't get involved much in local sports or the like, not like Hector did.'

The image of bullet holes peppered through the motel sign at the sportsground came to mind.

Pete continued. 'I just stepped away to call but Candace has him eating out of her hand. They are having a good laugh about his boxing days, I think. Colin is away from the pub until tonight and Albie is in his usual chair. We'll encourage him to talk about Janie a bit more. And get any names he remembers from the group which hung around with Jock.'

'Good. Reuben and I are about to walk down to Gordy's house, courtesy of an open gate.'

'Aw, you get all the fun jobs.'

'Until Betty shoots us or he comes home and kicks us out.'

'Yeah, but Gordy isn't exactly a suspect. Candace is giving me a look so I'll head back.'

'Hang on a sec... ask him if he has any photos of Hector. Or where we might find them.'

'Will do.' Pete rang off.

Reuben handed Liz her firearm. 'What are you thinking?'

'I don't know. There's a jumble of pieces which aren't meshing yet.'

'Let them mull. Nobody I know connects pieces better than you do, Liz.'

Jeff's face was a welcome sight even if it was only through the screen of Meg's phone. And even if that face was deeply creased by a frown.

'This is the kind of case I'd normally want to spend months on, Meg. Three suspicious deaths with a similar theme and location is not common. Add in the potential for a fourth body, but one with completely different markers, makes it forensically fascinating. Trace connecting some but not others. One entirely missing body. Three who miraculously,' he held up his fingers like quotation marks, 'were not identified. Evidence has been tampered with. There's a huge cover-up and it is intriguing.'

'While I agree, in the situation at hand we need to escalate everything which can be hurried. I can't identify the contents of either grave, and you've just told me that your lab experts can't either apart from seeing one coffin, as expected.'

'Well, yes, but I also told you there's a high likelihood that the other grave has a layer of some substance which is corrupting the images. Based upon the trace located belonging to Janie Swift or someone very close, I've advised Felix that exhumation is recommended. For both graves.'

'Reuben wants to take another look with the drone tonight.'

Jeff shook his head. 'Doubt it is worth doing. I know Reuben hopes the lack of light will boost the bounce-back but whatever is buried is best dug up.'

'I'll let Liz know.'

'I'm happy to join you and set up an on-site testing station.'

'Which you already know I have right here,' Meg said. 'I will say that Liz is giving a lot of thought to what the team needs if we do more remote cases. She'd better action my very excellent idea.'

'Let me guess. A coffee station.'

'And that is why we are friends.'

There was a tap on the door.

'Someone's at the door. Can you stay there a minute because I want to talk through the results from the pendant some more.'

'Just ring back, lovey.'

Meg was already on her feet. 'I'll be ten seconds.'

Jeff said something inaudible. If he was busy and needed to go then she'd do as he suggested.

About to open the door, she hesitated. 'Who is it?'

'Just me. Gordy. Really sorry to bother you, love, but I think I left a spanner in there when I was fixing a leaky faucet so you lot could move in. Do you mind if I check where I last saw it?'

She opened the door. Gordy grinned. 'I'll only be a sec.'

'No, stay there and I'll get it for you.'

'You sure? I was under the sink in the bathroom. Probably got up to check it was working and promptly forgot my tool.' He took a few steps and leaned his shoulder against the outside wall. 'Appreciate it.'

Meg hurried into the bathroom and opened the cabinet door, squatting to take a proper look. No spanner. Only loo paper. Straightening, she turned to leave and stopped dead.

Gordy was in the doorway.

'I asked you to wait outside the room.'

'I could. But I won't.'

Meg tried to push past. He slammed her backwards against the open door, pinning her arms and torso with his weight. She kicked at his legs and he laughed. Then a hand pushed her cheek hard onto the painted timber and a needle stabbed into her neck.

There was a needle mark on the body of the last man on the grave. Have you just killed me?

He kept his weight on her. She tried to call out for help and his hand whipped up to cover her mouth. His face was close to hers. His breath was foul. Her heartbeat was counting the minutes.

She could still get away. Trick him into thinking she was out.

I have to fight it.

The pressure of his weight came off. She swayed. Her legs

wouldn't move as his arm moved to around her waist, gently turning her until she could see herself in the bathroom mirror.

His voice was sad. 'You had no right to touch the sacred graves. But I would never harm a woman. I won't take your life but I imagine he will. He doesn't leave anything to chance. Keeps the evidence from prying eyes. Like yours.'

Meg's body was heavy... yet, weightless. Her reflection was sinking. Disappearing into nothingness.

34

The well-maintained front garden and first hundred metres of Gordon Brain's property gave way to neglect after it disappeared from the direct sight of the road. Potholes littered the long driveway and fallen trees were rotting on the ground. Liz stopped as they reached a bend.

'Is that the Carver's main house?' She pointed across the land to the left where a roof and chimneys were just visible.

'Looks it. Once we're done here we could get the drone up. Do a quick fly over.'

'Yes. All the buildings and down to the basin.'

They started walking again.

'If we're right about Jock and Skip being responsible for whatever happened to Janie, can you imagine living so close to them?' Reuben shook his head. 'Lenny Field must have needed the land enough to stay rather than take Hector and start over somewhere else.'

'But people don't start over. Not often, except in movies. Look at Vince Carter. He stayed in the cottage he'd shared with his wife after she died there. Raised their little girl there. And

Lyndall has stayed in the house she was taken from. Until recently, my sister Anna lived in a house filled with the saddest of memories.'

And I refused to move from my apartment after my darling niece was abducted right under my nose. For almost twenty years I waited for her to come home.

'Familiarity, I guess. And we're assuming Lenny knew it was them,' Reuben said. 'According to Albie, it was an open secret. Jock, Skip, and Skip's friend Neville. Others hung around with them, but those three were the ones he described as evil thugs.'

The house was modest and probably the original one built in the 70s. Brick, single story, tin roof. A carport to one side. Closed curtains.

'Meet you around the back.'

Liz veered to the right, crossing in front of several windows before the first corner. This one had two windows which again, had closed curtains. The stench of bleach reached her before she found the source a bit behind the house. There were two large bleach containers on their sides, pools of water around them, and a dribbling hose stuck into the neck of one.

'Must be what he had in his car the other day.' Reuben caught up. 'Chemicals of some sort but Pete and I figured it was part of cleaning the motel.'

'This is a lot of bleach. Can you see through that window?' Liz gestured to one which was too high for her.

It was high even for Reuben but he lifted himself on his toes to peer through a gap in the curtains. 'There's candles burning. Like, lots of them. Even near the corner of the curtains.'

'I'll message Meg and the hub to let them know we're entering the house forcibly for a credible fire danger. Better check in case anything's unlocked first.'

Liz tapped out the message and sent it then went the other way to Reuben, testing each window, and meeting at the front door.

'Boot job or I can run back to the BearCat for a lock kit.'

'Let's just get in.' Liz turned to the door and called out. 'Police. Open the door immediately or we'll enter forcibly.'

As expected there was no answer and one well-placed kick from Reuben had the door swing inwards.

'Police. We believe there is an imminent fire danger. Please come out through the front door. If you are not mobile, call out and we'll come and help you.' Liz was tired of waiting. 'Coming in now.'

Both drew their weapons.

Inside was dark. None of the lights worked. Using flashlights they worked their way through what was a very normal looking house with nothing out of ordinary, to the room with the candles. A lock and padlock made this room far from normal and they took a few steps back.

'We might take a better look from outside, Reuben. Grab a kitchen chair or two and let's see what's in here before we open this.'

It might be as simple as the place where Gordy kept all his financial information. His safe. Or something illegal but relatively harmless. Liz wasn't taking unnecessary chances. No risks. Take the time. Reduce the margin of error.

Chairs more or less stable on the ground outside the window, they climbed on them and shone flashlights in.

'Not wrong about the candles,' Liz said. 'What's on the wall? Are those photographs?'

'Too hard to see.'

'We might track Gordy down and get him to open this.'

Reuben was quiet as he returned the chairs, ending up in front of the door.

'What?'

'Why would he have candles burning in there? Doesn't it feel a bit... ritualistic?' He offered a small smile. 'What's one more broken door?'

'Alright. Get it open then we take our time going in.'

This one took more effort but once freed from its locks, Reuben gave it a nudge with his toe to fully open it. 'Looks okay, Liz. I'll go in first.'

About to tell him no, Liz pulled herself up. The time for being over-protective was past.

Taking photos on their phones as they entered, both were drawn to the large corkboard they'd seen through the window. Newspaper clippings, photographs, police reports... all surrounded one central image, a painting. It portrayed a teenaged girl sitting on a boulder, wildflowers in her hands and a smile on her face.

'Does the plaque say Janie?' Liz looked more closely. 'An angel lost but never forgotten. Janie Swift. My sacred sister.'

Reuben let out a long, slow whistle. 'This is a shrine to her.'

Liz gazed at the board. 'Look at those photos, Reuben. Police photos look like those we've seen from the first and second deaths but these ones show the faces. I think that is Jock Carver—' she pointed to one. 'See how he's holding the angel pendant?'

'And now we have faces for Meg to search. But my question is why here? Surely Gordy hasn't kept this room functioning as a shrine for a family he never knew?'

'Thailand.' The connection made, Liz's brain raced. 'Albie just told Pete and Candace that Hector Swift was heading to Thailand. And Erik Piper's background check had him in Thailand on several occasions and I think the most recent was a bit over ten years ago. What if they met there? But how would that even fit into this?'

Their flashlights roamed the board.

'That's us.' Reuben focused the light on a photo on the edge of the board. 'You and me when we stopped near Erik's pond. And you. I think that's Kath in the background near her patrol car.'

'From the day I arrived. And Meg. Oh, Reuben, look.' Liz's heart jumped. 'Meg outside her motel room. Meg at the first grave. Meg... where? In the bush somewhere?'

'That's where I followed her to. Across the road from the motel and she said she heard odd sounds and thought it was a kid being silly. But she was being watched this whole time.'

Liz dialled Meg's number. 'Come on, Meg. Pick up. Reuben get Pete back to the motel now.' The voicemail responded. 'Meg, lock yourself in the room. Inside the bathroom. Only open the door to one of us. You are in danger so do that then call me straight away.'

Reuben was already outside and Liz jogged with him up the driveway. Both were making calls as they went, Liz trying Meg again and Reuben speaking with Candace.

'Hang on a sec, Candace,' Reuben dropped to a fast walk. 'Liz?'

She hung up.

'They are on their way to the motel. Albie gave them a book about the region written in the early eighties which has photographs from sports clubs and some events and there are a couple of Neville Hunt as well as the Carver brothers.'

Liz's phone rang and she tapped without looking. 'Meg?'

'No, Jeff. Oh my lord, Liz. I was on a call with Meg and she answered her door and then I heard noises and I—'

'Slow down a bit. I'll put you on speaker so Reuben can hear.'

The gate was just ahead.

'Meg was talking to me but someone came to the door. She

said she'd only be a minute and I told her to call back when she was free but then I got a worried feeling and sang out to her not to open it. She didn't reply but I heard her speak to someone then a moment later she said, quite clearly, I asked you to wait outside the room.' His voice broke. 'There... there were noises. Then the door shut. Someone has hurt our Meg. Or taken her.'

'Have you spoken to Felix?' Reuben asked.

'I phoned you first.'

'We're going to the motel now, Jeff. Please go upstairs to the hub and stay there with the team. I'll speak to Felix. Okay?'

'Find her. Please find her.' Jeff ended the call.

A car turned into the driveway.

'It's Gordon,' Reuben shouted.

He raced across the few metres to the gate as the car backed at speed. Liz was right behind him as Gordon slammed the car out of reverse, swerving to avoid Reuben's desperate grab at the door handle. Liz had her firearm out and aimed at the tyres, taking a shot which missed before Reuben shouted again.

'Meg's in the backseat.'

Liz's arms dropped to her sides as she stood in the middle of the road watching the car drive away.

I've led you into this, Meg.

The BearCat roared into action and pulled up alongside Liz. She climbed in, pulling on her seatbelt as Reuben accelerated. The blue car turned left.

We're coming for you. Hold on, Meg. Hold on.

35

Pete slowly turned the handle on the door they used for their meetings. It was unlocked.

Candace was on the other side of the hire car, which he'd parked a few spaces up. He'd forbidden her to move and she'd nodded, the worry in her eyes matching that in his gut.

'Meg?'

Idiot. She's not here.

He kicked the door wide open, aiming his gun rapidly around the room then holstering it. Meg's phone was on the desk and he checked it. The call to Jeff was disconnected. Everything looked normal in here.

He stared at a half-drunk cup of coffee.

'Is it safe for me?' Candace peered in.

'Yes. I'll check the bathroom.'

The cabinet beneath the sink was open and tossed into a small bin was a syringe. 'Shit. Candace.'

'I'm here. Let me collect it. Can you grab a glove and evidence bag.'

Pete found a stash the team kept in the room and watched as she initially lifted the bin, then carefully picked up the syringe. The needle was uncapped and some liquid remained. She sniffed the end. 'I don't know.' Candace slid it into an evidence bag. 'We need to be cautious. I'll lock this in the safe.'

While she did that, Pete checked the computers. All were running background searches as usual.

'She had her watch on when we were here earlier,' Candace said. 'If she still does—'

'Good thinking.'

Pete went to open a tab on one of the computers but Candace picked up Meg's phone. 'This way is quicker.' He looked over her shoulder as she found the 'find a device' app and scrolled to 'watch'. A map popped up.

'She's moving down Brown Horse Road. In our direction. Stay here and keep monitoring.' Pete headed for the door. 'Lock it.'

'No, I'm coming with you.' Candace was right on his heels. 'I can monitor on the way and I'm not prepared to be a sitting duck if there's a second person involved in this.'

Of course, she was right. Pete had to get his head on straight instead of thinking about what he'd do to the person who'd taken Meg, once he rescued her.

As he started the motor a patrol car flew past, lights flashing but no sirens.

Candace craned her neck to see. 'We haven't notified them.'

'I know.'

'I'll call Liz.'

Pete pulled onto the road, the other car already a long away ahead and still moving fast.

'Candace?'

'Liz, we're both here. Have just left the motel and have

Meg's phone. We're tracking her via her watch along Brown Horse Road.' Candace's eyes were on the phone screen.

'She's in Gordon Brain's car. Reuben glimpsed her lying on the back seat.'

'Alive?' Pete's heart was just about leaping out of his chest.

'Unknown.'

'We found a used syringe in the bathroom,' Candace said. 'Possibly a barbiturate or something to subdue. If he's a ritualistic killer, he will have a system in place to follow.'

'Which we've ruined by being at his house.'

'Yes and no, Reuben. The photos you sent of the shrine is alarming but doesn't indicate he kills his victims on the property. It is more likely to be at or close to the graveyard. And Meg is different. The shrine refers to Janie as 'my sacred sister' so he may have a particular respect for females. He's going to need time to work out what to do.'

'There's a police patrol vehicle ahead of us. Passed the motel before we left going at high speed. I think... yes, it just turned onto the road to the church,' Pete said.

Candace zoomed in on the app. 'Meg's travelling east now. And more slowly.'

'Keep following the police car. Tell me if anything changes with Meg's location but otherwise we'll go to the church. Stay right out of sight. I'll ping the exact location of the BearCat, and Candace, you are to lock yourself in it. I need you to confirm that you understand my order.'

'I understand, Liz. Please stay safe.'

The phone call ended, Pete glanced at Candace. 'She's doing her job.'

'And doing it well.'

Pete swung into the road to the church and abruptly braked. 'Sorry. We're too close. Whether he saw us before or is being cautious...' He'd spotted taillights ahead near a curve. 'Got to be Hobson.'

He hated corrupt cops. Cross a line, sure, if it meant getting the worst types of criminal behind bars. But not police who protected the wicked. That Vince Carter once reported him for corruption still stung. It used to burn. And it was proved wrong.

'She's stationary, Pete. Behind the priest's residence. I'm sending that to Liz.'

'So Piper *is* involved. And Gordon Brain is who, exactly? A friend of Hector who is continuing what he started?'

'Or Hector.'

'We just saw pictures of him thanks to Albie. Other than the height they're nothing alike. Not even eye colour.' Pete slowed as they approached the church. The gate to the Piper place was wide open for the first time he'd ever seen. And there was no sign of Gordon's car or the patrol car. Or the BearCat.

'Liz sent a pin. Go through the church gate and swing left. Should be a bit of cover along the far fence.'

Wishing he had the BearCat rather than a lightweight SUV, Pete nursed it through dips and around trees until parking behind the other vehicle. Opening the back of the BearCat, he located a vest and a rifle and collected ammunition. 'Might take Meg's phone.'

'I've worked out the app which shows everyone. How do you want me to communicate?'

He put an earpiece in. 'This way is good. Liz and Reuben seem to have theirs as well as being kitted up. We're going to find Meg and bring her back safely. My worry is what she's drugged with.'

'I'll make a phone call to a friend who can help me work it out. Go.'

'No, you get in the front and lock the door first.'

By the time he'd closed up the back, she'd done as he asked, winding the window down enough to speak. 'As soon as its safe let me know and I'll come to Meg with the medi-kit.'

He nodded, then was jogging away under the extra weight of his gear. The rifle was loaded. He had comms. All he needed was a bad guy in his sights and the rest would take care of itself.

<h1 style="text-align:center">36</h1>

The back door of the church was ajar and from within, voices were raised enough to wake the dead.

Reuben wasn't prepared to risk putting his weight on the rotting timber of the small, covered verandah so waited as close as he dared, listening.

'You've gone too far this time. How do you expect me to protect you from this? A member of an elite team.'

Hobson.

'You don't need to, mate. Nobody knows I have her. The cameras around the church were disabled earlier. And once she's in the basin, they'll need to dredge it and who is going to do that? Unless you have a better place because it's your job to send her to her maker.'

Gordy. And she's still alive.

'No, I won't. It was never my job to do anything and I wish with all my heart I'd never helped you with Jock. You've ruined my life.'

'Ruined your life?' Gordy laughed. 'You were quite happy

to see him die. Helped me lure him here and held him while I extracted his confession. Then there was Skip.'

'And I told you after Jock it was done. Over for me.'

'But it can never be over for me.' Gordon's voice had changed. There was grief. 'Until the last Carver is in the ground. Until the last of Neville Hunt's family join him in a morgue. Then it is finished.'

Pete cautiously rounded a corner and Reuben gestured to the door and to be silent.

'You've completed what you set out to do all those years ago. Janie deserved better and you forced each of those mongrels to pray for forgiveness. If you release Betty and Bryant and disappear again, then nobody will come looking. There's no reason for you to go to prison. No reason for me either, Hector.'

Reuben's eyes shot to Pete's and he mouthed 'you heard that?' Pete nodded.

'You only care for yourself. If I hadn't kept what we recorded that night with Jock then you would have bailed on me. And it would have hurt me because you're my best friend. You and Erik are. Or it could be just me and Erik. If it comes to it.'

'You're threatening me? Me!' Hobson sounded furious. 'It wasn't you who destroyed evidence. It wasn't you who made sure anything identifying the bodies was buried so deep nobody could find it. What exactly do you think your new best friend will be useful for other than getting you in more trouble than you can imagine. No, mate. I'm done and I'm going to make sure you never threaten me again.'

Silence fell. Reuben wished he had eyes on the men. Storming in wasn't an option when at least Hobson was armed. Pete slowly backed away and pointed at himself and then the front of the church. Most likely he was going to ensure neither could leave by the front door.

And then we have them closed in and at the worst can keep them there until support arrives.

37

Meg looked so peaceful with her body relaxed on the soft grass and her head resting on Erik Piper's lap. Her glasses were missing and her shoes. He gently stroked her hair, talking to her too quietly for Liz to hear. It took a moment to see she was still breathing. The relief was physical and she had to hold herself rigid to stop herself from shaking.

Erik sat close to the pond in the shade of a large gum. He wore a long gown in white and around his neck was a heavy gold chain with an ornate crucifix. His feet were bare. At his side, on the ground, was a dagger.

'She's so close to perfect, this lovely angel.' He spoke audibly now. 'I've observed her working. So diligent and clever. And she's quite safe, if you were wondering.' His head lifted and he smiled at Liz. 'The drugs are fast acting but only last a short time. Did you know I was once a cosmetic surgeon? I had a particular interest in combining certain drugs in order to achieve different outcomes. Sometimes a subject needed to be more awake but not remember. I liked those ones.'

For a second Liz was frozen. She gazed at the dagger and realised it was actually a razor-sharp scalpel. Meg might be safe for now but one wrong move... Liz licked dry lips.

'That's how you know Gordy. Hector.'

The smile widened on Erik's face. 'Well done. And yes. He is my best work. My best *living* work, that is. And he changed my life as much as I changed his looks. His mission here, where angels abound, inspired me to upend my life and dedicate it to celebrating them. Angels, in all their forms. My childhood dream was not to become a surgeon. Nor a poet.' His fingers touched the crucifix. 'I chose a life serving God. Sadly, I was removed from the seminary in my first year. Apparently I have an... unstable nature.'

You are unhinged. And I'm not letting you lead me there.

'You met in Thailand? Hector?'

'He was desperate, poor man. We actually met at a bar. He wore a pendant with an angel I'd never seen. A few drinks and he'd told me his life story. Would you like to sit and I'll tell you?' One of his hands hovered in the direction of the scalpel.

Liz lowered herself onto the grass. She leaned over to look into the pond. 'It is deeper than I thought. And yes, I did notice your interest in angels.' Her hand slowly gestured to each of the ugly concrete creations and she deliberately almost fell into the pond. As she righted herself, she shuffled slightly closer. Still too far to reach Meg if he decided to act.

'I'm not stupid, detective. But I do like to tell the truth. You know that.'

'Yes, I do. You were honest about how you found the deceased man on the grave.'

He nodded and his hand returned to stroking Meg's hair.

'Hector had a problem. He didn't come right out and tell me about how he had extracted vengeance for dear Janie but he was ed and angry because he couldn't see a way to complete his promise to her. Did you know she died in the church? Three teenagers with evil hearts saw her as their prey. Hector remembers. You'd need to speak to him for the finer details but the priest found her and called her uncle. Janie died in their arms and they buried her in the grave beside her mother.'

And the crime buried with her. That poor girl.

Meg's eyes flickered open then immediately closed. It was impossible to know if she'd seen Liz or was even aware of her surroundings.

'I can't imagine how devastating that was for a child to see.'

'Oh it was far more than him seeing her die. The priest and his uncle colluded to cover the murder because the Carver family held all the power in the town. The church couldn't cope with the scandal and Lenny was frightened of losing Hector. But it was unforgiveable and Lenny became the first to pay for his sins.'

It wasn't suicide? Just how many people has he killed?

'You must be incredibly talented,' Liz said. 'I've seen photos of Hector when he was younger and there is not a chance I would have identified Gordy as the same man.'

The hair-stroking paused and the man's eyes narrowed. 'Best not that you flatter me for acts which the law considers reprehensible.'

'It was you who raised it, Erik. You called Gordy your best living work.'

'You were paying attention. And he is. Almost a year of surgery and recoveries. Painful but he never once complained. We became friends. His story inspired me and after he left Thailand, I went home to England but it was never the same. I like it here. The weather. Less people. The church gives me a strange sense of peace when I go through the front door and I have become its priest, in many ways. My days are spent among the dead and it is fitting.' He sighed heavily and gazed down at Meg. 'In another time, she would have become my next project. Truly a work of passion with someone so close to perfection. An angel of the highest order in the making.'

Where is everyone?

'Do you know where Father Bryant is, Erik?'

He looked at Liz again. 'Of course. He's with Betty Carver. They're waiting for Hector.'

A gunshot echoed in the distance.

Hundreds of birds rose from the trees with a cacophony of screeches.

Meg's eyes flew open and she rolled forward, off Erik, and kept rolling.

His hand grabbed for the scalpel and as another shot rang out, he fell backwards with a cry. Liz was on her knees, weapon drawn, Meg in her peripheral vision on the edge of the pond.

'Get face down on the ground and both hands behind your head.' Liz shouted the words as she stood.

Erik laughed and sobbed all in one and held up one hand. A finger was missing, shot right off, and blood began seeping down his palm and soaking into the white fabric of his gown.

She picked up the scalpel and backed away. 'I said to get on the ground.'

There were two more gunshots in the direction of the church and then a small squeal and splash from the pond. Meg disappeared beneath the surface. Liz tapped her earpiece.

'I have Meg but need help urgently at the pond.'

She threw herself into the water and submerged, grabbing an arm and kicking hard to get them both up. Meg's face broke the surface and she gasped for air. Liz pulled Meg against herself, keeping her head above water and dog-paddling them to the side. 'Help's coming, Meg. Hold on.'

With a splutter, Meg began kicking and then grabbed a clump of reeds, taking most of her weight off Liz.

'I'm not... a frigging... angel.'

Muscular arms reached down and lifted Meg as if she weighed nothing. Reuben carefully placed her on the ground then offered his hand to Liz, who was halfway out. She accepted it. Candace was racing toward them with a bag.

And Erik Piper was gone.

'They're both dead.'

Pete's heart finally was back to a normal beat. Liz's desperate call for help came when he was under fire from Hobson. It was minutes – might as well have been hours – before he knew Meg was safe. Alive.

Still sopping wet but brushing aside offers of a towel until she saw for herself what had happened, Liz squatted near the body of Sergeant Hobson. 'He was shooting at you.'

'Only because I'd told him to lower his weapon. He was determined to kill Gordy and he did, even after I shot him the first time. He chased Gordy out through the main door just as I came around to check it was locked.'

'But it wasn't.' Liz straightened.

'Someone had used a crowbar on it.'

They walked to the graves where police tape still fluttered in a breeze. A new body was face down, arms outstretched between both, at the end of a short trail of blood.

'Hector Swift. Reunited with Janie and their mum,' Liz said. 'Full circle.'

'He's wearing an angel pendant.'

A gift from his mother. *Love and protect each other, darling son.* He'd been eleven when his sister died in his arms. He'd spent a lifetime delivering his own brand of justice to her killers and anyone who'd covered their tracks.

'Are you okay, Lizzie?'

'Me? Be fine once I rinse bits of pond out of my hair.'

Reuben had brought the BearCat to the side of the church and was fussing over Meg. So was Candace. Both had her wrapped in blankets which she kept trying to unwrap and were offering water and asking her to lay down, rather than sit on the step.

There'd been a brief search for Erik with no sighting other than some drops of blood near the house. Once Operation Nobody's helicopter arrived with four tactical police on board, a proper search would find him. An older person who was injured and bleeding and barefoot was unlikely to evade them for long. Not with drones and a helicopter.

'I seriously do not need an ambulance! And where are my glasses and shoes?'

'At least she sounds back to normal,' Pete laughed. He didn't feel amused. He wanted to hug Meg and be the one fussing over her. Make sure she was really alright.

They reached the BearCat.

Meg looked at Liz and smiled. Then burst into tears.

Pete turned away as Liz put her arms around Meg, rapidly swallowing down the lump in his throat.

'We might set up a crime scene boundary.'

Reuben carried an open box of markers and he was blinking more than usual.

'Good idea. Ambulance should be here soon regardless of Meg's wishes. Make sure she's...'

'Yeah. Make sure.'

They glanced back at the BearCat. Candace was piling dry towels on the step and Meg had stopped crying and was trying again to unwrap the blankets. Liz was on a phone call.

'Gonna need a couple of shade tents,' Pete said. 'Protect the bodies. We'll get photographs. No more covering up evidence.'

'Waste of a good cop.' Reuben's head gestured toward Hobson's body.

'He was never a good cop. Us? We're the good guys.'

'And you, my friend, are the perfect example of a decent cop. Let's get this done.'

38

Two days later

The BearCat was packed and ready to leave. Operation Nobody wasn't needed for the massive job – expected to take months – of cleaning up the mess left by a corrupt officer, a revenge-driven serial killer, and a poet who had a much darker past than anyone would have imagined.

I only came to evaluate a cold case.

After being checked by paramedics, Meg was given the all-clear to return to Melbourne where she'd spent a night in hospital. A second helicopter had arrived to collect her and Candace, and unexpectedly, Felix had climbed out with an overnight bag. His first action was to go to Candace and put his arms around her. She'd hesitated then leaned against him. And before leaving, she'd told Liz that the friend they'd recently lost had been their wedding celebrant.

An hour ago, Reuben and Felix had left in the hire car. They'd drop it off in Ouyen then the remaining helicopter would collect them on its way back to Melbourne. A day and half of looking for Erik Piper was fruitless in spite of ground and air searches. The current thinking, based mostly on a second blood trail, was that he'd made it to Carver's Basin and drowned but Liz wasn't buying it. She had far too much experience with people who knew how to disappear. His phone was recovered from his house and contained hundreds of disturbing photographs, many from the events of the morning Neville Hunt was forced to beg for his life kneeling on Janie's grave. It hadn't taken long to identify the victims from the 80s as Jock and Skip Carver, thanks to Albie being willing to look at the long-hidden police photos.

They'd rescued Mr Bryant who'd been drugged and was locked in a room inside one of the Carver cottages. Betty Carver was deceased in another. The scare had opened the floodgates for the retired priest who was only too happy to confess to helping bury Janie and negotiating an arrangement between Lenny Field and the Carver family. His reward was financial. He'd eventually poured all the money into the Church as an anonymous donation.

Kath Connor was out of danger and expected to make a full recovery. Joy Reed was back at work and determined to help uncover all of Hobson's dirty secrets. His, and those in high places in the town who'd helped him.

It was peaceful here.

Pete wanted to take photographs of the dawn and they'd driven down to the water just as the sun peeked over the horizon. He wandered off to find the perfect spot while Liz strolled to the edge of the water.

We might have lost you, Meggie.

But they hadn't. *She* hadn't lost her. A breeze sent ripples across the water and Liz gazed at her reflection, just visible as the sky lightened. The fire was back in her belly and her mind was clear and ready to take on the next case. And the one after that.

'Gonna just admire yourself all day, or shall we go home?'

Liz began following Pete but then she stopped and scooped up a handful of red dirt. He turned to watch as she opened her palm and let the breeze scatter the ancient soil.

'I lost myself for a while, Pete.'

'Are you still lost, Lizzie?'

Touch the earth. Learn from it.

The last of the dirt returned to the ground.

'I'm ready to go home.'

About the Author

Phillipa lives just outside a beautiful town in country Victoria, Australia. She also lives in the many worlds of her imagination and stockpiles stories beside her laptop. She writes from the heart about love, dreams, secrets, discovery, the sea, the world as she knows it... or wishes it could be. She loves happy endings, heart-pounding suspense, and characters who stay with you long after the final page.

With a passion for music, the ocean, animals, nature, reading, and writing, she is often found in the vegetable garden pondering a new story.

Phillipa's website is www.phillipaclark.com

Also by Phillipa Nefri Clark

Detective Liz Moorland

Lest We Forgive

Lest Bridges Burn

Lest Tides Turn

Lest Nobody Lives

Lest Angels Weep

Last Known Contact

Rivers End Romantic Women's Fiction

The Stationmaster's Cottage

Jasmine Sea

The Secrets of Palmerston House

The Christmas Key

Taming the Wind

Temple River Romantic Women's Fiction

The Cottage at Whisper Lake

The Bookstore at Rivers End

The House at Angel's Beach

The Secrets of Willow Bay

The Lost Girl at Seahaven

Charlotte Dean Mysteries

Christmas Crime in Kingfisher Falls

Book Club Murder in Kingfisher Falls

Cold Case Murder in Kingfisher Falls

Plans for Murder in Kingfisher Falls

Festive Felony in Kingfisher Falls

Travelling Celebrant Mysteries

Of Marriage & Murder

Of Funerals & Feuds

Of Retreats & Revenge

Of Vines & Victims

Bindarra Creek Rural Fiction

A Perfect Danger

Tangled by Tinsel

Doctor Grok's Peculiar Shop Short Story Collection

Simple Words for Troubled Times

(Short non-fiction happiness and comfort book)

Acknowledgments

I absolutely loved writing *Lest Angels Weep* although it took so much longer than anticipated. Through it all, my wonderful readers have been nothing short of amazing with assurances that the delays would make it worth the wait. I truly hope that is the case and send heartfelt thanks to you all.

My editor (also a talented author) dropped everything to get to work with a tight turnaround and has done a terrific job. Susan Mackie - I love you!

The gorgeous Kerrie Paterson (who also writes amazing books) did much-needed research for me across a range of subjects.

Special thanks to my dear friend Cathy for insights and being a sounding board. I hope I did justice to Kath.

I put out a last minute call for early readers to help me find any anomalies or typos in addition to the usual processes of editing and proofreading. Thanks so much to Sally, Adelle, Sue, Cindy, and Heather.

www.ingramcontent.com/pod-product-compliance
Lightning Source LLC
Chambersburg PA
CBHW011926050726
47591CB00009B/2362